C0-ABX-154

SHORT STORIES
from the
OLD NORTH STATE

O. HENRY

PAUL GREEN

WILLIAM T. POLK

FRANCES GRAY PATTON

CHARLES W. CHESNUTT

OLIVE TILFORD DARGAN

JAMES BOYD

LUCY DANIELS

WILBUR DANIEL STEELE

BERNICE KELLY HARRIS

NOEL HOUSTON

DORIS BETTS

TOM WICKER

JOHN EHLE

THOMAS WOLFE

SHORT
STORIES
from the
OLD NORTH STATE

Edited by **RICHARD WALSER**

1959

CHAPEL HILL

THE UNIVERSITY OF NORTH CAROLINA PRESS

Shenandoah College Library
Dayton, Virginia

COPYRIGHT, 1959, BY

THE UNIVERSITY OF NORTH CAROLINA PRESS

Manufactured in the United States of America

The Library of Congress has cataloged this publication as follows:

Walser, Richard Gaither, 1908–   *ed.*
    Short stories from the Old North State. Chapel Hill,
University of North Carolina Press, 1959.

    288 p. 23 cm.

      1. Short stories, American—North Carolina.   ɪ. Title.

    PZ1.W167Sh   813.082   59–9609 ‡

    Library of Congress

813.082

PS
648
.S5
.S571
1959

PZ
1
.W167
Sh

Walser, Richard Gaither

Short stories from the
Old North State.

813.082 Wal14

813.082
WAL 14

Preface

TEN YEARS AGO, when *North Carolina in the Short Story* was proposed, both editor and publisher were unsure about the reception of an anthology of stories limited in setting and character to the boundaries of one state. The volume, however, soon found its place in schools, public libraries, and private collections. It is flattering, of course, that a second, similar book has been called for.

The present volume follows and complements the earlier one, whose fifteen selections attempted to reflect "those characteristics and features of life in North Carolina which had received significant artistic interpretation by writers of the short story." Neither collection may profess to present a full picture of the state, for, in their quiet way, authors choose material suitable for their talents and amenable to their craft. They are not geographers or sociologists or census-takers, but artists whose subjects are dictated by the interests of their minds and hearts.

There is, nevertheless, a sumptuous variety to choose from. O. Henry, Steele, Wolfe, and Mrs. Dargan write of the mountains, but only Mrs. Dargan is really concerned with the mountain people themselves. O. Henry tells of a brave experiment in his own life there, Steele uses the mountains merely as background for a serious comment on life, and Wolfe relates an incident from his family chronicle. The broad piedmont area of North Carolina provides material as diverse as Chesnutt's post-Civil War melodrama and the more contemporary urban scenes of Mrs. Betts and Miss Daniels. Polk's comedy and Boyd's story look gently and romantically into the past, while the years of the Depression are realistically presented by Tom Wicker and Paul Green. The characters in the stories by Mrs. Harris and Mrs. Patton give a reader the feeling of having walked right into a mid-state sitting room. Farther east, the coast of North Carolina during World War II is Noel Houston's setting. And John Ehle cleverly spans the distance from Asheville to Ocracoke. Actually, though, it is not so much a matter of section or decade. Each author has something to say about human beings and their reactions to life. That the characters happen to be North Carolinians within North Carolina is always secondary.

Of the fifteen writers in the 1948 book, ten are once more included, three of them (Boyd, Polk, Wolfe) with the same stories—stories which defied exclusion because of their classic quality. The other seven writers are represented by selections which are equally as expert as those in the earlier volume but which, it is hoped, will have more interest for present-day readers. The five "new" contributors are Ehle, Houston, Wicker, and two young writers still in their twenties, Mrs. Betts and Miss Daniels. Bernice Kelly Harris and Tom Wicker have been kind enough to allow the use of material previously unpublished.

With the revision and updating of the biographical headnotes, this book, excepting the three stories cited, is entirely new in everything but its purpose: to show that North Carolina has provided setting and inspiration for some of the most significant achievements in the American short story.

North Carolina State College   R. W.
Raleigh, 20 December 1958

Contents

SHORT STORIES
from the
OLD NORTH STATE

O. HENRY

WILLIAM SIDNEY PORTER, one of the most significant figures in the history of the American short story, was born in Greensboro, September 11, 1862. His father was a physician in the town, his mother an educated and gracious woman. She died when he was three years old; thereafter the boy was brought up and trained by his Aunt Lina Porter, who had built a one-room schoolhouse in the yard of her home on West Market Street. To it came the children of the neighborhood, and there on Friday nights young Porter, with chestnuts roasting and corn popping, took part in the collaborative storytelling, probably providing surprise endings to the tales started by others. His schooldays over, he began working in his Uncle Clark Porter's drugstore, where he learned pharmacy and in slack hours devoured the classics and drew cartoons of the customers. Often in the evenings he played the second fiddle with a group of serenaders who provided romantic moments for the students at the Greensboro Female College.

"I was born and raised in No'th Ca'lina," he once wrote, "and at 18 went to Texas and ran wild on the prairies." He had become wearied of the close confinement of the drugstore and was fleeing, too, his fear of tuberculosis. He worked on a ranch, served as a draftsman and journalist, then as a bank teller. Though he always maintained his innocence, he was indicted for embezzlement at the bank and escaped to Honduras. He returned to Texas the following year upon hearing of the serious illness of his wife, and later served three years in the penitentiary at Columbus,

Ohio. To pass the dull prison hours away, he began writing stories. Upon his release, he went to New York, where under the pseudonym of O. Henry he quickly established himself as the most popular short-story writer of the day. A majority of the 250 stories are set in New York, Texas, and Central America, though a few, notably "The Blackjack Bargainer," take place in North Carolina.

In 1907, he was married a second time in Asheville to a North Carolina woman, an old friend of his boyhood days. His health declined, and after two years in New York, he journeyed to the North Carolina mountains in the fall of 1909. He returned to New York on a business trip and died there on June 5. He is buried in Riverside Cemetery, Asheville.

Among the many biographies is *Alias O. Henry* (1957) by Gerald Langford. Helpful, too, is *O. Henry in North Carolina* (1957) by Cathleen Pike.

"Let Me Feel Your Pulse," his last story, is said to be the only one O. Henry wrote with strong autobiographical overtones. It is true that he had been drinking heavily and that he found a way out of his troubles similar to that described in the story. The typical, much-admired surprise ending has here an unexpected slant: hints allow the reader to understand how matters will turn out, and only the narrator seems to be ignorant of the trick being played on him. "Let Me Feel Your Pulse" was written in 1910 at Weaverville, the mountain home town of his wife.

Let Me Feel Your Pulse

O. HENRY

SO I WENT to a doctor.

"How long has it been since you took any alcohol into your system?" he asked.

Turning my head sidewise, I answered, "Oh, quite awhile."

He was a young doctor, somewhere between twenty and forty. He wore heliotrope socks, but he looked like Napoleon. I liked him immensely.

"Now," said he, "I am going to show you the effect of alcohol upon your circulation." I think it was "circulation" he said; though it may have been "advertising."

He bared my left arm to the elbow, brought out a bottle of whiskey, and gave me a drink. He began to look more like Napoleon. I began to like him better.

Then he put a tight compress on my upper arm, stopped my pulse with his fingers, and squeezed a rubber bulb connected with an apparatus on a stand that looked like a thermometer. The mercury jumped up and down without seeming to stop anywhere; but the doctor said it registered two hundred and thirty-seven or one hundred and sixty-five or some such number.

"Now," said he, "you see what alcohol does to the blood-pressure."

From *Sixes and Sevens* by O. Henry. Copyright, 1910, by Doubleday & Co., Inc. Reprinted by permission of the publisher.

"It's marvelous," said I, "but do you think it a sufficient test? Have one on me, and let's try the other arm." But, no!

Then he grasped my hand. I thought I was doomed and he was saying good-bye. But all he wanted to do was to jab a needle into the end of a finger and compare the red drop with a lot of fifty-cent poker chips that he had fastened to a card.

"It's the hæmoglobin test," he explained. "The color of your blood is wrong."

"Well," said I, "I know it should be blue; but this is a country of mix-ups. Some of my ancestors were cavaliers; but they got thick with some people on Nantucket Island, so——"

"I mean," said the doctor, "that the shade of red is too light."

"Oh," I said, "it's a case of matching instead of matches."

The doctor then pounded me severely in the region of the chest. When he did that I don't know whether he reminded me most of Napoleon or Battling or Lord Nelson. Then he looked grave and mentioned a string of grievances that the flesh is heir to—mostly ending in "itis." I immediately paid him fifteen dollars on account.

"Is or are it or some or any of them necessarily fatal?" I asked. I thought my connection with the matter justified my manifesting a certain amount of interest.

"All of them," he answered, cheerfully. "But their progress may be arrested. With care and proper continuous treatment you may live to be eighty-five or ninety."

I began to think of the doctor's bill. "Eighty-five would be sufficient, I am sure," was my comment. I paid him ten dollars more on account.

"The first thing to do," he said, with renewed animation, "is to find a sanitarium where you will get a complete rest for a while, and allow your nerves to get into a better

condition. I myself will go with you and select a suitable
one."

So he took me to a mad-house in the Catskills. It was on
a bare mountain frequented only by infrequent frequenters.
You could see nothing but stones and boulders, some
patches of snow, and scattered pine trees. The young physician in charge was most agreeable. He gave me a stimulant without applying a compress to the arm. It was
luncheon time, and we were invited to partake. There were
about twenty inmates at little tables in the dining room.
The young physician in charge came to our table and said:
"It is a custom with our guests not to regard themselves as
patients, but merely as tired ladies and gentlemen taking
a rest. Whatever slight maladies they may have are never
alluded to in conversation."

My doctor called loudly to a waitress to bring some
phosphoglycerate of lime hash, dog-bread, bromo-seltzer
pancakes, and nux vomica tea for my repast. Then a sound
arose like a sudden wind storm among pine trees. It was
produced by every guest in the room whispering loudly,
"Neurasthenia!"—except one man with a nose, whom I
distinctly heard say, "Chronic alcoholism." I hope to meet
him again. The physician in charge turned and walked
away.

An hour or so after luncheon he conducted us to the
workshop—say fifty yards from the house. Thither the
guests had been conducted by the physician in charge's
understudy and sponge-holder—a man with feet and a blue
sweater. He was so tall that I was not sure he had a face;
but the Armour Packing Company would have been delighted with his hands.

"Here," said the physician in charge, "our guests find
relaxation from past mental worries by devoting themselves
to physical labor—recreation, in reality."

There were turning-lathes, carpenters' outfits, clay-model-ing tools, spinning-wheels, weaving-frames, treadmills, bass drums, enlarged-crayon-portrait apparatuses, blacksmith forges, and everything, seemingly, that could interest the paying lunatic guests of a first-rate sanitarium.

"The lady making mud pies in the corner," whispered the physician in charge, "is no other than—Lulu Lulington, the authoress of the novel entitled 'Why Love Loves.' What she is doing now is simply to rest her mind after performing that piece of work."

I had seen the book. "Why doesn't she do it by writing another one instead?" I asked.

As you see, I wasn't as far gone as they thought I was.

"The gentleman pouring water through the funnel," continued the physician in charge, "is a Wall Street broker broken down from overwork."

I buttoned my coat.

Others he pointed out were architects playing with Noah's arks, ministers reading Darwin's "Theory of Evolution," lawyers sawing wood, tired-out society ladies talking Ibsen to the blue-sweatered sponge-holder, a neurotic millionaire lying asleep on the floor, and a prominent artist drawing a little red wagon around the room.

"You look pretty strong," said the physician in charge of me. "I think the best mental relaxation for you would be throwing small boulders over the mountainside and then bringing them up again."

I was a hundred yards away before my doctor overtook me.

"What's the matter?" he asked.

"The matter is," said I, "that there are no aeroplanes handy. So I am going to merrily and hastily jog the foot-pathway to yon station and catch the first unlimited-soft-coal express back to town."

"Well," said the doctor, "perhaps you are right. This

seems hardly the suitable place for you. But what you need is rest—absolute rest and exercise."

That night I went to a hotel in the city, and said to the clerk: "What I need is absolute rest and exercise. Can you give me a room with one of those tall folding beds in it, and a relay of bellboys to work it up and down while I rest?"

The clerk rubbed a speck off one of his finger nails and glanced sidewise at a tall man in a white hat sitting in the lobby. That man came over and asked me politely if I had seen the shrubbery at the west entrance. I had not, so he showed it to me and then looked me over.

"I thought you had 'em," he said, not unkindly, "but I guess you're all right. You'd better go see a doctor, old man."

A week afterward my doctor tested my blood pressure again without the preliminary stimulant. He looked to me a little less like Napoleon. And his socks were of a shade of tan that did not appeal to me.

"What you need," he decided, "is sea air and companionship."

"Would a mermaid—" I began; but he slipped on his professional manner.

"I myself," he said, "will take you to the Hotel Bonair off the coast of Long Island and see that you get in good shape. It is a quiet, comfortable resort where you will soon recuperate."

The Hotel Bonair proved to be a nine-hundred-room fashionable hostelry on an island off the main shore. Everybody who did not dress for dinner was shoved into a side dining room and given only a terrapin and champagne table d'hôte. The bay was a great stamping ground for wealthy yachtsmen. The *Corsair* anchored there the day we arrived. I saw Mr. Morgan standing on deck eating a cheese sandwich and gazing longingly at the hotel. Still, it was a very

inexpensive place. Nobody could afford to pay their prices.
When you went away you simply left your baggage, stole
a skiff, and beat it for the mainland in the night.

When I had been there one day I got a pad of mono-
grammed telegraph blanks at the clerk's desk and began
to wire to all my friends for get-away money. My doctor
and I played one game of croquet on the golf links and went
to sleep on the lawn.

When we got back to town a thought seemed to occur to
him suddenly. "By the way," he asked, "how do you feel?"

"Relieved of very much," I replied.

Now a consulting physician is different. He isn't exactly
sure whether he is to be paid or not, and this uncertainty
insures you either the most careful or the most careless
attention. My doctor took me to see a consulting physician.
He made a poor guess and gave me careful attention. I
liked him immensely. He put me through some coördina-
tion exercises.

"Have you a pain in the back of your head?" he asked.
I told him I had not.

"Shut your eyes," he ordered, "put your feet close together, and jump backward as far as you can."

I always was a good backward jumper with my eyes
shut, so I obeyed. My head struck the edge of the bathroom door, which had been left open and was only three
feet away. The doctor was very sorry. He had overlooked
the fact that the door was open. He closed it.

"Now touch your nose with your right forefinger," he
said.

"Where is it?" I asked.

"On your face," said he.

"I mean my right forefinger," I explained.

"Oh, excuse me," said he. He reopened the bathroom
door, and I took my finger out of the crack of it. After I
had performed the marvelous digito-nasal feat I said:

"I do not wish to deceive you as to symptoms, Doctor; I really have something like a pain in the back of my head." He ignored the symptom and examined my heart carefully with a latest-popular-air-penny-in-the-slot ear-trumpet. I felt like a ballad. "Now," he said, "gallop like a horse for about five minutes around the room."

I gave the best imitation I could of a disqualified Percheron being led out of Madison Square Garden. Then, without dropping in a penny, he listened to my chest again.

"No glanders in our family, Doc," I said.

The consulting physician held up his forefinger within three inches of my nose. "Look at my finger," he commanded.

"Did you ever try Pears'—" I began; but he went on with his test rapidly.

"Now look across the bay. At my finger. Across the bay. At my finger. At my finger. Across the bay. Across the bay. At my finger. Across the bay." This for about three minutes.

He explained that this was a test of the action of the brain. It seemed easy to me. I never once mistook his finger for the bay. I'll bet that if he had used the phrases: "Gaze, as it were, unpreoccupied, outward—or rather laterally—in the direction of the horizon, underlaid, so to speak, with the adjacent fluid inlet," and "Now, returning —or rather, in a manner, withdrawing your attention, bestow it upon my upraised digit"—I'll bet, I say, that Henry James himself could have passed the examination.

After asking me if I had ever had a grand uncle with curvature of the spine or a cousin with swelled ankles, the two doctors retired to the bathroom and sat on the edge of the bath tub for their consultation. I ate an apple, and gazed first at my finger and then across the bay.

The doctors came out looking grave. More: they looked tombstones and Tennessee-papers-please-copy. They wrote

out a diet list to which I was to be restricted. It had everything that I had ever heard of to eat on it, except snails.
And I never eat a snail unless it overtakes me and bites
me first.

"You must follow this diet strictly," said the doctors.

"I'd follow it a mile if I could get one-tenth of what's on
it," I answered.

"Of next importance," they went on, "is outdoor air
and exercise. And here is a prescription that will be of
great benefit to you."

Then all of us took something. They took their hats, and
I took my departure.

I went to a druggist and showed him the prescription.

"It will be $2.87 for an ounce bottle," he said.

"Will you give me a piece of your wrapping cord?" said I.

I made a hole in the prescription, ran the cord through
it, tied it around my neck, and tucked it inside. All of us
have a little superstition, and mine runs to a confidence in
amulets.

Of course there was nothing the matter with me, but I
was very ill. I couldn't work, sleep, eat, or bowl. The only
way I could get any sympathy was to go without shaving
for four days. Even then somebody would say: "Old man,
you look as hardy as a pine knot. Been up for a jaunt in
the Maine woods, eh?"

Then, suddenly, I remembered that I must have outdoor
air and exercise. So I went down South to John's. John is
an approximate relative by verdict of a preacher standing
with a little book in his hands in a bower of chrysanthe-
mums while a hundred thousand people looked on. John
has a country house seven miles from Pineville. It is at
an altitude and on the Blue Ridge Mountains in a state too
dignified to be dragged into this controversy. John is mica,
which is more valuable and clearer than gold.

He met me at Pineville, and we took the trolley car to his

home. It is a big, neighborless cottage on a hill surrounded by a hundred mountains. We got off at his little private station, where John's family and Amaryllis met and greeted us. Amaryllis looked at me a trifle anxiously.

A rabbit came bounding across the hill between us and the house. I threw down my suit-case and pursued it hotfoot. After I had run twenty yards and seen it disappear, I sat down on the grass and wept disconsolately.

"I can't catch a rabbit any more," I sobbed. "I'm of no further use in the world. I may as well be dead."

"Oh, what is it—what is it, Brother John?" I heard Amaryllis say.

"Nerves a little unstrung," said John, in his calm way. "Don't worry. Get up, you rabbit-chaser, and come on to the house before the biscuits get cold." It was about twilight, and the mountains came up nobly to Miss Murfree's descriptions of them.

Soon after dinner I announced that I believed I could sleep for a year or two, including legal holidays. So I was shown to a room as big and cool as a flower garden, where there was a bed as broad as a lawn. Soon afterward the remainder of the household retired, and then there fell upon the land a silence.

I had not heard a silence before in years. It was absolute. I raised myself on my elbow and listened to it. Sleep! I thought that if I only could hear a star twinkle or a blade of grass sharpen itself I could compose myself to rest. I thought once that I heard a sound like the sail of a cat-boat flapping as it veered about in a breeze, but I decided that it was probably only a tack in the carpet. Still I listened.

Suddenly some belated little bird alighted upon the window-sill, and, in what he no doubt considered sleepy tones, enunciated the noise generally translated as "cheep!"

I leaped into the air.

"Hey! what's the matter down there?" called John from his room above mine.

"Oh, nothing," I answered, "except that I accidentally bumped my head against the ceiling."

The next morning I went out on the porch and looked at the mountains. There were forty-seven of them in sight. I shuddered, went into the big hall sitting room of the house, selected "Pancoast's Family Practice of Medicine" from a bookcase, and began to read. John came in, took the book away from me, and led me outside. He has a farm of three hundred acres furnished with the usual complement of barns, mules, peasantry, and harrows with three front teeth broken off. I had seen such things in my childhood, and my heart began to sink.

Then John spoke of alfalfa, and I brightened at once.

"Oh, yes," said I, "wasn't she in the chorus of—let's see—"

"Green, you know," said John, "and tender, and you plow it under after the first season."

"I know," said I, "and the grass grows over her."

"Right," said John. "You know something about farming, after all."

"I know something of some farmers," said I, "and a sure scythe will mow them down some day."

On the way back to the house a beautiful and inexplicable creature walked across our path. I stopped, irresistibly fascinated, gazing at it. John waited patiently, smoking his cigarette. He is a modern farmer. After ten minutes he said: "Are you going to stand there looking at that chicken all day? Breakfast is nearly ready."

"A chicken?" said I.

"A white Orpington hen, if you want to particularize."

"A white Orpington hen?" I repeated, with intense interest. The fowl walked slowly away with graceful dignity, and I followed like a child after the Pied Piper. Five

minutes more were allowed me by John, and then he took
me by the sleeve and conducted me to breakfast.

After I had been there a week I began to grow alarmed.
I was sleeping and eating well and actually beginning to
enjoy life. For a man in my desperate condition that would
never do. So I sneaked down to the trolley-car station, took
the car for Pineville, and went to see one of the best
physicians in town. By this time I knew exactly what to
do when I needed medical treatment. I hung my hat on
the back of a chair, and said rapidly:

"Doctor, I have cirrhosis of the heart, indurated arteries,
neurasthenia, neuritis, acute indigestion, and convalescence.
I am going to live on a strict diet. I shall also take a tepid
bath at night and a cold one in the morning. I shall en-
deavor to be cheerful, and fix my mind on pleasant subjects.
In the way of drugs I intend to take a phosphorus pill
three times a day, preferably after meals, and a tonic composed of the tinctures of gentian, cinchona, calisaya, and
cardamon compound. Into each teaspoonful of this I
shall mix tincture of nux vomica, beginning with one drop
and increasing it a drop each day until the maximum dose
is reached. I shall drop this with a medicine-dropper, which
can be procured at a trifling cost at any pharmacy. Good-
morning."

I took my hat and walked out. After I had closed the
door I remembered something that I had forgotten to say.
I opened it again. The doctor had not moved from where he
had been sitting, but he gave a slightly nervous start when
he saw me again.

"I forgot to mention," said I, "that I shall also take
absolute rest and exercise."

After this consultation I felt much better. The reëstab-
lishing in my mind of the fact that I was hopelessly ill gave
me so much satisfaction that I almost became gloomy
again. There is nothing more alarming to a neurasthenic

than to feel himself growing well and cheerful.

John looked after me carefully. After I had evinced so much interest in his white Orpington chicken he tried his best to divert my mind, and was particular to lock his hen house of nights. Gradually the tonic mountain air, the wholesome food, and the daily walks among the hills so alleviated my malady that I became utterly wretched and despondent. I heard of a country doctor who lived in the mountains near-by. I went to see him and told him the whole story. He was a gray-bearded man with clear, blue, wrinkled eyes, in a home-made suit of gray jeans.

In order to save time I diagnosed my case, touched my nose with my right forefinger, struck myself below the knee to make my foot kick, sounded my chest, stuck out my tongue, and asked him the price of cemetery lots in Pineville.

He lit his pipe and looked at me for about three minutes. "Brother," he said, after a while, "you are in a mighty bad way. There's a chance for you to pull through, but it's a mighty slim one."

"What can it be?" I asked, eagerly. "I have taken arsenic and gold, phosphorus, exercise, nux vomica, hydrotherapeutic baths, rest, excitement, codeine, and aromatic spirits of ammonia. Is there anything left in the pharmacopœia?"

"Somewhere in these mountains," said the doctor, "there's a plant growing—a flowering plant that'll cure you, and it's about the only thing that will. It's of a kind that's as old as the world; but of late it's powerful scarce and hard to find. You and I will have to hunt it up. I'm not engaged in active practice now: I'm getting along in years; but I'll take your case. You'll have to come every day in the afternoon and help me hunt for this plant till we find it. The city doctors may know a lot about new scientific things, but they don't know much about the cures that nature carries around in her saddle bags."

So every day the old doctor and I hunted the cure-all plant among the mountains and valleys of the Blue Ridge. Together we toiled up steep heights so slippery with fallen autumn leaves that we had to catch every sapling and branch within our reach to save us from falling. We waded through gorges and chasms, breast-deep with laurel and ferns; we followed the banks of mountain streams for miles, we wound our way like Indians through brakes of pine— road side, hill side, river side, mountain side we explored in our search for the miraculous plant.

As the old doctor said, it must have grown scarce and hard to find. But we followed our quest. Day by day we plumbed the valleys, scaled the heights, and tramped the plateaus in search of the miraculous plant. Mountain-bred, he never seemed to tire. I often reached home too fatigued to do anything except fall into bed and sleep until morning. This we kept up for a month.

One evening after I had returned from a six-mile tramp with the old doctor, Amaryllis and I took a little walk under the trees near the road. We looked at the mountains drawing their royal-purple robes around them for their night's repose.

"I'm glad you're well again," she said. "When you first came you frightened me. I thought you were really ill."

"Well again!" I almost shrieked. "Do you know that I have only one chance in a thousand to live?"

Amaryllis looked at me in surprise. "Why," said she, "you are as strong as one of the plow-mules, and sleep ten or twelve hours every night, and you are eating us out of house and home. What more do you want?"

"I tell you," said I, "that unless we find the magic—that is, the plant we are looking for—in time, nothing can save me. The doctor tells me so."

"What doctor?"

"Doctor Tatum—the old doctor who lives halfway up Black Oak Mountain. Do you know him?"

"I have known him since I was able to talk. And is that where you go every day—is it he who takes you on these long walks and climbs that have brought back your health and strength? God bless the old doctor."

Just then the old doctor himself drove slowly down the road in his rickety old buggy. I waved my hand at him and shouted that I would be on hand the next day at the usual time. He stopped his horse and called to Amaryllis to come out to him. They talked for five minutes while I waited. Then the old doctor drove on.

When we got to the house Amaryllis lugged out an encyclopædia and sought a word in it. "The doctor said," she told me, "that you needn't call any more as a patient, but he'd be glad to see you any time as a friend. And then he told me to look up my name in the encyclopædia and tell you what it means. It seems to be the name of a genus of flowering plants, and also the name of a country girl in Theocritus and Virgil. What do you suppose the doctor meant by that?"

"I know what he meant," said I. "I know now."

A word to a brother who may have come under the spell of the unquiet Lady Neurasthenia.

The formula was true. Even though gropingly at times, the physicians of the walled cities had put their fingers upon the specific medicament.

And so for the exercise one is referred to good Doctor Tatum on Black Oak Mountain—take the road to your right at the Methodist meeting house in the pine-grove.

Absolute rest and exercise!

What rest more remedial than to sit with Amaryllis in the shade, and, with a sixth sense, read the wordless Theocritan idyl of the gold-bannered blue mountains marching orderly into the dormitories of the night?

PAUL GREEN

PAUL GREEN was born near Lillington in Harnett County
on March 17, 1894. His parents were descendants of
God-fearing English and Highland Scotch pioneers who
had settled the Cape Fear River country. After graduating
from Buies Creek Academy in 1914, he taught school for
two years; then he entered the University of North Carolina.
His college career was interrupted by his enlistment in the
army during World War I, and he spent the better part of
two years in Belgium and northern France. Back in Chapel
Hill, he received an A.B. degree in 1921 and later went
to Cornell University for graduate study. He returned to
the University of North Carolina as teacher of philosophy.
Identified with the Carolina Playmakers, he was already
gaining fame as a writer of short plays.

In 1927, he was awarded the Pulitzer Prize for the best
American play of the year, *In Abraham's Bosom*. His other
full-length dramas are *The Field God* (1927), *Tread the
Green Grass* (1929), *The House of Connelly* (1931), *Roll
Sweet Chariot* (1934), *Shroud My Body Down* (1935),
The Enchanted Maze (1935), *Johnny Johnson* (1936),
Native Son (1941, with Richard Wright), and an adapta-
tion of Ibsen's *Peer Gynt* (1951). He has published two
novels, *The Laughing Pioneer* (1932) and *This Body the
Earth* (1935). His essays on art, the theater, education,
and democracy are included in *The Hawthorn Tree* (1943),
Forever Growing (1945), *Dramatic Heritage* (1953), and
Drama and the Weather (1958).

Paul Green is best known for his symphonic dramas—
historical plays given in huge outdoor theaters: *The Lost*

Colony (since 1937) at Manteo; *The Highland Call*
(1939) at Fayetteville and Buies Creek; *The Common
Glory* (1948) at Williamsburg; *Faith of Our Fathers*
(1950) at Washington, D.C.; *Wilderness Road* (1953)
at Berea, Kentucky; *The Founders* (1957) at Jamestown;
and *The Confederacy* (1958) at Virginia Beach. There
have been several others.

In 1928, he was granted a Guggenheim Fellowship and
traveled in Germany and England for a year studying the
theater. He received a Litt.D. from Western Reverve University in 1941. In 1952, he was the first winner of the
Sir Walter Raleigh Award, given annually since then for
outstanding work in fiction by a North Carolinian. A
helpful biographical study is *Paul Green of Chapel Hill*
(1951) by Agatha Boyd Adams.

Three volumes of short stories by Paul Green have been
published: *Wide Fields* (1928); *Salvation of a String*
(1946), from which "Fine Wagon" is taken; and *Dog on
the Sun* (1949). "Fine Wagon," whose Chapel Hill setting
few readers will fail to identify, is an episode of the Depression years (it was first published in 1934). A sequel
to the story, "Sun Go Down," appeared in *Dog on the Sun*.

Fine Wagon

PAUL GREEN

1.

THE GREAT FOREST RANG as if with the clamor of
iron bells from the belfries of the trees. Standing on
the bank of the deep inky creek, Bobo strained with all his
might at his fishing pole. Down in the depths somewhere a
catfish big as a hog was hung on his hook and gradually
pulling him in. Lower and lower bent the pole and inch
by inch his bare feet slid in the slick mud. He felt himself
jerked headlong toward the sickish black water, when there
came a voice calling and a sudden soft breath blowing in
his ear. Whiff! And the great forest wheeled and turned
over, rushed toward him, by him. The bells were silent, and
in the flash of an eye the stream was gone and so were the
fishing pole and the fish.

"Wake up, son, wake up—it's already day." And he
felt a gentle hand diddling with his shoulder.—Who—
what?—Mammy. But he must sleep, sleep a little more.
And that fish—that great big fish!

"Wake up, sonny, your pa's done fed the mules."

He grunted and squirmed about under the quilts and
then sat up. Rubbing his scrawny dark fists in his eyes,

From *Salvation on a String* by Paul Green, published by Harper &
Brothers. Copyright, 1934, by Paul Green. By permission of the
author.

he blinked at the little brown woman who stood by the bed holding a wiggling lamp in her hand.

"Please, Mammy—please'm," he said. And then his eyelids drooped shut, he gaped and sank back slowly on the bed. Sweet sleepiness engulfed him instantly. Once more the edge of the great shadowy forest came moving toward him with its cool delicious shade, and once more he heard the lofty booming of the bells.

"Huh, so after all your proud bragging you done forgot you's going with your pappy?" the voice said.

He heard the words afar off. They meant nothing to him, they were empty sounds. But only for a moment. For then remembrance flooded into his mind and he sat quickly up. Today was the day and he was about to forget it. A sharp little rush of joy tickled somewhere in his chest behind his breastbone. He hopped out of bed as if a red fire coal had been dropped inside his drawers. Cramming his shirt-tail down in his trousers, he followed his mother into the kitchen. He hesitated before the basin of waiting chilly water, and then roaching up his shoulders, he soused his face down in his dipping cupped hands. "Whee—oo-oo," he chattered. Already Mammy was at the stove taking the sweet fried fat back out of the pan. And now heavy brogan shoes came clomp-clomping along the porch, and Pappy entered—a tall grave black man.

"Morning, Bobo."

"Morning, Pappy," he answered, his scrubbed face coming out of the ragged bundle of towel.

"You done got that sleepy out'n them eyes—unh?"

"Yessuh, I'se all loud awake."

"That's a boy."

"When's we going, Pappy?"

"Mmn—now not too big a swivet. We got to swallow a bite of grub fust." And Pappy sat down to the table with his hat on, as he did when he had a pushing job ahead.

Mammy hurried the cornbread from the stove and put it in front of him.

"Come on, Bobo," she said, but Bobo had already dived under her arm and onto his bench. She stood still at the end of the table with the dishcloth in her hand ready to get the coffee pot while Pappy bent his head over. "Make us thankful for what we're 'bout to receive," he mumbled, "and bless us all for time to come."

"Amen," Bobo whispered fervently.

Nobody in the world could cook like Mammy. How good that fat back tasted, and the molasses and the bread! And then—what's that? He couldn't believe his eyes, as she came and set a cup of steaming coffee by his plate.

"Seeing how cold it is and you going off to work same like a man," she said.

His eyes were brimming with thanks as he poured his saucer full of the dark stuff—dark as the water in that creek where the big fish stayed. Then he blew on it with a great oof the way Pappy did to cool it.

"Warm you up inside?" his father asked.

"It do that," he answered gulping it down with the noise of a small horse drinking water.

He gobbled his bread and meat, trying to keep up with Pappy, and in a few minutes breakfast was over. Mammy took Pappy's extra old coat from the wall and brought it to him.

"It'll be mightly cold riding out on that wagon, son," she said as she slipped it on him.

"Come on," said Pappy, and they hurried out of the house toward the barn. There in the gray morning light their fine wagon stood with its long tongue hanging out. It wasn't new like a white folks' wagon, but it was mighty nice just the same. He and Pappy had worked on it hard the day before, spiking up the loose spokes and driving wedges under the tires to tighten them for the heavy

loads they'd have to haul. And with the new pine board seat
laid across the body it stood waiting to ride.

Pappy had bought the wagon on a credit at a sale a few
days before for eight dollars. It would come in handy
hauling stuff for the professors up in town, and in a week
or two they would make enough to pay for it. After that
they'd keep on hauling. Pappy had needed a wagon.
When he came home a few weeks before bringing old
blind Mary to match with the other mule Suke, he had
set his mind on something to hitch both of them to.
He had traded a dog and gun and two or three dollars for
old Mary, and it'd take a lot of hauling to get the money
together to pay for the wagon. But shucks, Pappy was
stepping on in the world, he was smart. Didn't Mammy say
so yesterday at supper—that there weren't nobody smart
like him. And she had kissed Pappy, feeling fine about
how things were going.

Last night Pappy had said, "Honey, I got me a job
right off the bat. 'Fessor up there in town met me on the
street today and said he had some wood to haul down
where he's gonna build his chillun's swimming pool and
could I haul it. 'Could I do it?' I says, 'Can't nobody do it
better. I got me a fine wagon and a first-class team.' That's
the way it goes in this world. You get ready for the job
and the job gets ready for you. I says, 'I got a boy Bobo
growing like a weed, and all muscling up. Me and him
both'll be back heah, suh, tomorrow.' "

These things ran through Bobo's mind as he padded
along toward the barn trying to keep up with his father's
long stride.

"Yessuh, put me at a stick of wood and I'll tote my end,"
he said out loud.

"Huh, what's that?" Pappy asked, looking down at him
but never slackening his pace.

"I mean—mean I'se gonna sho' work hard."

And Pappy looked out toward the glad morning star, laughed a great laugh and patted him on the shoulder.

"How much that man gonna pay me, Pappy?" he inquired as they slid open the stable door.

"I bet a whole ten cents, that's what you'd better charge him."

Ten cents! And there'd be other ten centses—nearly every day there would, for they would be so good at hauling that all the 'fessors would be asking them to do jobs. Ten cents a day! His little skinny hand slid down into his pocket as if he already expected to find a piece of hard round money there. And once more, as had happened several times during the last day and night, the bright picture of a new fishing hook and line gleamed for an instant in his mind. But he was cunning, he'd not mention that yet. But he knew where they could be got though. Up there in town in the hardware store—all with red corks and plenty of good lead sinkers.

"You try your stuff at bridling Suke," Pappy said, "this here new mule is kinder—er—mulish."

And pridefully Bobo opened the door and went in with the bridle in his hand. Old Suke stood with her head down as if expecting him, and slick as that old Syrian peddler he put the bridle on her and led her from the stall. Then the business of harnessing and getting the bellyband and the hamestring tight. It didn't matter if Pappy did come around and retie the hamestring when he'd just managed to pull it together, for the hames were fitting snug in the collar and Pappy said that was doing fine as a fiddle.

"Them's stout hamestrings too," said Pappy, "Joe Ed let me cut 'em from that bull hide of hisn."

"I bet they'll hold—hold near'bout a lion," Bobo spoke up.

"Or a' elevint," said Pappy.

"Or a steam engine," Bobo chuckled.

"Yeh, they'll hold—hold till the cows come home. And that britchin', that's a real piece of scrimptious handiwork." And Pappy surveyed the old ragged strips of bed ticking he had sewed together to help finish off the harness.

By this time the light of dawn had spread upward from the east across the sky, wide and spangled like a great peacock's tail, and Bobo wasn't afraid at all as he went into the loft and threw down two bundles of fodder for the mules' dinner. And now Mammy came out of the house bringing lunch wrapped up in a paper for her two menfolks. So everything was ready at last and not a bit too soon, for the smiling face of the sun was already peeping up over the edge of the world.

"You all be smart," Mammy called out as they climbed up into the wagon and sat down on the plank seat side by side. Pappy thudded his rope whip through the air with a great flourish, and off they went.

"We'll be home right around sundown!" he shouted back, "and me'n Bobo wants us a real bait of that fat side meat all fried and ready!"

"We'll be home at sundown!" Bobo repeated loudly, sticking his hand up out of his father's old coat sleeve in a little crooked gesture, half a wave and half a salute. He had seen the white boys stick their hands up like that at the college campus. And Mammy waved back at him, standing there by the gate with the new sun shining in her face.

2.

They drove on down the dead-weeded lane and soon came into the high road. To the right and to the left stretched the sparkly frosty fields, and yonder in the distance the sun-fired church spires of the white man's town stuck up above the wooded hill. The steel wagon tires made little harsh gritty sounds as they drove along.

"Don't this wagon run good, Bobo?"

"It sho' do, Pappy."

"It orter—I was up and give it a good greasing whilst you was snoozing."

"You'da woke me up I'da been there and holp you."

"Then tiahs cries a little, but they's tight as a drum, ain't they?"

"Tight as Dick's hatband. We sho' put the fixing on 'em, Pappy."

"Yeh, didn't we?"

"Git up there, Suke—you, Mary," Bobo chirped in his manful way. They were now mounting the hill, the air was sharp and biting, and Bobo had to clamp his jaws tight, his teeth were chattering so. But he'd never let Pappy know. They rode on in silence awhile. Bobo could see from Pappy's thoughtful face he was thinking of something. Maybe planning out the big work ahead and he didn't want to talk. A gang of robins flew across over his head going north. He watched them till they were little jumping eye specks low in the sky. It would turn warm soon— today, tomorrow. It always turned warm after a heavy frost like this one. The robins knew—they were smart like people. And they were going north.

Soon they were rolling along the asphalt street of the town, and for the moment Bobo feared the wagon wheels made too loud a sound. Every shop was closed, every place deserted. It was too early for the white folks to be up. They were different from colored folks who had to be out to get a soon start. Already some of the women cooks were on their way to work—their arms in front of them, their elbows gripped in the palm of each enclosing hand. It was cold and they walked in a hurry. Their shoes made a clock-clock on the hard sidewalks.

"Ain't everything quiet—like somebody asleep?" Bobo half whispered.

"Yeh," Pappy replied, "sleep. That's what's the matter with people, Bobo. They all sleep too much. Now look at you and me—we's up and doing."

"That's right," Bobo agreed soberly. And Pappy continued with feeling in his voice—"By the time other folks start to work we done done half a day. That's what gets a man ahead. He that rises 'fore the sun is the man what gets the most work done."

And now they were passing by the big gray granite building that was the great bank where the white men went in and out during the day, hauling in their money and putting it away. Bushels and bushels of yellow dollars and white dollars and bales of greenbacks they kept stored away there. That was where all the money came from to buy the things that people needed. That's where the money would come from to pay him and Pappy for their hauling. And to the left there was the hardware store where they kept all kinds of blades, and knives and hooks—fishhooks. Well, when spring came again——

Next, down there by the drugstore, was the blue and white sign of the telegraph office shut up and waiting. In a few hours it would be open, and folks would go in there and write things on a slip of paper, and a man would tap on a little handle, and them taps would be words that went out along wires and 'way to New York and maybe across the world through a pipe under the sea. Lord, Lord, weren't people smart!—Smart. But he was smart too, today he was.

Bobo had always been frightened by the big buildings and goings on when he'd come up town to buy five cents worth of snuff or ten cents worth of fat back for Mammy and Pappy. But this morning he looked at the houses and stores with bolder eyes. He felt more at home among them today. He was a workingman now, and nobody ever bothered a workingman—not even big boys that liked to

pick on you and throw your cap up and lodge it in a tree.
He had something to do now, work for the white folks,
and that made everything right. The white folks wouldn't
allow no foolishness with any of their help.

In a few minutes they had gone through the village to the
outer edge and came where a little alley turned off from the
main street and down a hill into a new development.

"Is we 'bout got there yit, Pappy?"

"Yeh, right down yonder is where 'Fessor lives," and
he pulled the heads of the mules into the alley. "He's
got a lot of wood cut 'way down below his house there and
he wants it hauled up to put in his cellar."

"Looks like a sort of rough place down there," Bobo
said, straining his eyes ahead of him.

"Sho', but we's the men to get that wood up and out'n it,
ain't we, Bobo?"

"Is that," Bobo spoke up strongly and briskly.

"And he's going to pay us a dollar a cawd to move it. He
said he had ten or twelve cawds down there."

"How much is a cawd, Pappy?"

And now they were turning off to the left down a little
rock path that skirted around and away from the professor's
house. What a house that was, all white and pretty shining
there among the bare trees. And how many chimneys did
it have, and the windows with green blinds! Bobo almost
caught his breath—there on the porch sat a big red bicycle.
That must belong to one of the chillun, but he didn't mind
how many bicycles the chillun had now 'cause some of these
days he would—that too maybe—not a new one—no—no
—just an old one.

"Well a cawd of wood is a pile 'bout ten feet long and as
high as your head and you get a dollar for moving it," said
Pappy. "Yeh, ten or twelve of 'em. I bet we near'bout
will move six or eight of them cawds today, and that's six
or eight dollars."

"Look out there, Pappy!"

"Sho," his father gravely replied as he pulled on the plow line reins and stopped the mules, for the wagon was going down the hill and almost pushing the collars up over their heads. "I better tighten up them britchin' strops a little bit," he said. Holding to the lines, he climbed down and scotched the wheel with a rock. In a few minutes he had tightened the straps of bed ticking and was ready to go.

"Does you think you mought drive some?"

"Lemme," Bobo answered eagerly.

Handing over the reins, Pappy got behind the wagon and held it back as the mules moved down the hill. What a strong man Pappy was there pulling on the coupling pole like as if it had been the wagon's tail, and the mules had to push a little bit against the collar now that he was holding back so sharp.

3.

They finally got safely down to the little wooded hollow where the firewood was piled in great heaps, and they did no damage at all other than tearing off a patch of bark from a sugar-maple tree with the wagon hub. After much backing and sliding the rear end of the wagon around, by pushing and jerking on the coupling pole, they got set near a pile of wood and began to load it. It was a fine mixture of oak and pine cut in the proper lengths for the professor's fireplace, and Bobo liked to work at it, it looked so nice. Already he could feel how it would pop and burn, making a warm blaze to keep the chillun snug at night—there with their studying and their books and playing with their toys. He heaved piece after piece up into the open body trying to match his father. Talk about being smart— huh, with a few days of this stuff he'd put a muscle in his arm like a big mice running under his skin.

"All right," Pappy called, "try the end of that thing."

And Bobo took hold of the big black log of solid hickory
all ready to show his strength.   Then they heard a heavy
voice calling down from the house above, and looking up
Bobo saw a man wearing some kind of a gown standing by
the porch railing with his hair all rumpled.

"Who's that?" Bobo asked, letting go of the log and
stopping still as a post.

"S-sh, that's 'Fessor," Pappy said.

"Hey, what you doing down there?" the professor called.
And Pappy even as far away as he was pulled off his hat
quickly and bowed respectfully.

"Morning, 'Fessor," he answered in a low voice and
smiled same as if 'Fessor was right in front of him.

"Morning, suh," Bobo whispered pulling off his hat like-
wise.

"You make enough racket to wake up the neighborhood," said the figure on the porch.

"Yessuh," Pappy began and then fumbled a bit for his
words. "We thought we'd get an early start, suh."

"Well, you have that, it's just seven o'clock."

"Yessuh," and Pappy bowed again.

"Well, go on and be as quiet as possible. Haul the wood
around to the cellar door. I'll come out a little later."

"Yessuh," said Pappy again, still holding his hat in his
hand.

The figure on the porch looked around at the world,
yawned and retired into the house. Pappy and Bobo
waited a moment and then went on with their loading but
this time slow and careful-like, laying each piece of wood
gently in the wagon as if they were packing eggs.

"Why do he do that?" Bobo at last timidly inquired.

"Who you mean do what?" his father asked in a low
stern voice.

"The man up there in that big house—'Fessor."

Something seemed to be bothering Pappy, for he laid

down his piece of wood and looked at Bobo. "Why you ask that?"

"He kept looking around at the earf and up at the sky. It ain't going to snow, is it?"

"Oh," said Pappy as if he had been thinking of something else. And then he turned back to loading the wood again, and Bobo turned back also. But they decided to leave the big hickory log until the next load.

"Must be some kinder big man, ain't he," Bobo said presently, "living in that big house with all these woods around?"

"He's a 'fessor—teaches boys and gals. That's what 'fessor means." Pappy was silent a bit and then went on as if to himself, "He a mighty big man, and plenty of things to worry his mind. I heard some folks say he a big man," and now Pappy looked carefully about him.

"Huh?" said Bobo.

"Do what?" and Pappy seized a piece of oak and lifted it aloft.

"Yeh, do what, Pappy?"

"Don't ask so many questions. 'Fessor wants his wood hauled, he going to pay for it and we going to haul it. He a big man, he stand mighty high. I hear 'em say he writes books and play pieces and makes money enough—enough to burn." And surveying the pile of wood on the wagon, he added, "Looks like we 'bout got a load."

"What do he write about, Pappy?"

"Huh?"

" 'Fessor. Do he write tales like what Mammy read from a book that time?"

Pappy suddenly snickered and looked around at him in a way he didn't understand. Then he said, "Say he writes books and things about the colored folks."

"Sho'?"

"Sho'."

"And do the colored folks read 'em?"

"Shet your mouth and go 'way," Pappy answered. And snickering again, he went on. "White folks buy 'em and read 'em 'way off yonder. That's how he gets so much money to build his house and this heah swimming pool."

Now Pappy's hand went into his pocket, and Bobo watched it like a hawk. How long had he been waiting for that. This time it was true, he was going to do it. And sure enough Pappy pulled out a twist of homemade tobacco and bit off a big chew. Bobo edged up to him, waiting. For a moment the twist hesitated in Pappy's hand, and then he pinched off a big crumb and handed it to him. Bobo's skinny black paw darted out and seized it quick as a bat catching a bug. He stuck it in his mouth, rolled it around with his tongue and settled it over on one side making his jaw push out.

"Well I spec's we better start up the hill with this," and Pappy gathered up the reins. Suke and Mary who had stood drooping in their tracks suddenly woke as if a swarm of hornets had come up out of the ground at them. At Pappy's first word Suke gave a lunge forward and old blind Mary gave a lunge backward. "Get up there," he said, whopping Mary a blow on the rump with his whip. And now she sprang forward and Suke stood still. "You Suke!" he shouted. And quicker than hailing out of the sky the blows of the whip danced from one mule to the other. With a rattle and groaning of the wheels the heavy load began to move up the stony hill, and Pappy winked at Bobo as much as to say, "Ain't that pulling for you?"

As they swung around into the little road, the rear wheel hooked the sugar maple again. "Whoa," said Pappy, and just in time, for the coupling pole was bent like a sick cow's tail. The mules stopped, slumped down in their tracks and began to gnaw the dead scattering brown oak leaves that hung from a branch above their heads. Suddenly the creaky twanging of a screen door opening sounded across the hollow. Bobo looked out toward the house and saw the professor partly dressed standing on the porch again.

"There he is again, Pappy," he said, clutching his father's arm.

"Whoa," said Pappy softly to the mules.

"Heigh," said the professor, "didn't I tell you to keep quiet down there?"

Pappy's hat was already off in his hands again as he answered gently, "Yessuh, yessuh, we's just getting started, 'Fessor, and we"—Pappy looked down at Bobo as if asking him what to say.

"Haven't you hung your wheel in that maple tree?" the professor called, and Bobo saw him sliding his suspenders on his shoulders in a quick nervous jerk.

"He's coming down here, Pappy," he whispered.

"No suh," answered Pappy, "we just giving the mules a little breathing space, suh!"

"Well, see that you don't hurt anything." And once more the professor gave that look around him and turned back into the house.

After much prying and straining, they shoved the wheel loose from the tree, but not until another great gleaming gap of bark had been torn off in the process. When they had got the load farther up the hill, they scotched the wheels and went back. Pappy grabbed up a handful of dirt, smeared it over the scars so that no one would notice them, and Bobo ran about picking up the pieces of bark which he hid under the fallen leaves. Then they returned to the wagon and rode out onto the high ground. They drove proudly around back of the house and stopped near the cellar door.

"Look a-there, Pappy," Bobo whispered, horrified, pointing to one of the rear wheels. The wedges had fallen out

from under the tire and the old wheel stood all twisted
and crank-sided.

"Oh, that wheel'll stand up," said Pappy lightly, eyeing it.
"We'll get unloaded and then take a rock and drive that
tire back on." And climbing down, he wrapped the reins
tight around a front hub so the mules couldn't get at the
spirea bushes. Bobo passed the wood piece by piece to his
father who took it in armfuls quietly down into the cellar.
By this time the people in the house were astir, and Bobo
could see into the kitchen where Miss Sally the cook,
wearing some kind of fancy lace thing on her head, was
preparing breakfast. The smell of coffee and bacon came
out to him and he sniffed the air hungrily like a little dog.
And now the professor reappeared, his face clean-shaven
and his hair brushed. He came up to the wagon and looked
sharply at the load. Bobo tried to keep his mind on his
work handing down the wood to his father below, but he
could smell the clear pine-winey stuff the professor had used
for shaving. It filled the air, getting into his mouth and
nostrils so wonderful and strong that he could taste it.

"You'll never move that wood with such a turnout as
that," said the professor a little shortly and abruptly. "Look
at that wheel!"

"Yessuh," answered Pappy, as he laid his hat on the
ground beside him. "We'll fix that up in a minute, suh, the
wedge just fell out."

"Yes, I see it did. How are you, son?" His voice was
suddenly kind.

"Fine, thanky, suh," Bobo choked, almost speechless at
being addressed by the mighty man who lived in such a
house and had cooks and bicycles and automobiles and a
big furnace thing down there in the cellar that kept the
house warm.

"What's your name?" But now Bobo had lost his tongue.

"His name's Roosevelt, suh, but we calls him Bobo," answered Pappy gravely.

"H'm," said the professor softly. "And pile the wood straight back against the coal bin, will you?"

"Yessuh, we's fixing it up fine and dandy."

"And you can turn around down there next to the garage."

"Yessuh."

"What have you got in your mouth, son?" But Bobo could only stare at the professor with wide frightened eyes. "Don't you know chewing tobacco at your age will stunt you and keep you from growing up? Why, you're nothing but a baby." And once more the professor looked inquiringly about the world and up at the sky as he turned to re-enter the house.

4.

At last the load was stored away. And after much knocking and wedging down at the garage, the old wheel was strengthened, and they returned to the woods. But now it seemed the mules had decided not to do any more work that day. They kept twisting and turning about and sticking out their heads trying to get at the dead leaves. And when after a lot of trouble the wagon was finally backed and skewed around to another pile of wood, old Mary suddenly began to kick and lunge in the harness. Pappy seesawed on the reins and spanked her with the whip, and only after she had torn the britching off and burst one of his prized hamestrings did he finally get her quieted. All the while Bobo kept looking up toward the house expecting the professor to come charging out yelling at them. His heart was in his mouth, and he breathed again when at last the britching was mended, the hamestring retied and everything ready for the loading to begin. This time Pappy pitched the wood boldly into the wagon. The white folks were up and having breakfast, and the chatter of children was heard in the house. It didn't make any difference about noise now.

"We better not put such a heavy load on this time, had we, Pappy?"

"No, we ain't going to load up furder'n to the brim," he replied. And when they were ready once more, Pappy mounted briskly to the top of the seat and gave the word for the mules to go. Bobo started following behind, but old Mary acted like Satan was in her. She lunged forward, broke the hamestring again and ran straight out of the harness. And before Pappy could do a thing she had turned herself completely around and stood facing them with her white, sightless eyes as if laughing at them. Pappy suddenly lost his temper, and leaning far over with his rope whip, struck her a knock in the face. She reared up on her hind feet, and giving a great jump, left the harness behind her.

"Look out, look out, Pappy!" Bobo squealed in fright.

Pappy sprang down from the wagon, and with a strong hold upon the reins kept old Mary from getting entirely loose and running away. And now from the porch Bobo heard the dreaded voice again.

"What is the matter down there?"

Bobo didn't dare look up, for he knew the professor was coming down the hill. And in a minute there he stood beside them. Without a word Pappy dropped his whip on the ground and began straightening out the harness, and old Mary started greedily eating the dead leaves again. Suddenly the professor broke into a low laugh, and Bobo shook in his tracks. Somehow that laugh made him feel queer and trembly.

"Why in the name of mercy did you come trying to haul wood with such a mess as this?" the professor said.

"Yessuh, yessuh, but—" Pappy began.

"But nothing," the professor replied irritably and sharply,

and he took a step backward and surveyed the wagon and the team. Then his voice was kind again. "Here, son, you hold her head and let's see what we can do." The professor took off his fine coat and undid his white collar and set to work tying up the britching and rehitching the traces on old Mary.

"You sho' knows your stuff 'bout mules, 'Fessor," Pappy broke in presently, standing there pinching a dead twig in pieces between his fingers.

"I was raised on a farm."

"Do tell, suh."

"And I learned not to starve a mule to death and not to try to haul wood with the harness and wagon falling to bits," he added.

Pappy was silent.

Bobo stood looking on, every now and then spitting in noiseless excitement off to one side. He watched the deft movements of the professor as if mesmerized, and his gaze traveled to his father, who stood all shamed and humbled with his hat off. A queer lump rose up from his breast and stuck in his throat, and he swallowed quickly. Then he began sputtering, trying to get back the wad of tobacco that had gone down behind his breastbone. Gritting his teeth, he blinked and shook the tears out of his eyes, making little choking noises in his throat.

"What's the matter with you, son?" queried the professor, staring at him.

"Nothing," he answered quickly.

"You look sick. Have you had any breakfast?"

"Yessuh."

"Yessuh, we both et a big bait of good coffee and side meat 'fore we come off," Pappy said, coming over and timidly offering to help fasten the breast chains.

"You wait, I'll drive for you," said the professor. And clucking kindly to the mules, he jigged the reins gently.

The wagon slowly began to move. The professor walked along as the mules pulled on up the hill, and then blam, that old rear wheel struck a stone hidden by the leaves, and with a moaning groan it collapsed. And now once more the professor gave his queer laugh. He stood a moment looking at the reins in his hand, and then throwing them down took out some money and handed it to Pappy. "Here's a dollar, though you've not earned fifty cents," he said.

"Thanky suh, thanky suh," said Pappy, wiping his hand on his coat and humbly taking the money.

Without a word the professor turned and strode off toward the house. When he had gone a little distance, he turned and called, "Take your bundle of trash and clear out, I'll get somebody else to haul my wood! I'm sorry." With that he was gone.

Bobo stood looking at the ground. He could see the toes of his father's ragged shoes in front of him. Finally the shoes moved, and he heard his father say, "I reckon we just about as well quit and go home, son." And then he heard another voice saying—a woman's voice up on the porch—"What's the matter, Harvey?" and the professor replying, "The same old story, Nan—My God, these everlasting Negroes—poverty—trifling! Come on, let's finish our breakfast." And the door of the great house slammed shut like the jaws of a steel trap.

Pappy slowly began unloading the wood and laying it gently and heavily on the ground. All the while Bobo stood by without moving. His hands and arms hung down by his sides. He made no effort to help Pappy or do anything, but just stood there. "Come on, boy," Pappy said harshly.

5.

When they had finished unloading, Pappy tied a limb to the coupling pole under the axle, and the old broken wheel was loaded into the wagon body. Then they climbed up into the wagon. And the mules now, as if glad to be free of work, moved quickly up the hill and back into the main highway. Through the town they rode, the old limb dragging under the wheel-less end of the axle. People looked out from the houses as they passed, and a group of white school children playing tag on the sidewalk stopped and pointed at them. Bobo sat on the seat by Pappy looking straight ahead, and Pappy was looking straight ahead too. When they neared the business section of the village, Pappy turned off and went along a side street. And soon they came to the other edge of the town and descended the hill.

When they rode up near the yard gate, Mammy unbent from her sweeping by the door and stared at them.

"Why you back so early?" she called. "I ain't got a speck of dinner ready. Eyh, and look what's happened to your wagon wheel!"

"Shet your mouth, woman!" Pappy roared.

Jumping down from his seat, Bobo entered the yard.

"We don't want no dinner," he heard his father's rough brutal voice shout behind him.

"What's the matter, son?" Mammy said.

"Nothing, nothing," he gulped. And catching hold of her apron, he began to sob.

"Dry up!" Pappy yelled after him, but Bobo sobbed and sobbed.

"What's happened, son?" Mammy said, smoothing his woolly head with her hand.

"Nothing, nothing." he spluttered. And then a dreadful thumping and squealing began in the edge of the yard. But Bobo didn't look up. There was no need to. For even with his face buried in his mother's apron and his eyes stuck shut with tears he could see a skinny black man there by the woodpile beating old Mary with an ax helve, and that black man was Pappy—and he was ragged and pitiful and weak.

WILLIAM T. POLK

BACK IN 1930, William T. Polk was once described as a lawyer who spent his time "writing poetry, deeds, criticism, contracts, and stories." During the period in which he was mayor of Warrenton, the town claimed him as the only mayor in America who was also a professional writer of short stories.

William Tannahill Polk was born in Warrenton on March 12, 1896. He was the son of Tasker Polk, a prominent lawyer of the day, and grandnephew of President James K. Polk. At the University of North Carolina, from which he graduated in 1917, he was a member of Phi Beta Kappa and editor of *The Tar Heel*, student newspaper. During World War I, he enlisted as a private in the army and rose to second lieutenant. In 1919, he went to Columbia University to take courses in journalism, but the following year transferred to Harvard to study law. There he became a close friend of Thomas Wolfe. In 1922, he began practicing law in Warrenton. While on a world cruise in 1931, he met and later married Marion Campbell Gunn of Canada. There were two daughters.

Polk was the first chairman of the Citizens' Library Movement, an organization created to encourage the establishment of county libraries; in 1936, he served as president of the State Literary and Historical Association. As mayor of Warrenton, he sought to preserve the beauty of the historic town and instituted a city board of planning. On January 1, 1942, he left Warrenton and became associate editor of the *Greensboro Daily News*. He died suddenly in Washington, D.C., on October 16, 1955, and is buried in Warrenton.

Though he had contributed many poems, stories, and articles to various publications, his first book was *Southern Accent: From Uncle Remus to Oak Ridge* (1953), emphasizing two separate Souths—the old agricultural region and the new industrial one. He treated his subject with a careful mixture of the humorous and the serious.

Humorous and serious, too, were his short stories, most of them about the black-and-white, agrarian, aristocratic section of North Carolina where he grew up. They were posthumously published as *The Fallen Angel and Other Stories* (1956). Tom Wicker wrote that the stories possess "an evocative genius like that of the old storytellers who handed down history by the fireside to children who could not have remembered dates or understood documents but who would never forget the flavor and sound and the sense of legend."

First published in *Story* in 1935, "The Fallen Angel and the Hunter's Moon" has the glow of legend about it. The time is in the 1870's; the town Hastings is the author's name for Warrenton. But to be truthful, the "serious" is somewhat lacking in this hilarious story of Uncle Hal and his "pack of girls."

The Fallen Angel and the Hunter's Moon

WILLIAM T. POLK

WHAT, you don't remember your Uncle Hal! Pshaw, boy, you're as bad as these people that never had delirium tremens—"you ain't been nowhere and you ain't seen nothing." Ah, Lord, they broke the mold when they made him. No, that's right, you wouldn't remember him, he died—yes, and went to hell—ten years before you were born, and if you ever get down there yourself—as you probably will if you're like most of these young folks nowadays—and see a big, bald-headed, black-bearded man following a pack of hounds after a fox over those brimstone bogs with sparks flying off his tail like a comet, that will be your Uncle Hal.

He was a great hunter and a savigorous man in his prime, boy, and many's the time I've been sitting on Main Street in Hastings when somebody would say, "Look out, here comes Hal Hawkins!" and folks would begin shutting up their stores, and pretty soon you would hear the damnedest hullabaloo, hounds baying, horns blowing, and lickety-split here would come your Uncle Hal down the road in the midst of a hundred hounds, sitting on his black horse Nimrod, with his bald head red as a lobster, his little blue eyes snapping,

From *The Fallen Angel and Other Stories* by William Polk. Copyright, 1956, by The University of North Carolina Press.

his big ears flapping in the wind and his black beard floating over his shoulder like a muffler. Sometimes he'd ride in the barroom and order drinks for everybody, sometimes he'd ride through the court house and shoot a few holes in the ceiling, and then again he'd just go through town like a bat out of Hades. 'Y-God, he was a *win*-chester! Try to stop him? No, who would try it? He and Sheriff Jones fought in the same company in the War—Sharpsburg, the Wilderness, Gettysburg—and so everybody simply sat back and thanked God for the excitement. People had more sense in those days.

Well, when your Uncle got sort of old, he had to close his flour mill—the fact is the mill was sold under mortgage, times were so tight then that the only way people could pay him was in wheat and about the time he'd get it ground up along would come some poor devil needing flour for his family and your Uncle Hal would give it to him, so he went broke. He was one of those natural-born extravagant people, never could do anything without overdoing it. Do you know what he gave my mother for a wedding present? A barrel of cream. It's a good thing he didn't think about giving her pepper.

After Hal left the mill, he went to live with his sister, Hannah, who heired the old Hawkins home, Esmeralda. Everybody knew they wouldn't get along together. They were opposites in everything except their high tempers and their cussing abilities. Cousin Hannah was all for skimping and saving, and she was a great temperance worker. Finally they had a big fuss and Hal moved out. It was about Hal's dogs. The Hawkinses always have been fools about dogs, but Hal was the worst of them all. Many's the time I've heard my mother tell about those dogs. Hal would take them with him wherever he went. If he visited your house for a week or a month or two like people used to do, here would come that pack of hounds with him—there was a hundred if there was a one, well, fifty anyway—and it would take all of a Negro's time carrying trays of bread to feed them.

They were mostly females. Hal had an idea that they were better hunters and more intelligent than males. And they were beautiful hounds—wonderful hunters with sleek bodies, not fat but fast and rangy and supple as cats, with sweet clear voices like opera singers. Hal called them his girls and gave them highfalutin names like Creole Belle, Camille, Ophelia, Cordelia, Desdemona, and Helenella. If you were a stranger you'd never know they were dogs, to hear him talk.

The fact is he treated all dogs about the same as people. Did you ever hear about the time he had the fight with Wollett's bulldog? That's another story as the writers say, leaving you to think they've got a fine story up their sleeves but you'll never know what it is. I don't like that way of doing, so I'll tell you the story about the bulldog, though the main story is about the tableau at Cousin Hannah's, and don't you forget it.

Well, one Saturday night when your Uncle Hal was stopping at Cam Stevenson's, he and Cam decided to go to town and see what was the fun. Did you ever know Cam? Every time he'd see you, he'd say, "What's the fun? What's all the fun?" Your Uncle Hal thought they might run into some fun in town, so he stuck his pistol in his belt and his razor in his vest pocket and they set out.

It was a full moonlight night and they walked down the road arm in arm laughing and talking. When they got opposite Wollett's farm, they heard an almighty barking and down the path to the road came the bulldog with his white hair bristling on his back. Cam said his hair stood up too, and he took to a tree. He yelled at Hal to run, but Hal just stood still facing the dog and pulled out his pistol. Nobody would have blamed him for shooting the dog. He was a

ferocious critter, and had pretty nearly killed several people
and Wollett had been ordered by the law to muzzle him or
chloroform him.

When the dog saw Hal standing still he stopped running
and began walking towards him, his front legs being so
bowed and so short, Cam says, that he looked like he was
pushing himself in a wheelbarrow. "You want to fight?"
Hal yelled. The dog growled and snarled and his teeth shone
in the moonlight like a tiger's. "All right," said Hal, "I won't
take any advantage of you. I'll fight you fair and square."
He took the pistol by the barrel and threw it away. "Fair
and square!" he said. Then he took out his razor and threw
that away. Cam said he was so overcome he couldn't make
a sound. The dog came on very slowly, raising each foot
gently and putting it down delicately, still snarling. Hal got
down on his hands and knees and hollered, "Come on, you
jimmie-jawed devil!" And the dog sprang on him.

Many's the time I've heard Cam tell about it. "I'll pledge
you my word," he would say, "I never saw such a dog-fight
in my life. The air was full of howls and yells and curses and
pieces of hair and bits of skin, and the ground looked like
somebody had been digging for buried treasure. Sometimes
the bulldog would be on top and sometimes Hal. Finally
the dog broke away and ran home on three legs limping and
howling. I hoorayed for Hal and fell out of the tree. I'm the
biggest liar that ever lived if Hal hadn't caught the dog's
foot in his mouth and pretty nigh bit it off!"

Fair play and good grit, that was your Uncle Hal all over.
He was a gentleman of the old South if ever I saw one. And
he had mighty delicate feelings. So you see he couldn't stand
your Aunt Hannah speaking disrespectfully to his dogs, calling them "lousy, flea-bitten varmints," beating them with
brooms when they came in the house, and telling him that
he'd have to get rid of them or she'd get rid of him. Finally
they had such a bodacious fuss that the old Hawkins house

rocked and shivered with their cussing. After that Hal went to live with Charlie Gregory.

Some folks do say that they fussed over a bushel of wheat, but I think it was the dogs. To be sure, your Aunt Hannah did bring suit against Hal, her own brother, in court, for a bushel of wheat. The court, though, decided that she owed Hal the bushel. And the judge ordered her to deliver it to Hal in person.

Was she mad? She told Judge Montcastle what she thought of him and dared him to put her in jail for contempt. He ordered the sheriff to take her in custody, but let me tell you, boy, Sheriff Jones would no more have touched a hair of her head than he would have grabbed a roaring lion by the mane or a cobra by the hood.

Next day, though, sure enough, Cousin Hannah took the bushel of wheat to Charlie's house. Hal was on the porch. She hoisted the sack on her shoulder and poured the wheat out on the floor. "There's your infernal wheat, Brother Hal," she said, "and I hope you go to hell and stay there a thousand years for every grain of wheat in that bushel!"

Charlie ran a store and he was one of these people who are the salt of the earth, sandy-haired, pink-cheeked, getting fat, nearing thirty, never saying much but always ready to do anybody a good turn. His father died when he was a boy and he ran the store and supported his mother and sister. It was after his mother died and his sister got married that he asked old man Hal to live with him and stay in the store with him.

That store was something, boy. Charlie sold everything there—overcoats, bananas, ice cream, bandannas, night-shirts, red peppers, shoestrings, guns, kerosene oil—there was mighty few things you couldn't get there, that is, if he liked you. If he didn't, he'd sit in the back office playing backgammon with your Uncle Hal and you would wait until you were black in the face.

Jim Caldwell, a mighty mannerable field hand, told me once that he was waiting in the store one day to buy a can of sardines—but of course he wouldn't say anything or make any noise until Charlie and Hal had finished their game—when a big colored boy just back from up North breezed in and when he didn't get any service he began tapping on the counter with a nickel. When that didn't get results he tapped louder and louder.

Finally your Uncle Hal came boiling out. "What in the name of heaven do you mean by that racket?" "I *did* want to buy something," said the boy, mighty uppity, "but I've changed my mind." "You'd better change it back," said Hal picking up a baseball bat and catching him by the collar, "and say what you want." So the boy bought a cake of soap. Then Hal turned to Jim Caldwell and said, "All right, Jim, what is it for you?" By that time Jim was so scared that he couldn't think what it was he came in to get, but he knew it wouldn't do to say, "Nothing." So he bought the first thing his eye lighted on, which was a horse collar, though he didn't have any more horse than you have.

Ah, Lord, boy, they don't run stores like that nowadays. Your Uncle Hal kept the store books for a while, and I'll bet they were the most original set of books any mercantile establishment ever had. One item I remember was "Fishing tackel 25 cts." And who do you reckon he had it charged to? "Unknown colored boy."

One day Hal noticed that Charlie seemed worried and restless. He lost four backgammon games hand-running out of pure carelessness.

"What's the matter, Charlie?"

"Nothing."

But when a woman came in asking for a dozen eggs and Charlie gave her a parasol, Hal was enough of a psychologist to know that something was wrong. "What the hell's the matter, old man?" he asked. And Charlie said, "*She* is in town, Cousin Hal." (He called him "cousin" though they weren't any kin that I know of.)

"Who?"

"Louise," said Charlie, dark and gloomy.

Louise Maxwell he was talking about. She lived in New York. Her father—one of the Perquimans Maxwells, you know—moved to New York after the War and got to be head of the Cotton Exchange. Louise came down every summer or so for a week's visit to her cousin who was none other than your Aunt Hannah. She was a girl now would make you thank God for the use of your eyes—a fine figger of a woman, none of your sickly, fainty-fit, spindle-shank, sensitive plants, but a good hundred and fifty pounds of pure beauty—straight as an Indian, with black hair and blue eyes, a little sharp-tempered and out-spoken maybe, but kind-hearted and with the sweetest mouth—no, you couldn't understand, they don't make women like her nowadays. And Charlie, he was crazy in love with her.

"Great Jehovah!" said Hal, dipping himself a drink out of the barrel, "what are you moping around for? You've got the inside track, haven't you?"

"I thought so, last summer," Charlie sighed, "but I don't know now. It looks like—like I've sort of lost out."

"Lost out? Who to?"

Charlie turned red. "Leonine Montrose." He swallowed. It wasn't easy to say.

"Leonine Montrose? Don't tell me that." Hal hit the table so hard with his fist that the backgammon counters flew all over the floor. "That ape with a name out of a book? That goggle-eyed perch that claims to come from Louisiana? That—"

All this was just your Uncle's way of talking. Montrose was a good-looking young fellow, something like the pictures of Byron, seemed to have plenty of money, and came to the All-Healing Springs near Hastings every summer. To be sure nobody knew for certain just who his people were or where he came from or how he got his money, but I think the mystery made him all the more romantic to the ladies.

"He won the tournament yesterday," said Charlie sadly.

Do you know what a tournament is, boy? No, you never saw one. You young folks don't know how to have a good time nowadays.

A tournament was a great shakes in my day. The young men would fix up like knights and get on their horses with lances in their hands and ride in a circle trying to catch the ring on their lances and the one that got the most rings had the honor of crowning his lady the Queen of Love and Beauty. All the girls would be there looking on, of course, and to be crowned was equal to an engagement at least. "He won the tournament," said Charlie mighty down in the mouth, "and he crowned Louise Queen of Love and Beauty."

Hal tugged at his beard with both hands. The situation was serious. "Leonine Montrose!" he snorted. "He's a damned imposter, I'll bet my pack of girls he is. Where did he come from, where did he git his money, do you reckon he ever saw Louisiana? Mark my words, he's a scalawag, a rascal, a carpet-bagger, or something."

"Your sister, Cousin Hannah, is all for him," said Charlie. "She thinks he's fine. She thinks he's the son of a lord."

"Son of a what?"

"Son of a lord."

"Son of a lord but the Lord knows who!" Hal spat so vigorously that he almost overturned the big brass spittoon. He hitched up his trousers, put on his coat, got his hat and dipped his glass in the whiskey barrel.

"Where are you going, Cousin Hal?"

"I'm going to see that girl and stop all this tomfoolery."

"No, don't. Whatever you say about Leonine, it won't do any good. It'll make matters worse."

"I won't mention him then. I'll tell her what a fine fellow you are." Hal took another drink.

"No don't do that for God's sake. You don't hardly know her." Charlie foresaw trouble, but he was too late. Hal was out and gone.

When Hal rolled in about an hour later hiccuping consistently, Charlie feared the worst. But Hal gave a rose-colored report. He had seen the lady—"yes, she was—hic! —most remarkable girl—hup!—told her what a good man she was about to lose—yes, she was interested—asked a lot of questions about you—hiccup!"

Pretty shortly a colored boy came in with a note from Miss Maxwell.

"Now then, Charlie," said Hal, "didn't I tell you—hic!— I'd fix things all right for you?"

Charlie ripped the note from its envelope. It read:

Mr. Charles Gregory:
In vino veritas. Your friend, Mr. Hawkins, has told me of your girls, Creole Belle and the rest. I beg to be excused from competing with a harem. You need not attempt to see me again.
                              Miss Louise Maxwell.

Charlie stared at the letter dumbfounded. "What does she mean—girls?—harem? Look here, Cousin Hal, did you say anything to her about your pack of hounds?"

"Well yes, I think I did say something—hic!—about the girls."

"And you told her how good I was to them, how much I liked them?"

"I may have."

"But did you tell her they were *dogs*?"

Hal studied the letter. "Hellfire, I don't know that I told her in so many words. Everybody knows my dogs."

"She doesn't. She's only here a week or so a year. How can we *prove* to her you were talking about dogs?"

"I'll straighten that—hippup!—out," said Hal. He wrote on the back of the note, *"When I said girls I meant dogs,"* and sent the boy away with it.

When the boy returned half an hour later with the same note, Charlie noticed that Louise had written under Hal's reply: *"I dare say you make no distinctions."*

Charlie stared at the floor. "I reckon it's all over."

"Oh, no, Charlie—huccup!—do you think I'm going to let her do you like this?"

"Well, what are you going to do about it?"

"I don't know yet. I'll have to think. I'm going fox-hunting—huc!—I can think better when I'm hunting."

"I'll never see her again, Cousin Hal."

"Yes, you will—at the tableau—hec!—tomorrow night."

"And your sister Hannah will be announcing Louise's engagement to Leonine Montrose at that," said Charlie bitterly.

"I'll be—hip!—if she will," said Hal and he fell asleep with his head on the counter.

The next night, though, he was out hunting and thinking. That was the night of the tableau. A fine full moon—the hunter's moon, we used to call it—shone down on the old Hawkins home at the end of its long straight walk bordered by thick boxbush on both sides. It was one of those old Southern mansions with white columns that you read about with a big front door and a hall as wide as one of your city houses nowadays. That night the hall was filled with people. The chairs were arranged to leave an aisle in the middle of the hall. A calico curtain towards the rear screened the back part of it, and behind that the actors were fixing up for the tableau.

You could see through the open front door that everybody that was anybody was there. It was a fairly warm night, and the leg o' mutton shoulders of the ladies bobbed up and down as they fanned themselves. The gentlemen wore tight pants, high collars, big cravats and coats buttoned up almost to their Adam's apples.

Your Cousin Hannah was proud of that crowd. The quality was there all right—Preacher Pettigrew, Senator Ranson, old Lawyer Eaton, Mrs. Post Office Johnson, Mr. Dromgoole the schoolmaster, bunches of young ladies fluttering and whispering, a few squirming children, young Doctor Mat Jenkins, who had been to New York and seen things, Major Littlejohn, the Misses Turner, and old Doctor Sam Williams, who always wore a shawl fastened in front with a pin. The main question agitating the audience was whether this tableau could come up to the one last year at the town hall when *Maud Muller* was shown with a real horse on the stage.

Cousin Hannah bustled around behind the scenes, censoring the costumes, fixing some refreshments and ordering everybody around. A tableau was a sight of trouble and it cost a lot, she was thinking. She did hope things would "pass off nicely." She felt almost too good. Louise had at last decided to accept Leonine Montrose and the engagement would be announced after the last scene.

Things went smoothly enough. Judge Stewart pulled back the curtain and the spectators rose a little out of their seats to get a good look at the first tableau, *Chisel in Hand Stood the Sculptor Boy,* showing George Threewits with upraised chisel and mallet about to begin carving the lovely Dorothea Branch who looked a little apprehensive in spite of her voluminous draperies.

Next came *Love or Lucre,* a scene which disclosed Miss Helen Watson standing with reluctant feet between the poor but honest young Wallace Perry and the rich city slicker, Coley Price, gaudy in borrowed rings, stick pin and watch chain, while in the background the Prescott baby with a bow and arrow in a bower of roses and lilies represented Cupid. Doctor Jenkins said that this scene in beauty and dramatic interest rivaled anything on the New York stage.

Then came two comic scenes: *Bonaparte Crossing the Rhine,* which was a backbone of a herring placed crossways of a watermelon rind; and *Cinderella and the Glass Slipper,* in which Sid Alston dressed as a woman with a big bustle ran in with a tray full of glasses and slipped up and broke them.

But the grand finale, the tableau of tableaux, the scene on which your Aunt Hannah had set her heart to beat even the famous *Maud Muller* one was yet to come. It would have a moral and religious meaning. She had made up this tableau herself. It was called *The Drunkard's Damnation.* The idea was this. The Drunkard, played by Charlie, was to stagger in, ragged, muddy, red-nosed, wild-haired, wild-eyed, in the last stages of drink. Just as he would pull a bottle out of his pocket and raise it to his lips, an angel would fly in, white-robed, white-winged, with the word *Temperance* written in large gilt letters on a ribbon across her bosom. The angel was to be Louise, and she would stretch out her hands pleadingly to the Drunkard. Considering her wing-spread, she was obviously too plump for successful flight, but she would fly in and out by means of an arrangement of ropes and pulleys hid from the audience. To Leonine Montrose your Aunt Hannah had assigned the job of elevating the precious burden and engineering the flight. He had the responsibility of keeping the angel safely aloft by holding tight to the rope.

Poor Charlie was to be so sunk in sin that he would scorn the angel's help. He would shake his bottle at her, drink it down and die in agony.

When the time came for *The Drunkard's Damnation,* Cousin Hannah was watching from a seat on the front row. I felt afraid for Charlie. It would take a pretty good actor, you know, to play that part.

Well, Charlie staggered in. He lurched to the front of the

stage, teetered on the edge, staggered back. It was real act-
ing or real drunkenness. Then the angel floated in—white
wings, white robes, her curly black hair down her back and
those Langtry bangs in front—she was a seductive-looking
angel if ever I saw one. Charlie gazed at her and registered
tragedy. He raised the bottle and drained it. The D.T.'s got
him. He gnashed his teeth and foamed at the mouth. The
horrors came at him and he almost made you see them—at
first it was maybe a mouse or a candlefly, then worms,
wolves, tigers, an avalanche of snakes and a rain of devilfish.
Charlie's eyes were wide with terror and his hands were
plucking and pulling and warding them off.

You could feel a shiver run through the audience and
everything was silent.

Then suddenly there was a noise, a scurrying, rushing,
howling noise, like the first rumbling of a volcano or the
whining of a cyclone or the yells of damned souls escaping
from hell with Cerberus after them. Was it real? I wondered for a moment. It sounded like it came from the front
yard. Then through the front door and down the aisle shot
a dark ball of fur like a black bolt of lightning pursued by a
hundred howling demons — ooouuurrr! — ooouuurrr! —
ooorooroo!—ooorooroo!—ooorowooo!—ooorowrow! Not
dogs of war but Hal Hawkins' pack of fox hounds, overturn-
ing chairs, leaping over heads, huddling like a football team,
scurrying back and forth, swarming down the aisle, dashing
between legs, leaping, bounding, jumping, high-jumping,
broad-jumping, hurdling, doubling, dodging, and mortally
howling!

Your Aunt Hannah had a double-duck-fit. She let out a
yell of rage and, for the first time in her life, fainted. She
knew that her brother Hal had turned that fox loose with
the dogs behind him at the far end of the boxbush walk.

And then, as if there wasn't enough excitement, there
was a creaking of ropes and pulleys. The angel started fall-

ing! There was a surprised expression on her face and what
she said would have sounded like a cuss-word coming from
anybody but an angel. But Charlie was there on the spot.
He dropped the bottle, took one step and stood with arms
out-stretched. Yes, he caught the angel. Luckily the ropes
slowed her down some. Charlie staggered in earnest when
he caught her, his legs bent under the strain and he almost
sat down. He did sink on one knee, but he held to the
angel and finally straightened up.

A black-bearded figure stepped from behind some scenery
and pulled the curtains to, screening the angel in the drunkard's arms. Louise stepped out of the ropes and out of
Charlie's grasp. She was mad for getting let down in such an
undignified manner. She peeped behind the backdrop and
called, "Leonine," in no uncertain tone. No answer. He had
disappeared. In fact, he didn't turn up for two weeks.
"What happened to that idiot?" she asked. Your Uncle Hal
handed her a piece of paper that he picked up from the floor
"Maybe this note I sent him had something to do with it,"
he said, handing it to her. She read it: *"Leonine Montrose
—All is discovered. Fly at once.* BLOODHOUNDS *are on
your trail.* A FRIEND."

"But how did you know he would run away?" she asked.

"There are mighty few people that won't run away when
you tell them 'all is discovered,' " said Hal.

"Are they bloodhounds?"

"No, they are my girls."

"Your girls?"

"Yes. Louise, don't you remember my telling you about
my girls?"

"But Cousin Hannah told me you were talking about
your—your real girls—yours and Charlie's." Her eyes were
big with surprise. "You didn't tell me they were dogs."

"Here, I'll show them to you." He sang out, "Camille,"
in that deep voice of his, and in trotted a black-and-white

spotted hound, looking very proud. "Ophelia!" A slim black-and-tan hound entered with a roast chicken in her mouth. The girls had evidently been raiding the kitchen. "Creole Belle!" And there came a beautiful dog, with dark red hair, long-eared, melancholy-eyed, with a ham-bone in her jaws.

"Creole Belle!" said Louise and the dog went to her.

Hal called the others and they came in, some with food in their mouths and some with satisfied expressions and greasy chops. One brought in half a chocolate cake.

Hal looked at them and said solemnly: "Girls, meet your new Mistress, Louise Gregory." And the hounds regarded her with large grave eyes.

Louise laughed and blushed, yes she did. "Charlie, can you forgive me," her eyes shone as she held out her hands to him, "for being such a fool?"

"My angel!" he said, taking her in his arms.

"A fallen angel!" she was both laughing and crying. "Would you want a fallen angel?"

A little colored boy scrambled through the curtain. "Look out, Marse Hal, you and Marse Charlie," he said, "Miss Hannah, she's a-coming to!"

"Louise," said Charlie, "I can't leave you. Will you come with me?"

She frowned a bit, trying to think, and then she smiled straight at him. "Yes, I will," she said.

Your Uncle Hal blew a blast on his horn. "Come on!" he shouted and they followed him out the back way. I went to the kitchen window. And that was a sight I'll never forget, boy—Charlie on Nimrod's black back with the angel on the saddle before him riding slowly over the shining grass under the hunter's moon toward Preacher Burton's, with your Uncle Hal leading the way in the midst of his dogs, sounding his horn and cutting a few capers like the great god Pan come to life again.

FRANCES GRAY PATTON

FRANCES GRAY PATTON was born in Raleigh on March 19, 1906. Writing was always a commonplace activity in the Gray family. Her father, Robert Lilly Gray, was one of the best known editors in the South in his time, and at present she has two brothers who are newspapermen. After local schooling and a year at Duke University, she went to the University of North Carolina, where it is interesting to note that her mother, Mary MacRae, had been the first coed. While at Chapel Hill, Frances Gray's principal interest was the Carolina Playmakers. As a sophomore, she wrote "The Beaded Buckle," later published in one of the folkplay anthologies prepared by F. H. Koch and one of the most popular comedies in the Playmakers' repertory. During her college years, she spent the summers in Cincinnati as an actor in a stock company. In 1927, she was married to Dr. Lewis Patton, professor of English at Duke, and settled down in Durham to rear her family, a son and twin daughters.

As the children grew older, she began to write once again. Her poems appeared in the *Saturday Review of Literature* and the New York *Herald Tribune,* and in 1944, her first published short story won the second prize in a contest conducted by the *Kenyon Review* and Doubleday, Doran and Company. From over a thousand entries only two prizes were given. This story, "A Piece of Bread," appeared in the *O. Henry Memorial Award Prize Stories of 1945.* Other stories have been published in *Harper's,* the *Ladies' Home Journal,* and especially the *New Yorker.*

She is the author of three books, each of which won

the Sir Walter Raleigh Award for the outstanding work of fiction by a North Carolinian during the season of its publication. Two were collections of short stories: *The Finer Things of Life* (1951), which includes "Grade 5B and the Well-Fed Rat," and *A Piece of Luck* (1955). Her novel *Good Morning, Miss Dove* (1954) was not only a Book-of-the-Month Club selection but was also made into a successful motion picture.

Mrs. Patton has taught creative writing at Salem College, the Woman's College in Greensboro, and the University in Chapel Hill. She still lives, however, just off the Duke University campus in Durham.

"Grade 5B and the Well-Fed Rat" shows the author at her urbane best. Mrs. Patton is never guilty of moralizing and preaching, but perhaps in this story she has something rather definite to say to those who live in a *very* scientific age.

Grade 5B and the Well-Fed Rat

FRANCES GRAY PATTON

"DEAR PARENT," said the mimeographed letter from the Parent-Teacher's Association of the Oaklawn School, "In this atomic age the future safety of civilization depends upon a truly scientific atmosphere. The boys and girls of today will be the men and women of tomorrow. At our meeting, Wednesday November 14, Miss Oates' grade, 5B-1, will take over the program to show we parents how our little folk are progressing in this direction."

Mrs. Potter sighed when she read it. Her daughter, Elinor, was in grade 5B-1.

Mrs. Potter made a point of staying away from schools. They depressed her. The very odor of their halls was an undertow to her spirits. It sucked her back into that nervous dullness of childhood from which she, by the grace of time, had thankfully escaped.

Her first two children were boys. They seemed fond of their mother, and not abnormally ashamed of her. They accompanied her on bird-walks in the woods, and sometimes even to a movie—though they did not sit with her there because, they explained, they could see better from the front row. They talked openly to her about sex and

From *The Finer Things of Life* by Frances Gray Patton. Copyright, 1951, by Frances Gray Patton. Used by permission of Dodd, Mead & Company, Inc.

tropical fish and airplane motor frequency. But they did
not discuss their school affairs. And on the rare occasions
when she was obliged to come to their school (to bring
forgotten notebooks, for instance, or raincoats when the
weather had changed unexpectedly), their embarrassment
was pathetic. They greeted her vaguely, like people who
"know the face, but can't recall the name." It suited Mrs.
Potter.

But Elinor was different. To Elinor school was the stuff
of life, and she brought it home with her. She remembered in detail the appearance of her teachers. She discovered, somehow, their private histories and philosophies.
She recounted everything at the dinner table.

"Miss Oates had lipstick on her teeth again today,"
Elinor would remark. "It was probably her mother's fault.
Miss Oates lives with this old, old mother, and sometimes
she beats Miss Oates to the bathroom in the morning and
she stays in there so long—you know how old people are!
—that Miss Oates doesn't have time to fix herself up before school. Poor Miss Oates! I don't like lipstick on
teeth."

Or she would lean forward, pudding spoon halfway to
her mouth, and announce solemnly:

"Miss Bangs, our new music teacher, loves God. She
really *loves* Him."

Elinor liked, also, to share her homework with her family.
Her eyes shone as she recited the multiplication table or
the trials of the Jamestown Colony. Her voice was full
of proud emotion when she read her compositions aloud.
One of these ended with a fine, confident flourish:

"After reading this chapter in *Tales of Distant Lands*,"
declared Elinor, "I know that if I woke up tomorrow
morning in the middle of the Desert of Sahara, I would
feel perfectly at home."

(She probably would at that, thought Mrs. Potter. Anybody who feels at home in a public school would feel at home anywhere.)

It was entertaining. It might have been entirely charming if Elinor had not begun urging her mother to visit the school. Other mothers came all the time; wasn't her mother interested in education?

"Miss Oates thinks the school and the home should co-operate," said Elinor. "And besides," she added, "everybody wants to see you. I've told them you look like a pin-up girl."

This bit of flattery was irresistible. Mrs. Potter, though well-preserved, was on the shady side of thirty-five. She promised Elinor that next time her class was on the program she would attend the P.-T.A. meeting. It had seemed then something faraway and rather unlikely to happen.

Now, with the letter in her hand, she knew she was caught.

On the morning of the appointed Wednesday Mrs. Potter awoke with a heaviness, like a cold, undigested pancake, on her stomach. Then she heard her husband, Professor Potter, gargling in the bathroom and she took heart. Maybe, she thought, he was coming down with a strep throat, and she would have to stay home and nurse him. But he said he was all right—he was just gargling as a precaution because there were some colds among his students.

"I guess this is it," she said bleakly, and went down to the kitchen to start the cereal.

Elinor was too excited to eat much breakfast. She was to make the longest speech of all. She had not said the speech at home because she wanted it to be a surprise for her mother, and now she was afraid she didn't know it. She stared down at her plate and kept mumbling something about rats.

"Mama," one of the boys said at last, "don't let her

go crazy right here at the breakfast table. She takes my appetite away."

"Suppose I forget something," said Elinor, trembling, "before those thousands of people!"

"I don't suppose there'll be many people," murmured Mrs. Potter soothingly.

It was the wrong thing to say.

"You mean we won't have a good audience?" demanded Elinor. In a gesture of despair she clapped her hand to her head. "My hair!" she moaned, holding out a yellow wisp in her fingers. "Oh, I wish I had some glamour. I have to get up there on that stage—without any glamour!"

She moaned again as she gathered up her books. But it was a moan, Mrs. Potter knew, made half of ecstasy.

"Wear your new girdle, Mama," said Elinor, "and use enough lipstick. Don't get it on your teeth."

Before the meeting Mrs. Potter went downtown for a shampoo and a manicure. She disliked painted finger-nails, but this time she permitted the manicurist to give her a brilliant polish called *Frozen Flame*. She was not going to let Elinor down. Then she went to a department store where she bought a red rayon carnation to pin on her coat. She thought she looked very nice. She almost believed she was going to enjoy the meeting.

After all, she told herself, her attitude of aloofness toward her children's education was self-indulgent and anti-social. More than that, it was ignorant; it was based upon some infantile fixation of her own. Times had changed. The public school must have changed with them, and—witness Elinor's enthusiasm—for the better.

But when she went into the school it did not smell very different. It did not look different, either. The walls were painted the same pale tan—a faintly nauseating color —and on the wall the same peasant girl still listened to her lark. As she walked down the concrete hall Mrs. Potter heard the echo of her own footsteps tapping behind her, like some hopeless monotony that would shadow her all her life.

At the door of the auditorium she was welcomed by Miss Oates. Her teeth, Mrs. Potter saw with relief, were clean as the proverbial hound's. Miss Oates, when Mrs. Potter introduced herself, exclaimed in evident surprise: "Are you *Elinor's* mother?" She gave her a long look, equally appraising and disappointed.

Mrs. Potter found a seat among the score of other mothers who were, she saw, as carefuly coifed, as resolutely complacent as she herself. There was time only for the briefest interchange of compliments on one another's "darling children" before Miss Bangs began playing the piano. (Mrs. Potter found herself thinking irreverently that God might have rewarded that lady's devotion with the gift of greater talent!) Thirty children filed out upon the stage, singing "We march, we march, to vic-to-ree," in fresh, tuneless voices.

The children all looked healthy and clean. The boys wore white shirts and dark knickers. The bright, starched dresses of the girls belled out like field flowers. Their eyes were steady and serious, as if some transcendent emotion arose to sweep the least trace of frivolity from them. They made a touching picture.

Her Elinor, Mrs. Potter observed, was pale. She looked as if she had been crying and had just washed her face. But she seemed composed. She stood primly, with her hands crossed, like little limp fish, over her middle. When she caught her mother's glance, she shot her a swift, tremulous smile.

Miss Oates mounted the rostrum. She was a thin, tall woman. She curved her body a little from the waist, as if to reduce the impression of its length. She fingered her pearls as she talked, and her features assumed the languid lines of patronizing whimsy. But her prominent blue eyes were coy and restless. Mrs. Potter felt sorry for her, and sorry, too, that she did not like her.

"*Ave!*" said Miss Oates cheerfully. "In this day of racial unrest and the atom bomb—"

Mrs. Potter shivered. Suddenly the pretty children on the platform looked unsubstantial, doomed, like the over-bright figures in a nightmare. What earthly relevance had the race problem to the matter in hand, and why drag in the bomb at this juncture? The woman was a plain fool. Mrs. Potter bowed her head in vicarious shame.

"In this atomic age," Miss Oates continued, "this time of changing val-yews, we must dare to change our meth-ods also. Therefore, when the fifth graders took up the study of nutrition, we did not give them dead books, but live, vibrant material. The Health Department kindly do-nated two white rats. We named one of them Wiffles, and the other one Squiffles."

She paused, smiling graciously. The audience made a sound that Mrs. Potter supposed might be called "an ap-preciative titter."

"Wiffles," said Miss Oates, "had his private cage, and Squiffles had his. But while Wiffles was fed milk and eggs and vegetable stew, Mr. Squiffles received only cookies and coca-cola. At first we thought Squiffles was the lucky rat, but we soon changed our minds. Wiffles began to look like a great big Marine sergeant, and Squiffles was just a poor little 4-F. But I'm going to let our young scientists tell you the rest. I know you want to hear, in their own little words, just what they've learned with their honest, inquiring little minds. So, ladies and gentlemen," here she dimpled at the principal, a bald, sleepy-looking man, "and mothers of the fifth grade, I want to introduce some-body you already know—The Class of Five B One."

Miss Oates retired into the wings. Everybody clapped. A stout, pink-cheeked boy came forward. He gave his bulging pants a hitch, and began to talk in a challenging monotone.

"In this atomic age," he said, "we must all be scientists."

Mrs. Potter did not listen closely to him. She did not pay much attention, either, to the girl who maintained that, since the discovery of the airplane and the atom bomb, it was necessary to learn the rules of health. Mrs. Potter was waiting for Elinor.

Elinor, whose job was to sum up the results of the class experiment, was the last to speak. Mrs. Potter thought she was infinitely better than the others. In the first place, she looked exactly the way a ten-year-old girl ought to look. Even her straight hair, with its bothersome cowlick, had all the weedy grace of childhood; it made the ringlets of the other girls look artificial. And she spoke her piece in a rapid, businesslike way, without any hesitation or any fancy frills.

"The characteristics of the well-fed rat," said Elinor, "are different from the characteristics of the poorly-fed rat. The well-fed rat is heavier. The fur of the well-fed rat is soft and creamy. The poorly-fed rat has sore eyes, and his fur is very ratty. The poorly-fed rat is maladjusted, and he also has a bad disposition. He is ready to dart out of his cage whenever the door is opened. The well-fed rat has a calm, kind disposition. He is contented with his surroundings and does not wish to leave his cage. His tail is pink and waxy."

After the program was over Mrs. Potter stayed to congratulate Miss Oates upon the performance of her pupils. The children were marching off the stage through a back door, but Elinor darted from the line (like the poorly-fed rat, thought Mrs. Potter), and bounced over the footlights to her mother's side. Miss Oates came down, too, but by the steps.

"We're glad to see Mummy, aren't we, Elinor?" she said. There was something subtly menacing in her tone.

"It was really remarkable, Miss Oates," said Mrs. Potter. "I'm sure *we* were never so poised in the fifth grade." Then, in an attempt to add a friendly, adult note to the conversation, she added flippantly: "But it's sad, isn't it, that the well-fed rat liked his cage. Is the desire for freedom only the desire for food?"

Miss Oates curved her lips slightly. It was the sort of smile, Mrs. Potter remembered, that teachers kept for parents who tried to be clever.

"That's what the chart told us," Elinor said. "It said the well-fed rat liked his cage. It wasn't that way with our Wiffles."

She gulped on the last word. Miss Oates gave her an uneasy look.

"But, Elinor," said Mrs. Potter, "I thought you said in your report—"

"You see, Mrs. Potter," said Miss Oates, "the Health Department furnished us with a chart on rat nutrition to help us find our facts, but the rats didn't always co-operate. Squiffles, *our* poorly-fed rat, just cowered in a corner—"

"With a blank expression on his face," said Elinor contemptuously.

"—while Wiffles, who was supposed to feel all comfy, was forever trying to get out. Once he did escape, didn't he, Elinor?"

"Yes, Miss Oates," said Elinor, "and bit the blood out of Randy Adams when he caught him."

"We disinfected Randy's finger with iodine," Miss Oates said quickly.

Mrs. Potter was honestly puzzled.

"I thought," she said, "that the class just observed the rats first-hand, and drew its own conclusions."

"That's right," said Miss Oates patiently, "we observed them for a month. We fed and weighed them every day. Then, with the chart as a guide, we made out our reports."

"I see," said Mrs. Potter. But she wondered if she did.

"But," said Miss Oates, "when we compared our findings with those on the chart we saw that something, somewhere, had gone wrong. Maybe there was something funny about the rats to begin with. Or maybe we didn't follow directions properly. I don't know." She shrugged helplessly. "Frankly, I've never been good at science. I was always more the esthetic type."

"I know," said Mrs. Potter vaguely.

"Anyhow," said Miss Oates, "our results weren't exactly what we'd expected. We had promised to give this program and we simply didn't have time to do the experiment all over again. But we knew from the Health Department what facts we *ought* to have found, so— well, we just decided to take the bull by the horns and go ahead and find them! In this atomic age, we can't afford to be narrow about facts, can we? I mean we have to realize their broader implications. And after all," she finished, on a note of inspiration, "things often don't turn out right the first time—even at Oak Ridge."

"Indeed they don't," agreed Mrs. Potter.

"Now," said Miss Oates briskly, "I've dissipated long enough. I must go see what my class is doing. I believe in trusting children, you know. In times like these they have to learn self-reliance. And then I check up on them. Elinor, would you like to spend five whole minutes alone with Mummy? Be sure to ask her to come again."

"Maybe Elinor could show me the rats," suggested Mrs. Potter.

A glint of something like exasperation shone in Miss Oates' eyes.

"I do wish she could," she said, "but the truth is we've had a minor tragedy in our midst. When we took the covers off the cages this morning we found something that made us all feel dreadfully blue." She pursed her mouth ruefully and dropped her voice. "The well-fed rat was dead."

She began to back off with her eyes fixed warily on Elinor.

"Bye-bye," she said, and was gone.

"I hate her," said Elinor, grinding her words between her teeth. "She is a cold, black-hearted woman."

Mrs. Potter was dismayed.

"Oh no, darling—you don't!" she cried. "You don't *hate* anybody."

"I hate Miss Oates," said Elinor flatly. "She wouldn't even let us have a funeral for him."

"But she was so busy," said Mrs. Potter. "And she has that poor old mother!"

"I feel sorry for Miss Oates' mother," said Elinor. "Imagine thinking you were going to have a nice baby, and it turning out to be Miss Oates! She has no feeling for children or rats or anything. Mama, I loved Wiffles. He was a sweet rat."

"Maybe he's happy somewhere," said Mrs. Potter. It seemed the only thing to say.

"He didn't look happy," said Elinor. "He looked awful dead. He was lying on his back with his feet up in the air. His body was still warm." She began to sob quietly. "We wanted to cremate him like we read in the paper Jerome Kern was cremated. We were going to build a funeral pyre on the playground, and dance around it

singing hymns. But ole Quaker Oats wouldn't let us. Do
you know what she said?"

"What did she say?" asked Mrs. Potter, aware of an
ignominious sympathy for Miss Oates.

"She said: 'In this atomic age we have no time to play
funeral with rats.' And then—" Elinor's voice shook with
grief and scorn—"she picked him up, by the pink, waxy
tail, and gave him to the janitor."

Mrs. Potter kissed Elinor and patted her on the shoulder.
She wiped her wet cheeks with a handkerchief.

"I guess you'll have to go now, baby," she said. "It was
a lovely program, anyhow." She fished a nickel out of her
purse. "After school get yourself an ice-cream cone—or a
coca-cola."

As she saw Elinor's face brighten, Mrs. Potter felt like
crying. The quick shift of a child's mood, like sunlight
running up the beach on the heels of a cloud, had always
been a thing to move her deeply. She had an impulse to
snatch Elinor out of these cloisters of pious confusion and
set her free in the simple light of day. But of course she
did no such thing. She only smiled and watched her little
girl skip jauntily off to Miss Oates' home room.

And a minute later when she, herself, walked down the
hall, Mrs. Potter felt comforted. The old smell of chalk
and peanuts, the hollow, reverberating sound of her own
shoes, the pastoral rapture—expressed in sepia—of Mil-
let's rustic, all managed to put reality smugly in its place.
Life seemed inept and innocent and debonair. Even the
split atom lost its terrors for the moment and became just
something people talked about at P.-T.A. meetings.

CHARLES W. CHESNUTT

CHESNUTT is generally conceded to be the first Negro writer to employ the short story as a serious medium of artistic expression. In *To Make a Poet Black*, J. Saunders Redding states that Chesnutt was "a transitional figure. He drew together the various post-Civil War tendencies in Negro creative literature and translated them into the most worthy prose fiction that the Negro has produced."

Though born in Cleveland, Ohio, June 20, 1858, Chesnutt was of North Carolina parentage. During the war, his father served as a soldier in the Northern army. When the boy was eight years old, the family returned to North Carolina, where Chesnutt completed his education. For nine years, he was a teacher in the Negro schools of the state. In 1880, at the age of twenty-two, he became principal of the State Normal School in Fayetteville. In 1883, he was in New York as a reporter. After working for a while in the office of a railroad company, he began to study law and, in 1887, was admitted to the Cleveland bar. In that year, he established his home in Cleveland, where he practiced law the remainder of his life. Following the success of his books, he spent much time on the lecture platform as a reader of his dialect stories. In 1928, he won the Spingarn Achievement Award "for his pioneer work as a literary artist depicting the life and struggle of Americans of Negro descent." This gold medal is given annually to the Negro who is judged as having contributed most significantly to his chosen field. Chesnutt died on November 15, 1932.

He is best remembered for the seven dialect stories in

The Conjure Woman (1899), plantation tales written in the Uncle Remus tradition and told from the point of view of the white man who has respect and tolerance for the picturesque Negro slave. In *The Wife of His Youth and Other Stories of the Color Line* (1901), from which "Cicely's Dream" is taken, Chesnutt turned from the good-humored Negro legends and struck out at the problems of his people both North and South. *The House Behind the Cedars* (1900), *The Marrow of Tradition* (1901), and *The Colonel's Dream* (1905) are novels dealing with race relations in North Carolina. The first is a tragedy of a beautiful girl of mixed blood, the second treats the Wilmington Race Riots of 1898, and the third is Chesnutt's agonized cry against those who willfully prevent the Negro's few white friends from helping him.

Charles Waddell Chesnutt: Pioneer of the Color Line (1952) is a biography written by the author's daughter Helen M. Chesnutt, who made full use of her father's letters and journals.

"Cicely's Dream" takes the reader back to the topsy-turvy times at the end of the Civil War when neither race in the South had found its direction. The lost soldier, the Negro girl, and the Northern schoolmistress are caught up in a situation not of their making. Chesnutt gives the plot a melodramatic twist which is characteristic of his color-line stories. Though the author disguises his setting, it is, of course Fayetteville.

Cicely's Dream

CHARLES W. CHESNUTT

I

THE OLD WOMAN STOOD at the back door of the cabin, shading her eyes with her hand, and looking across the vegetable garden that ran up to the very door. Beyond the garden she saw, bathed in the sunlight, a field of corn, just in the ear, stretching for half a mile, its yellow, pollen-laden tassels over-topping the dark green mass of broad glistening blades; and in the distance, through the faint morning haze of evaporating dew, the line of the woods, of a still darker green, meeting the clear blue of the summer sky. Old Dinah saw, going down the path, a tall, brown girl, in a homespun frock, swinging a slat-bonnet in one hand and a splint basket in the other.

"Oh, Cicely!" she called.

The girl turned and answered in a resonant voice, vibrating with youth and life,—

"Yes, granny!"

"Be sho' and pick a good mess er peas, chile, fer yo' gran'daddy's gwine ter be home ter dinner ter-day."

The old woman stood a moment longer and then turned to go into the house. What she had not seen was that the girl was not only young, but lithe and shapely as a sculptor's model; that her bare feet seemed to spurn the

By permission of Helen M. Chesnutt.

earth as they struck it; that though brown, she was not so brown but that her cheek was darkly red with the blood of another race than that which gave her her name and station in life; and the old woman did not see that Cicely's face was as comely as her figure was superb, and that her eyes were dreamy with vague yearnings.

Cicely climbed the low fence between the garden and the cornfield, and started down one of the long rows leading directly away from the house. Old Needham was a good ploughman, and straight as an arrow ran the furrow between the rows of corn, until it vanished in the distant perspective. The peas were planted beside alternate hills of corn, the corn-stalks serving as supports for the climbing pea-vines. The vines nearest the house had been picked more or less clear of the long green pods, and Cicely walked down the row for a quarter of a mile, to where the peas were more plentiful. And as she walked she thought of her dream of the night before.

She had dreamed a beautiful dream. The fact that it was a beautiful dream, a delightful dream, her memory retained very vividly. She was troubled because she could not remember just what her dream had been about. Of one other fact she was certain, that in her dream she had found something, and that her happiness had been bound up with the thing she had found. As she walked down the corn-row she ran over in her mind the various things with which she had always associated happiness. Had she found a gold ring? No, it was not a gold ring—of that she felt sure. Was it a soft, curly plume for her hat? She had seen town people with them, and had indulged in daydreams on the subject; but it was not a feather. Was it a bright-colored silk dress? No; as much as she had always wanted one, it was not a silk dress. For an instant, in a dream, she had tasted some great and novel happiness, and when she awoke it was dashed from her lips, and she could not even enjoy the memory of it, except in a vague, indefinite, and tantalizing way.

Cicely was troubled, too, because dreams were serious things. Dreams had certain meanings, most of them, and some dreams went by contraries. If her dream had been a prophecy of some good thing, she had by forgetting it lost the pleasure of anticipation. If her dream had been one of those that go by contraries, the warning would be in vain, because she would not know against what evil to provide. So, with a sigh, Cicely said to herself that it was a troubled world, more or less; and having come to a promising point, began to pick the tenderest pea-pods and throw them into her basket.

By the time she had reached the end of the line the basket was nearly full. Glancing toward the pine woods beyond the rail fence, she saw a brier bush loaded with large, luscious blackberries. Cicely was fond of black-berries, so she set her basket down, climbed the fence, and was soon busily engaged in gathering the fruit, de-licious even in its wild state.

She had soon eaten all she cared for. But the berries were still numerous, and it occurred to her that her grand-daddy would like a blackberry pudding for dinner. Catch-ing up her apron, and using it as a receptacle for the berries, she had gathered scarcely more than a handful when she heard a groan.

Cicely was not timid, and her curiosity being aroused by the sound, she stood erect and remained in a listening atti-tude. In a moment the sound was repeated, and, gauging the point from which it came, she plunged resolutely into the thick underbrush of the forest. She had gone but a few yards when she stopped short with an exclamation of sur-prise and concern.

Upon the ground, under the shadow of the towering pines, a man lay at full length,—a young man, several years under thirty, apparently, so far as his age could be guessed from a face that wore a short soft beard, and was so begrimed with dust and incrusted with blood that little could be seen of the underlying integument. What was visible showed a skin browned by nature or by exposure. His hands were of even a darker brown, almost as dark as Cicely's own. A tangled mass of very curly black hair, matted with burs, dank with dew, and clotted with blood, fell partly over his forehead, on the edge of which, extending back into the hair, an ugly scalp wound was gaping, and, though apparently not just inflicted, was still bleeding slowly, as though reluctant to stop, in spite of the coagulation that had almost closed it.

Cicely with a glance took in all this and more. But, first of all, she saw the man was wounded and bleeding, and the nurse latent in all womankind awoke in her to the requirements of the situation. She knew there was a spring a few rods away, and ran swiftly to it. There was usually a gourd at the spring, but now it was gone. Pouring out the blackberries in a little heap where they could be found again, she took off her apron, dipped one end of it into the spring, and ran back to the wounded man. The apron was clean, and she squeezed a little stream of water from it into the man's mouth. He swallowed it with avidity. Cicely then knelt by his side, and with the wet end of her apron washed the blood from the wound lightly, and the dust from the man's face. Then she looked at her apron a moment, debating whether she should tear it or not.

"I'm feared granny'll be mad," she said to herself. "I reckon I'll jes' use de whole apron."

So she bound the apron around his head as well as she could, and then sat down a moment on a fallen tree trunk, to think what she should do next. The man already seemed more comfortable; he had ceased moaning, and lay quiet, though breathing heavily.

"What shall I do with that man?" she reflected. "I don' know whether he's a w'ite man or a black man. Ef he's a w'ite man, I oughter go an' tell de w'ite folks up at de big house, an' dey'd take keer of 'im. If he's a black man, I oughter go tell granny. He don' look lack a black man somehow er nuther, an' yet he don' look lack a wi'te man; he's too dahk, an' his hair's too curly. But I mus' do somethin' wid 'im. He can't be lef' here ter die in de woods all by hisse'f. Reckon I'll go an' tell granny."

She scaled the fence, caught up the basket of peas from where she had left it, and ran, lightly and swiftly as a deer, toward the house. Her short skirt did not impede her progress, and in a few minutes she had covered the half mile and was at the cabin door, a slight heaving of her full and yet youthful breast being the only sign of any unusual exertion.

Her story was told in a moment. The old woman took down a black bottle from a high shelf, and set out with Cicely across the cornfield, toward the wounded man.

As they went through the corn Cicely recalled part of her dream. She had dreamed that under some strange circumstances—what they had been was still obscure—she had met a young man—a young man whiter than she and yet not all white—and that he had loved her and courted her and married her. Her dream had been all the sweeter because in it she had first tasted the sweetness of love, and she had not recalled it before because only in her dream had she known or thought of love as something supremely desirable.

With the memory of her dream, however, her fears revived. Dreams were solemn things. To Cicely the fabric of a vision was by no means baseless. Her trouble arose from her not being able to recall, though she was well versed in dream-lore, just what event was foreshadowed by a dream of finding a wounded man. If the wounded

man were of her own race, her dream would thus far have
been realized, and having met the young man, the other
joys might be expected to follow. If he should turn out to
be a white man, then her dream was clearly one of the kind
that go by contraries, and she could expect only sorrow and
trouble and pain as the proper sequences of this fateful
discovery.

II

The two women reached the fence that separated the
cornfield from the pine woods.

"How is I gwine ter git ovuh dat fence, chile?" asked
the old woman.

"Wait a minute, granny," said Cicely; "I'll take it down."

It was only an eight-rail fence, and it was a matter of
but a few minutes for the girl to lift down and lay to either
side the ends of the rails that formed one of the angles.
This done, the old woman easily stepped across the remaining two or three rails. It was only a moment before
they stood by the wounded man. He was lying still, breathing regularly, and seemingly asleep.

"What is he, granny," asked the girl anxiously, "a w'ite
man, or not?"

Old Dinah pushed back the matted hair from the
wounded man's brow, and looked at the skin beneath. It
was fairer there, but yet of a decided brown. She raised
his hand, pushed back the tattered sleeve from his wrist,
and then she laid his hand down gently.

"Mos' lackly he's a mulatter man f'om up de country
somewhar. He don' look lack dese yer niggers roun' yere,
ner yet lack a w'ite man. But de po' boy's in a bad fix,
w'ateber he is, an' I 'spec's we bettah do w'at we kin fer
'im, an' w'en he comes to he'll tell us w'at he is—er w'at he
calls hisse'f. Hol' 'is head up, chile, an' I'll po' a drop er dis
yer liquor down his th'oat; dat 'll bring 'im to quicker
'n anything e'se I knows."

Cicely lifted the sick man's head, and Dinah poured a few drops of the whiskey between his teeth. He swallowed it readily enough. In a few minutes he opened his eyes and stared blankly at the two women. Cicely saw that his eyes were large and black, and glistening with fever.

"How you feelin', suh?" asked the old woman.

There was no answer.

"Is you feelin' bettah now?"

The wounded man kept on staring blankly. Suddenly he essayed to put his hand to his head, gave a deep groan, and fell back again unconscious.

"He's gone ag'in," said Dinah. "I reckon we'll hafter tote 'im up ter de house and take keer er 'im dere. W'ite folks would n't want ter fool wid a nigger man, an' we doan know who his folks is. He's outer his head an' will be fer some time yet, an' we can't tell nuthin' 'bout 'im tel he comes ter his senses."

Cicely lifted the wounded man by the arms and shoulders. She was strong, with the strength of youth and a sturdy race. The man was pitifully emaciated; how much, the two women had not suspected until they raised him. They had no difficulty whatever, except for the awkwardness of such a burden, in lifting him over the fence and carrying him through the cornfield to the cabin.

They laid him on Cicely's bed in the little lean-to shed that formed a room separate from the main apartment of the cabin. The old woman sent Cicely to cook the dinner, while she gave her own attention exclusively to the still unconscious man. She brought water and washed him as though he were a child.

"Po' boy," she said, "he doan feel lack he's be'n eatin' nuff to feed a sparrer. He 'pears ter be mos' starved ter def."

She washed his wound more carefully, made some lint, —the art was well known in the sixties,—and dressed his wound with a fair degree of skill.

"Somebody must 'a' be'n tryin' ter put yo' light out, chile," she muttered to herself as she adjusted the bandage around his head. "A little higher er a little lower, an' you wouldn' 'a' be'n yere ter tell de tale. Dem clo's," she argued, lifting the tattered garments she had removed from her patient, "don' b'long 'roun' yere. Dat kinder weavin' come f'om down to'ds Souf Ca'lina. I wish Needham 'u'd come erlong. He kin tell who dis man is, an' all erbout 'im."

She made a bowl of gruel, and fed it, drop by drop, to the sick man. This roused him somewhat from his stupor, but when Dinah thought he had enough of the gruel, and stopped feeding him, he closed his eyes again and relapsed into a heavy sleep that was so closely akin to unconsciousness as to be scarcely distinguishable from it.

When old Needham came home at noon, his wife, who had been anxiously awaiting his return, told him in a few words the story of Cicely's discovery and of the subsequent events.

Needham inspected the stranger with a professional eye. He had been something of a plantation doctor in his day, and was known far and wide for his knowledge of simple remedies. The negroes all around, as well as many of the poorer white people, came to him for the treatment of common ailments.

"He's got a fevuh," he said, after feeling the patient's pulse and laying his hand on his brow, "an we'll hafter gib 'im some yarb tea an' nuss 'im tel de fevuh w'ars off. I 'spec'," he added, "dat I knows whar dis boy come f'om. He's mos' lackly one er dem bright mulatters, f'om Robeson County—some of 'em call deyse'ves Croatan Injins—w'at's been conscripted an' sent ter wu'k on de fo'tifications down at Wimbleton er some'er's er nuther, an' done 'scaped, and got mos' killed gittin' erway, an' wuz n' none too well fed befo', an' nigh 'bout starved ter def sence. We'll hafter hide dis man, er e'se we is lackly ter git inter trouble ou'se'ves by harb'rin' 'im. Ef dey ketch 'im yere, dey's liable ter take 'im out an' shoot 'im—an' des ez lackly us too."

Cicely was listening with bated breath.

"Oh, gran'daddy," she cried with trembling voice, "don' let 'em ketch 'im! Hide 'im somewhar."

"I reckon we'll leave 'im yere fer a day er so. Ef he had come f'om roun' yere I'd be skeered ter keep 'im, fer de w'ite folks 'u'd prob'ly be lookin' fer 'im. But I knows ev'ybody w'at's be'n conscripted fer ten miles 'roun', an' dis yere boy don' b'long in dis neighborhood. W'en 'e gits so 'e kin he'p 'isse'f we'll put 'im up in de lof' an' hide 'im till de Yankees come. Fer dey're comin', sho'. I dremp' las' night dey wuz close ter han', and I hears de w'ite folks talkin' ter deyse'ves 'bout it. An' de time is comin' w'en de good Lawd gwine ter set his people free, an' it ain' gwine ter be long, nuther."

Needham's prophecy proved true. In less than a week the Confederate garrison evacuated the arsenal in the neighboring town of Patesville, blew up the buildings, destroyed the ordnance and stores, and retreated across the Cape Fear River, burning the river bridge behind them,—two acts of war afterwards unjustly attributed to General Sherman's army, which followed close upon the heels of the retreating Confederates.

When there was no longer any fear for the stranger's safety, no more pains were taken to conceal him. His wound had healed rapidly, and in a week he had been able with some help to climb up the ladder into the loft. In all this time, however, though apparently conscious, he had said no word to any one, nor had he seemed to comprehend a word that was spoken to him.

Cicely had been his constant attendant. After the first day, during which her granny had nursed him, she had sat by his bedside, had fanned his fevered brow, had held food

and water and medicine to his lips. When it was safe
for him to come down from the loft and sit in a chair under
a spreading oak, Cicely supported him until he was strong
enough to walk about the yard. When his strength had
increased sufficiently to permit of greater exertion, she
accompanied him on long rambles in the fields and woods.

In spite of his gain in physical strength, the newcomer
changed very little in other respects. For a long time he
neither spoke nor smiled. To questions put to him he simply
gave no reply, but looked at his questioner with the blank
unconsciousness of an infant. By and by he began to
recognize Cicely, and to smile at her approach. The next
step in returning consciousness was but another manifesta-
tion of the same sentiment. When Cicely would leave him
he would look his regret, and be restless and uneasy until
she returned.

The family were at a loss what to call him. To any
inquiry as to his name he answered no more than to other
questions.

"He come jes' befo' Sherman," said Needham, after a
few weeks, "lack John de Baptis' befo' de Lawd. I reckon
we bettah call 'im John."

So they called him John. He soon learned the name.
As time went on Cicely found that he was quick at learning
things. She taught him to speak her own negro English,
which he pronounced with absolute fidelity to her intona-
tions; so that barring the quality of his voice, his speech was
an echo of Cicely's own.

The summer wore away and the autumn came. John
and Cicely wandered in the woods together and gathered
walnuts, and chinquapins and wild grapes. When harvest
time came, they worked in the fields side by side,—
plucked the corn, pulled the fodder, and gathered the dried
peas from the yellow pea-vines. Cicely was a phenomenal
cottonpicker, and John accompanied her to the fields and

stayed by her hours at a time, though occasionally he would complain of his head, and sit under a tree and rest part of the day while Cicely worked, the two keeping one another always in sight.

They did not have a great deal of intercourse with other people. Young men came to the cabin sometimes to see Cicely, but when they found her entirely absorbed in the stranger they ceased their visits. For a time Cicely kept him away, as much as possible, from others, because she did not wish them to see that there was anything wrong about him. This was her motive at first, but after a while she kept him to herself simply because she was happier so. He was hers—hers alone. She had found him, as Pharaoh's daughter had found Moses in the bulrushes; she had taught him to speak, to think, to love. She had not taught him to remember; she would not have wished him to; she would have been jealous of any past to which he might have proved bound by other ties. Her dream so far had come true. She had found him; he loved her. The rest of it would as surely follow, and that before long. For dreams were serious things, and time had proved hers to have been not a presage of misfortune, but one of the beneficent visions that are sent, that we may enjoy by anticipation the good things that are in store for us.

III

But a short interval of time elapsed after the passage of the warlike host that swept through North Carolina, until there appeared upon the scene the vanguard of a second army, which came to bring light and the fruits of liberty to a land which slavery and the havoc of war had brought to ruin. It is fashionable to assume that those who undertook the political rehabilitation of the Southern States merely rounded out the ruin that the war had wrought— merely ploughed up the desolate land and sowed it with salt.

Perhaps the gentler judgments of the future may recognize that their task was a difficult one, and that wiser and honester men might have failed as egregiously. It may even, in time, be conceded that some good came out of the carpet-bag governments, as, for instance, the establishment of a system of popular education in the former slave States. Where it had been a crime to teach people to read or write, a schoolhouse dotted every hillside, and the State provided education for rich and poor, for white and black alike. Let us lay at least this token upon the grave of the carpet-baggers. The evil they did lives after them, and the statute of limitations does not seem to run against it. It is but just that we should not forget the good.

Long, however, before the work of political reconstruction had begun, a brigade of Yankee schoolmasters and schoolma'ams had invaded Dixie, and one of the latter had opened a Freedman's Bureau School in the town of Patesville, about four miles from Needham Green's cabin on the neighboring sandhills.

It had been quite a surprise to Miss Chandler's Boston friends when she had announced her intention of going South to teach the freedmen. Rich, accomplished, beautiful, and a social favorite, she was giving up the comforts and luxuries of Northern life to go among hostile strangers, where her associates would be mostly ignorant negroes. Perhaps she might meet occasionally an officer of some Federal garrison, or a traveler from the North; but to all intents and purposes her friends considered her as going into voluntary exile. But heroism was not rare in those days, and Martha Chandler was only one of the great multitude whose hearts went out toward an oppressed race, and who freely poured out their talents, their money, their lives,—whatever God had given them,—in the sublime and not unfruitful effort to transform three millions of slaves into intelligent freemen. Miss Chandler's friends knew, too, that she had met a great sorrow, and more than suspected that out of it had grown her determination to go South.

When Cicely Green heard that a school for colored people had been opened at Patesville she combed her hair, put on her Sunday frock and such bits of finery as she possessed, and set out for town early the next Monday morning.

There were many who came to learn the new gospel of education, which was to be the cure for all the freedmen's ills. The old and gray-haired, the full-grown man and woman, the toddling infant,—they came to acquire the new and wonderful learning that was to make them the equals of the white people. It was the teacher's task, by no means an easy one, to select from this incongruous mass the most promising material, and to distribute among them the second-hand books and clothing that were sent, largely by her Boston friends, to aid her in her work; to find out what they knew, to classify them by their intelligence rather than by their knowledge, for they were all lamentably ignorant. Some among them were the children of parents who had been free before the war, and of these some few could read and one or two could write. One paragon, who could repeat the multiplication table, was immediately promoted to the position of pupil teacher.

Miss Chandler took a liking to the tall girl who had come so far to sit under her instruction. There was a fine, free air in her bearing, a lightness in her step, a sparkle in her eye, that spoke of good blood,—whether fused by nature in its own alembic, out of material despised and spurned of men, or whether some obscure ancestral strain, the teacher could not tell. The girl proved intelligent and learned rapidly, indeed seemed almost feverishly anxious to learn. She was quiet, and was, though utterly untrained, instinctively polite, and profited from the first day by the example of her teacher's quiet elegance. The teacher dressed in simple black. When Cicely came

back to school the second day, she had left off her glass
beads and her red ribbon, and had arranged her hair as
nearly like the teacher's as her skill and its quality would
permit.

The teacher was touched by these efforts at imitation,
and by the intense devotion Cicely soon manifested toward
her. It was not a sycophantic, troublesome devotion, that
made itself a burden to its object. It found expression in
little things done rather than in any words the girl said.
To the degree that the attraction was mutual, Martha recognized in it a sort of freemasonry of temperament that drew
them together in spite of the differences between them.
Martha felt sometimes, in the vague way that one specu-
lates about the impossible, that if she were brown, and had
been brought up in North Carolina, she would be like
Cicely; and that if Cicely's ancestors had come over in
the Mayflower, and Cicely had been reared on Beacon
Street, in the shadow of the State House dome, Cicely would
have been very much like herself.

Miss Chandler was lonely sometimes. Her duties kept her
occupied all day. On Sunday she taught a Bible class in
the schoolroom. Correspondence with bureau officials and
friends at home furnished her with additional occupation.
At times, nevertheless, she felt a longing for the company
of women of her own race; but the white ladies of the
town did not call, even in the most formal way, upon the
Yankee school-teacher. Miss Chandler was therefore fain
to do the best she could with such companionship as was
available. She took Cicely to her home occasionally, and
asked her once to stay all night. Thinking, however, that
she detected a reluctance on the girl's part to remain away
from home, she did not repeat her invitation.

Cicely, indeed, was filling a double rôle. The learning
acquired from Miss Chandler she imparted to John at
home. Every evening, by the light of the pine-knots blazing

on Needham's ample hearth, she taught John to read the
simple words she had learned during the day. Why she did
not take him to school she had never asked herself; there
were several other pupils as old as he seemed to be.
Perhaps she still thought it necessary to protect him from
curious remark. He worked with Needham by day, and she
could see him at night, and all of Saturdays and Sundays.
Perhaps it was the jealous selfishness of love. She had found
him; he was hers. In the spring, when school was over,
her granny had said that she might marry him. Till then
her dream would not yet have come true, and she must
keep him to herself. And yet she did not wish him to lose
this golden key to the avenues of opportunity. She would
not take him to school, but she would teach him each
day all that she herself had learned. He was not difficult
to teach, but learned, indeed, with what seemed to Cicely
marvelous ease,—always, however, by her lead, and never
of his own initiative. For while he could do a man's work,
he was in most things but a child, without a child's curiosity.
His love for Cicely appeared the only thing for which he
needed no suggestion; and even that possessed an element
of childish dependence that would have seemed, to minds
trained to thoughtful observation, infinitely pathetic.

The spring came and cotton-planting time. The children
began to drop out of Miss Chandler's school one by one,
as their services were required at home. Cicely was among
those who intended to remain in school until the term
closed with the "exhibition," in which she was assigned a
leading part. She had selected her recitation, or "speech,"
from among half a dozen poems that her teacher had
suggested, and to memorizing it she devoted considerable
time and study. The exhibition, as the first of its kind, was
sure to be a notable event. The parents and friends of
the children were invited to attend, and a colored church,
recently erected,—the largest available building,—was

secured as the place where the exercises should take place.

On the morning of the eventful day, uncle Needham, assisted by John, harnessed the mule to the two-wheeled cart, on which a couple of splint-bottomed chairs were fastened to accommodate Dinah and Cicely. John put on his best clothes,—an ill-fitting suit of blue jeans,—a round wool hat, a pair of coarse brogans, a homespun shirt, and a bright blue necktie. Cicely wore her best frock, a red ribbon at her throat, another in her hair, and carried a bunch of flowers in her hand. Uncle Needham and aunt Dinah were also in holiday array. Needham and John took their seats on opposite sides of the cart-frame, with their feet dangling down, and thus the equipage set out leisurely for the town.

Cicely had long looked forward impatiently to this day. She was going to marry John the next week, and then her dream would have come entirely true. But even this anticipated happiness did not overshadow the importance of the present occasion, which would be an epoch in her life, a day of joy and triumph. She knew her speech perfectly, and timidity was not one of her weaknesses. She knew that the red ribbons set off her dark beauty effectively, and that her dress fitted neatly the curves of her shapely figure. She confidently expected to win the first prize, a large morocco-covered Bible, offered by Miss Chandler for the best exercise.

Cicely and her companions soon arrived at Patesville. Their entrance into the church made quite a sensation, for Cicely was not only an acknowledged belle, but a general favorite, and to John there attached a tinge of mystery which inspired a respect not bestowed upon those who had grown up in the neighborhood. Cicely secured a seat in the front part of the church, next to the aisle, in the place reserved for the pupils. As the house was already partly filled by townspeople when the party from the country arrived, Needham and his wife and John were forced to content themselves with places somewhat in the rear of the room, from which they could see and hear what took place on the platform, but where they were not at all conspicuously visible to those at the front of the church.

The schoolmistress had not yet arrived, and order was preserved in the audience by two of the elder pupils, adorned with large rosettes of red, white, and blue, who ushered the most important vistors to the seats reserved for them. A national flag was gracefully draped over the platform, and under it hung a lithograph of the Great Emancipator, for it was thus these people thought of him. He had saved the Union, but the Union had never meant anything good to them. He had proclaimed liberty to the captive, which meant all to them; and to them he was and would ever be the Great Emancipator.

The schoolmistress came in at a rear door and took her seat upon the platform. Martha was dressed in white; for once she had laid aside the sombre garb in which alone she had been seen since her arrival at Patesville. She wore a yellow rose at her throat, a bunch of jasmine in her belt. A sense of responsibility for the success of the exhibition had deepened the habitual seriousness of her face, yet she greeted the audience with a smile.

"Don' Miss Chan'ler look sweet," whispered the little girls to one another, devouring her beauty with sparkling eyes, their lips parted over a wealth of ivory.

"De Lawd will bress dat chile," said one old woman, in soliloquy. "I t'ank de good Marster I's libbed ter see dis day."

Even envy could not hide its noisome head: a pretty quadroon whispered to her neighbor:—

"I don't b'liebe she's natch'ly ez white ez dat. I 'spec'

she's be'n powd'rin'! An' I know all dat hair can't be her'n; she's got on a switch, sho's you bawn."

"You knows dat ain' so, Ma'y 'Liza Smif," rejoined the other, with a look of stern disapproval; "you *knows* dat ain' so. You'd gib yo' everlastin' soul 'f you wuz ez white ez Miss Chan'ler, en yo' ha'r wuz ez long ez her'n."

"By Jove, Maxwell!" exclaimed a young officer, who belonged to the Federal garrison stationed in the town, "but that girl is a beauty." The speaker and a companion were in fatigue uniform, and had merely dropped in for an hour between garrison duty. The ushers had wished to give them seats on the platform, but they had declined, thinking that perhaps their presence there might embarrass the teacher. They sought rather to avoid observation by sitting behind a pillar in the rear of the room, around which they could see without attracting undue attention.

"To think," the lieutenant went on, "of that Junonian figure, those lustrous orbs, that golden coronal, that flower of Northern civilization, being wasted on these barbarians!" The speaker uttered an exaggerated but suppressed groan.

His companion, a young man of cleanshaven face and serious aspect, nodded assent, but whispered reprovingly,—

" 'Sh! some one will hear you. The exercises are going to begin."

When Miss Chandler stepped forward to announce the hymn to be sung by the school as the first exercise, every eye in the room was fixed upon her, except John's, which saw only Cicely. When the teacher had uttered a few words, he looked up to her, and from that moment did not take his eyes off Martha's face.

After the singing, a little girl, dressed in white, crossed by ribbons of red and blue, recited with much spirit a patriotic poem.

When Martha announced the third exercise, John's face took on a more than usually animated expression, and there was a perceptible deepening of the troubled look in his eyes, never entirely absent since Cicely had found him in the woods.

A little yellow boy, with long curls, and a frightened air, next ascended the platform.

"Now, Jimmie, be a man, and speak right out," whispered his teacher, tapping his arm reassuringly with her fan as he passed her.

Jimmie essayed to recite the lines so familiar to a past generation of schoolchildren:—

> "I knew a widow very poor,
>   Who four small children had;
> The eldest was but six years old,
>   A gentle, modest lad."

He ducked his head hurriedly in a futile attempt at a bow; then, following instructions previously given him, fixed his eyes upon a large cardboard motto hanging on the rear wall of the room, which admonished him in bright red letters to

" ALWAYS SPEAK THE TRUTH,"

and started off with assumed confidence—

> "I knew a widow very poor,
>   Who"—

At this point, drawn by an irresistible impulse, his eyes sought the level of the audience. Ah, fatal blunder! He stammered, but with an effort raised his eyes and began again:

> "I knew a widow very poor,
>   Who four"—

Again his treacherous eyes fell, and his little remaining self-possession utterly forsook him. He made one more despairing effort:—

> "I knew a widow very poor,
>   Who four small"—

and then, bursting into tears, turned and fled amid a murmur of sympathy.

Jimmie's inglorious retreat was covered by the singing in chorus of "The Star-spangled Banner," after which Cicely came forward to recite her poem.

"By Jove, Maxwell!" whispered the young officer, who was evidently a connoisseur of female beauty, "that isn't bad for a bronze Venus. I'll tell you"—

" 'Sh!" said the other. "Keep still."

When Cicely finished her recitation, the young officers began to applaud, but stopped suddenly in some confusion as they realized that they were the only ones in the audience so engaged. The colored people had either not learned how to express their approval in orthodox fashion, or else their respect for the sacred character of the edifice forbade any such demonstration. Their enthusiasm found vent, however, in a subdued murmur, emphasized by numerous nods and winks and suppressed exclamations. During the singing that followed Cicely's recitation the two officers quietly withdrew, their duties calling them away at this hour.

At the close of the exercises, a committee on prizes met in the vestibule, and unanimously decided that Cicely Green was entitled to the first prize. Proudly erect, with sparkling eyes and cheeks flushed with victory, Cicely advanced to the platform to receive the coveted reward. As she turned away, her eyes, shining with gratified vanity, sought those of her lover.

John sat bent slightly forward in an attitude of strained attention; and Cicely's triumph lost half its value when she saw that it was not at her, but at Miss Chandler, that his look was directed. Though she watched him thenceforward, not one glance did he vouchsafe to his jealous sweetheart, and never for an instant withdrew his eyes from Martha, or relaxed the unnatural intentness of his gaze. The imprisoned mind, stirred to unwonted efforts, was

struggling for liberty; and from Martha had come the first
ray of outer light that had penetrated its dungeon.

Before the audience was dismissed, the teacher rose
to bid her school farewell. Her intention was to take
a vacation of three months; but what might happen in that
time she did not know, and there were duties at home of
such apparent urgency as to render her return to North
Carolina at least doubtful; so that in her own heart her
au revoir sounded very much like a farewell.

She spoke to them of the hopeful progress they had
made, and praised them for their eager desire to learn.
She told them of the serious duties of life, and of the use
they should make of their acquirements. With prophetic
finger she pointed them to the upward way which they must
climb with patient feet to raise themselves out of the depths.

Then, an unusual thing with her, she spoke of herself.
Her heart was full; it was with difficulty that she maintained her composure; for the faces that confronted her
were kindly faces, and not critical, and some of them she
had learned to love right well.

"I am going away from you, my children," she said;
"but before I go I want to tell you how I came to be in
North Carolina; so that if I have been able to do anything
here among you for which you might feel inclined, in your
good nature, to thank me, you may thank not me alone,
but another who came before me, and whose work I have
but taken up where *he* laid it down. I had a friend,—
a dear friend,—why should I be ashamed to say it?—
a lover, to whom I was to be married,—as I hope all you
girls may some day be happily married. His country needed
him, and I gave him up. He came to fight for the Union
and for Freedom, for he believed that all men are brothers.
He did not come back again—he gave up his life for you.
Could I do less than he? I came to the land that he
sanctified by his death, and I have tried in my weak

way to tend the plant he watered with his blood, and which, in the fullness of time, will blossom forth into the perfect flower of liberty."

She could say no more, and as the whole audience thrilled in sympathy with her emotion, there was a hoarse cry from the men's side of the room, and John forced his way to the aisle and rushed forward to the platform.

"Martha! Martha!"

"Arthur! O Arthur!"

Pent-up love burst the flood-gates of despair and oblivion, and caught these two young hearts in its torrent. Captain Arthur Carey, of the 1st Massachusetts, long since reported missing, and mourned as dead, was restored to reason and to his world.

It seemed to him but yesterday that he had escaped from the Confederate prison at Salisbury; that in an encounter with a guard he had received a wound in the head; that he had wandered on in the woods, keeping himself alive by means of wild berries, with now and then a piece of bread or a potato from a friendly negro. It seemed but the night before that he had laid himself down, tortured with fever, weak from loss of blood, and with no hope that he would ever rise again. From that moment his memory of the past was a blank until he recognized Martha on the platform and took up again the thread of his former existence where it had been broken off.

And Cicely? Well, there is often another woman, and Cicely, all unwittingly to Carey or to Martha, had been the other woman. For, after all, her beautiful dream had been one of the kind that go by contraries.

OLIVE TILFORD DARGAN

It is unusual for a writer to be successful in more than one type of composition. Olive Tilford Dargan has made a name for herself in four: drama, poetry, the novel, and the short story. *Semiramis and Other Plays* (1904), *Lords and Lovers* (1906), and *The Mortal Gods* (1912) are closet dramas on Biblical and historical subjects. *Pathflower* (1914), *The Cycle's Rim* (1916), and *Lute and Furrow* (1922) are volumes of poetry. In 1925, she published a book of short stories, *Highland Annals*. Then, under the pen name of Fielding Burke, she wrote three novels, *Call Home the Heart* (1932), *A Stone Came Rolling* (1935), and *Sons of the Stranger* (1947). In 1941, *Highland Annals* was revised and issued under the title *From My Highest Hill*.

She was born of Virginia stock in Grayson County, Kentucky, near the town of Leitchfield. After teaching school in Arkansas, Missouri, Texas, and in Canada, she studied at Peabody College in Tennessee and at Radcliffe in Massachusetts. During her Radcliffe days, she met Pegram Dargan, a Harvard student from South Carolina, and they were married. For six years, they lived in New York; then they moved to western North Carolina seeking health and, as she says, "the magic of mountains." In 1916, Pegram Dargan was drowned on a Cuban voyage; and soon afterwards Mrs. Dargan returned to her Swain County acres, Horizon Farm, twelve miles from Bryson City, where she lived the life of a dirt farmer. Except for frequent visits to Europe, she remained there till 1925, when she moved to Bluebonnet Lodge in West Asheville.

Mrs. Dargan has received many honors. She is a charter member of the Poetry Society of America. In 1916, *The Cycle's Rim* won the $500 prize awarded by the Southern Society of New York for the best book by a Southern writer. The following year the University of North Carolina conferred upon her the honorary degree of Litt.D.

For a while in the 1950's, it looked as though Mrs. Dargan had forsaken her pen. Then it was revealed that for more than a decade she had been writing poetry. A new volume of verse, *The Spotted Hawk,* was published in 1958.

"Evvie: Somewhat Married" is probably a portrait drawn from life. Its action dates from the time Mrs. Dargan lived in the Great Smoky Mountains. First introduced into literature in a poem from *Lute and Furrow,* the heroine is too real not to have once walked and breathed. At any rate, one can judge from this one story alone why Olive Tilford Dargan has been acclaimed as the writer of fiction who has most faithfully interpreted the North Carolina mountain people.

Evvie: Somewhat Married

OLIVE TILFORD DARGAN

THE KANES were a deserving family tainted with in-
articulate ambition. I was glad to have them as rather
distant neighbors instead of tenants. Evvie, the oldest child,
possessed beauty of the artless kind that stirs even the hurried passer-by with a feeling of responsibility. As a tenant's
daughter she would have troubled my sleep. Her mother,
Angeline Kane, sometimes stopped to see me when trudging
to Beebread for supplies, or on her way to visit some member of the Merlin clan. My typewriter seemed to have a
hypnotic effect on Angeline. I did not understand this until
the day that she came in with Evvie.

"She hain't strong, Evvie. I kain't get her to stay with a
hoe long enough fer me to go in an' cook dinner. I say
to her, 'Evvie, you take my place an' let me go in,' an' she'll
try fer a bit, but her poppie'll notice her drappin' back an'
drawin' her breath hard, an' he'll say, 'You run along now
an' he'p yer mother,' an' in she'll come. So I've got in the
way of lettin' her handle the dinner by herse'f an' I stay
with the hoe."

"But she can't be more than ten," I said.

"She's twelve, an' that's nigh to a woman. Cleve
Saunders kain't pass our place now 'thout peekin' around
fer Evvie."

From *From My Highest Hill* by Olive Tilford Dargan, published by
J. B. Lippincott Co. Copyright, 1925, 1941, by Olive Tilford Dargan.

I expected Evvie to drop her head or wriggle behind a chair; but her chiselled chin was high, and her eyes darkened as easily as twilight water.

Mrs. Kane's glance swerved again to my typewriter, and her heart tumbled out as she said: "I been thinkin' maybe you could learn Evvie to write on that."

"If she is so much help to you," I answered, snatching at the first defense, "why not keep her at home until she is married?"

"That's the trouble—her marryin'. She'll disappint any boy around here. They all expect a woman to take a hand in makin' the livin', through crop-time anyway. An' Evvie kain't hold out. If she could learn to work on *that,* an' get a job in town, like as not some boy out there 'ud take a notion to her, an' town boys don't want their wives to work. 'Tain't expected of 'em to do more 'n the cookin' an' housework an' sewin', an' that wouldn't be too hard on Evvie."

Evvie had stepped into the yard. It was a habit with her, I found, to vanish as if for charming asides with herself and reappear with no sign of absence upon her. I reminded her mother that there might be children to care for in addition to the occupations mentioned.

" 'Course there would, but she'd have *them* anywheres, an' she'd better have 'em where life is easier'n it is here."

"No doubt. What is her school grade?"

"She's got to the fifth reader. She ain't for'd in her books, smart-lookin' as she is."

"Bring her to me when she finishes the seventh grade, and we'll see."

The mother's face grew long. "She ain't fitten fer school," she said. "She's had to quit walkin' so fur, 'count o' that wheezin' in her chest that ketches her when she climbs up the mountain. Her poppie had to meet her halfway down an' carry her up pick-a-back. She's too big fer that now, an' he says she knows enough. He's awful proud o' Evvie. She reads the paper to him ever' week. She's as smart as Annie Dills who learned to write on one o' them things an's makin' twelve dollars a week in Asheville."

I held out that skill on the machine would be useless without more schooling behind it. Evvie, who had shown no interest in her future, revealed no disappointment. She was a flower and had implicit faith in the sun. But there was a touch of desperation in Mrs. Kane's voice as she took her leave. I tried to believe with Evvie in the reliability of sunshine.

A year later Evvie was "talkin' " to Cleve Saunders. He was a good boy who here and there had learned the carpenter's trade. Occasionally he would go to Asheville to work on a job, and then a weekly letter would come to Evvie. I approved of Cleve, but Evvie was only thirteen, and though vividly and perfectly moulded as a woman, she was small for her years. I protested to Mrs. Kane.

"I ain't goin' to let her git married 'fore she's fifteen," the mother assured me. "Not if I can he'p it. Ef she had some work to keep her mind on—"

"I've a friend," I said, as I stepped between Mrs. Kane and my typewriter, "who would like a helper with her children. It would be a good home for Evvie and she would have nothing to do but play."

"You mean anybody'd pay her fer playin'?"

"With children. And Evvie is fine with her little brothers and sisters." (I'll make Sue Waters take her, said I to myself.)

"Where'd the place be?"

"It's on a big farm near Knoxville."

"It'll cost a heap to go, an' we ain't got nary calf we can sell now."

"My friend will send the money for her fare, and Evvie can pay it back if she stays."

Mrs. Kane threw up her head with almost as fine an air as Evvie herself.

"If she don't stay, I'll pay it back if it takes ever' egg fer a year," she said.

We thought it settled; but before I could sufficiently browbeat Sue Waters, Evvie's mother came to me with a face that was gray and pinched.

"I reckon," she said, "Evvie kain't go till next year. I shore thought I was through with babies, but there's another comin', an' Evvie's all the he'p I've got."

During preparations for Evvie's setting forth, I had seen more of her than usual, and had detected signs of a quick temper that gave me uneasy visions of her amid the Waters brood. Also I feared that her ideas of equality, as natural to her as the ground under her feet, might give some trouble. If little Margaret Waters should receive a piano for her birthday, Evvie would expect the same or "just as good." Sue Waters, having taken her degree in the right subjects, would of course comprehend, but could hardly supply the piano. My relief was almost as deep as my concern when Mrs. Kane made her joyless announcement.

"Perhaps it is better to wait," said I. "Evvie will be older and larger by a year."

"I dunno as that's better," said the mother. "She's a woman to the bone, an' a year'll seem a long time."

"Your husband's two orphan nieces are coming to live with you. Won't they be help enough? And you can let Evvie go?"

"Dolph's sister, in Beebread, says she's goin' to keep the girls till they get through first year High. Says by that time they'll be proud enough to want to finish school an' won't mind walkin' up an' down the mountain. She's sent Dolph's grandmother to us, 'stead of Amy an' Sue."

"His grandmother! But she's so old. What a burden for you!"

"She's only ninety-two, an' no trouble at all. Kain't get around much, but she's as keen in her mind as a sang-hoe. I wish you'd come over to see her. She likes to see folks. Says her hands may be still, but her eyes ain't."

I went to see Rebecca Kane, and found her to be a bright challenge to old age. No snuff, no pipe. "All I want for comfort," she said, "is a sheep-skin in my chair." Her twisted hands lay in her lap like small helpless birds, but her eyes had surrendered nothing.

Mrs. Kane told me that Evvie was receiving letters from Cleve Saunders which she wouldn't let anybody read.

"There's more signs around here than that," said Rebecca. "Last Sunday she put on that mail-order dress Dolph give her for her birthday, an' them hound-tongue shoes her cousin sent her, an' went around dreamin' on her feet. When she went to the branch-spout for kittle-water that her mother was waitin' for, she fergot to come back. A gal kain't have the weddin' day on her mind an' hide it."

"It will never do," I burst out. "She's only thirteen. Cleve Saunders ought to know better!"

"She's fourteen in two months," corrected Rebecca. "An' nobody can lay out a gal's road. Life has a lot to do with livin'. More'n we have."

But I did not give up my plan. Though I left the mountains before the year was out, and was gone several months, I arranged by correspondence for Evvie to go to Sue Waters as soon as conditions in the Kane home permitted. She was to write to Mrs. Waters, and money for the journey would be sent to her. As the train taking me home pulled into the village, I thought of Evvie as safe with Sue Waters, and I felt that I had helped to rob the hills of a flower that should have belonged to them utterly. A woman sharing my seat was giving me the news. I did not hear much of it, but finally caught the words, "An' Evvie got married."

I gave a start as if I would snatch the child to dry land.

Then I made my conscience comfortable. "Cleve will take good care of her," I said.

" 'Tain't Cleve," replied the woman. "It's that young feller from Mossy Creek. Judd Mason."

II

I had heard of him; a mountain buck, big and good-looking. He had never worked except to make little patches of corn that he could turn into whiskey. As soon as I saw Evvie I asked how she happened to marry Judd.

"I was goin' to the Post Office," she said, "with a letter to Mrs. Waters, tellin' her to send the money an' I'd come right on, when I met Judd an' he turned an' walked down the road with me. He begged me not to send the letter. I'd find it hard, he said, out there with strange folks who wouldn't keer nothin' fer me, an' I'd better let him look after me right. I was afraid to go so fur from home, an' Judd—he talked good. He said it 'ud be fine fer us to grow old 'longside o' one another like Aunt Marthy an' Uncle Maje Green. They're 'most up to ninety an' kaint none o' their childern get 'em to break up an' quit livin' to theirsevs."

"Where was Cleve?"

"Over in Asheville workin'. He was goin' to meet me an' put me on the Knoxville train. He lost his job, goin' to the train fer a week. I wrote to tell him I wasn't comin', but Judd lost the letter an' forgot to tell me about it. Cleve got another job though. Anybody'll give Cleve work."

"And Judd has been as good as his talk, I suppose."

Evvie swung her head to one side as if she forbade it to droop. "It'll be all right as soon as we get to oursevs. We're livin' with poppie an' mommie an' they's so many younguns at home Judd gets pouty sometimes. I kain't fix good things to eat when they's so many, an' Judd'll leave the table when he don't like what's on it."

Notwithstanding Evvie's hope, it was nearly a year be-

fore they moved to themselves. Her parents, with a home
already overflowing with small, unprofitable humanity,
would have sheltered the young pair and their expected
baby without a murmur, preferring to break their bowed
backs than breach the custom of welcome for all. But
Judd was growing restless for his old occupation, and Evvie
wanted her baby to be born in her own home. I could
see, however, that she was frightened, and would have
chosen to stay with her mother if she could have given up
the hope she had built on getting Judd to herself.

Mrs. Kane, with her heart breaking over Evvie, took
what relief she could from the exodus.

"I could stand Judd," she told me, "if it wasn't fer his
poutin'. Our folks, the Twillers and the Kanes, don't pout.
We git mad an' blow off, and that's all of it. Judd'll hang
on an' pout till my bones rub sore. I was gettin' so edgy it's
jest as well they're gone."

I went once to see Evvie after she moved. There was a
trail down the western side of the ridge on which I lived
that would bring me to Judd's cabin at the end of four
miles; and there was a wagon-road down the eastern side
which would take me eleven miles around the foot of the
ridge. I chose the trail and went down alone.

On the ridge top the sun had seemed to be of eternal
brightness; but I descended strangely into an unlit world.
The intervale below me was much narrower than the usual
valley where a settlement lies; and it was almost cut in
halves by a huge spur that was bounded on either side by a
stream of water. The two streams, Nighthawk Branch and
Mossy Creek, united at the toe of the spur. I took the trail
up Mossy Creek, as I had been told to do, and walked along
in sound of the water, but getting no glimpse of it through
the smothering laurel. It was the first time that water
running behind green leaves had left me untouched by a
mysterious joy; the first time that I had ever thought of

the laurel as somber. Its dark radiance seemed like a warning from Nature ready to spring and regain an inimical kingdom. I was half in sympathy with the Highlander who regarded it merely as a thing to fight or let contemptuously alone. My old admiration for the Greeks came rushing back. What a redoubtable imagination it was that, in the credulous youth and fear-time of the world, could draw all terror from the forest and people it with creatures of play and light!

The trail led me into a cove, away from the quavering incantation of the water, but the laurel went darkly with me, heavily mingled with kalmia that choked the trees and wrenched at their life with its curling arms.

"The shack's on northy land," Mrs. Kane had said to me, "an' the la'r'l is so blustery it 'ud tangle a wild hog."

I knew why the original settler had chosen such a spot, in spite of his aversion to "thicketty patches." In the stifling cove it would be difficult to find a hidden "still." This made the place highly desirable in the eyes of the latest tenant, Judd. I had known Evvie only on sunny hilltops, and I wondered what "living under the mountain," as the natives put it, had done to her spirit. I recalled Mrs. Kane's remark after her first visit to Evvie. "Seemed like I had to keep wipin' at the shadders all the time I's there." Evvie must be very tired, I thought, of wiping at the shadows.

The trees rose more freely and I came to a clearing. On a hill opposite me, which faced the east, was a cornfield, two or three acres in size. This, thanks to a low gap in the near-by ridge, received a few hours of morning sunlight. In the hollow below stood the shack where Evvie lived. I found her in bed with one of Judd's sisters in sullen attendance.

"She's in bed 'bout every other day," the sister said, "an' Judd's always havin' to come over the branch fer one of us to wait on her."

"I can get up to-morr' sure," said Evvie, but the faint remark only sent her attendant's nose a little higher.

Evvie was strange to see. Her eyes, dark and burning, clung devouringly to a face that already had lost all flesh.

"Where is Judd?" I asked.

The sister was silent, but Evvie flushed and said that he had gone to try to kill her a squirrel. "I ain't eat nothing all day," she said. "I been thinkin' 'bout the devil tryin' to ketch Amos Britton one night last week."

I thought she was delirious, but her companion gloatingly explained that the devil had indeed made an effort to capture Amos alive.

"It's 'cause he killed Wes Baxter in a fight a year ago, an' ain't never gone to church ner been prayed over. He went huntin' with Jim Webster Thursday night, an' something took after 'em, they couldn't tell what. Jim broke away an' run home, but Amos got behind a tree to shoot it, an' it knocked his gun down an' run him round an' round the tree fer hours. Then all at oncet daylight was comin' an' the thing wa'n't there. Amos said it run on two feet, near as he could make out, an' kep' flappin' a tail. He's so skeered he ain't stuck his nose out o' the house sence he got home."

"Do you reckon it 'uz the devil, Mis' Dolly?" asked Evvie, as if sanity hung on my answer.

"Of course not, Evvie. The man was drunk probably."

"He wa'nt drunk," interposed the sister. "It run him round an' round the tree, an' he could feel its breath on his neck hot as fire."

I moved toward the water-bucket, and courtesy demanded that she should go to the spring for fresh water. She disappeared and the room lost its spirit of combat. With swimming head—how far were we from the Greeks and the bright gods of the woods?—I did what I could to reassure Evvie.

"I ain't afeard when Judd is here," she said. "Judd ain't afeard o' nothin'. He'll stay at home more when the baby comes. Don't men always think a lot o' their babies, Mis' Dolly?"

I lied vigorously, and Evvie was smiling when the sister-in-law returned. She was smiling when I left, for I had promised that her mother would come next day and stay a week.

I went home by way of the Kanes, and fortunately found Jane Drake there. She was in the yard hulling a bushel of walnuts to take home and store for Christmas. Jane was never caught unprepared for the holiday raids of her swarming grandchildren. Yes, she would take care of the Kane household, "but not more'n till Saturday, 'count o' meetin' at Stecoah." And Mrs. Kane hurried down the dark mountain trail to her daughter, not waiting for next day.

Evvie had chosen a thorny bed, and homespun philosophy would have her lie on it. That was Jane Drake's conclusion, as she brandished a fork over a skillet of meat she was frying for supper. But old Rebecca's eyes snapped.

"Evvie ain't tied to no bed," she said sharply. "Life ain't much more'n climbin' out of mistakes. If you make one a-marryin' that ain't no reason for not comin' from under it."

"I don't want no daughter o' mine leavin' her husband an' runnin' back to him," said Dolph.

"Nobody said anything about her runnin' back. Evvie ain't overly smart, but she knows enough to stay outen the fire after she's set in it once."

I left the house, assured of strong moral support from Rebecca if I tried to free Evvie from Judd's clutches. But before ways or means could be devised, a surprise gripped the mountain and I was drawn into the circle of agitation. . . . When life resumed its even flow again, Evvie's boy was two weeks old.

In the secluded hollows of the mountains birth goes
the indifferent way of Nature; gliding as the seasons for the
most part, but too often ruthless, confounding as storm.
Evvie, so fragile and so young, barely lived. I went once
more to the shack, going down the mountain trail with
Mrs. Kane and little Tommie, taking old Bill, the mule,
to help us climb back. Mrs. Mason met us at the door.
As soon as the customary greetings were over, the mother-
in-law put in her very just complaint.

"Law, I'm glad you got here. I kain't spen' my time
waitin' on a girl 'at won't try to sit up an' her baby two
weeks old. Won't eat nothin' nuther, makes no difference
what I fix. I baked her some loaf bread, an' put lasses on
it, an' some butter I brought from home, an' she won't
tech it. She'll not git well till she tries to, an' I kain't
wait round fer her to make up her mind. All my own work
is pilin' up, an' I've got to be at it. You know how it is,
Mis' Kane. You kain't stay here all the time no more'n I
can."

As on my first visit, I asked, "Where is Judd?" and
received the same information. "He's gone out to kill a
squirrel."

Evvie, who was lying with her eyes shut, said with
startling vigor, "He's been gone since yesterday."

Judd's mother looked toward the bed with snapping
eyes. "You kain't expect a man to lay round home forever
waitin' fer a woman to git up. I've had ten younguns an'
I never stayed in bed more'n nine days with ary one of 'em.
In two weeks I was out in the crap, if it was crap time, doin'
my part. But Evvie, she's as tender as a butterweed. An'
that's hard on Judd."

There was a big crack in the cabin near Evvie's bed.
Her eyes sought the opening in a manner that told me she
often found mental escape that way. It was obvious that
her last hope was crushed. The baby had come, but had

wrought no miracle. She knew, and all of us knew, that Judd was out on a bootlegging adventure; but it was not to be admitted in look or speech.

Evvie gazed through the crack, seeing nothing but the face of a hill that seemed about to fall on to the cabin. She stared as if her eyes would tunnel through it, and a delirious flare came over her face.

"Take that hill away, mommie," she said, in a fret.

Mrs. Kane surprised me. "I kain't take hit away, Evvie —but I can take you over hit," she said, making aspirates in her clear determination. "Can't you set up on ol' Bill? Tommie'll ride behind you an' hold you on. I'll tote the baby, Mis' Dolly'll lead Bill, an' we'll get you home."

Evvie hardly knew there was a baby, but she caught at the word home. "Oh, mommie, I can set up!"

"Set up an' ride a mule!" cried Mrs. Mason. "An' me here slaverin' fer ye, an' ye makin' out ye couldn't move!"

I made no protest; for I recalled an incident of the days before Evvie's marriage. She had been ill, and her mother had sent hurriedly for me. I went, accompanied by a friend from the region of grand opera and fever-thermometers, who happened to be in the highlands. She applied her thermometer and found that Evvie's fever was running high. We fumbled about with improvised ministrations until Evvie asked for a "flitter." Mrs. Kane was mainly worried because the child had eaten nothing since the day before, and when I saw her face light up at Evvie's request, I hastily withdrew with my friend.

"Why did you leave?" she asked. "The child may be killed. Her mother may be ignorant enough to give her that fritter, or whatever she calls it."

"Yes, she is going to get the flitter, and that is why I left. I had to take your disruptive civilized mind off the current. I want Evvie to live."

The next day my friend returned to the Kanes, expecting

to find a house in mourning. Evvie was sitting on the porch stringing beans. Mrs. Kane's face was luminous.

"Evvie got better right away," she explained, "soon as she et them three flitters I give her."

Remembering that result, and seeing the glaze of resolution on her mother's face, I meekly became a party to the process of getting Evvie out of the hollow. We formed under Mrs. Kane's direction: I first, leading the mule, and Evvie in the saddle, leaning back on Tommie's shoulder, quite safe with his strong little arms about her waist. Mrs. Kane followed, carrying the baby. And so Evvie came home.

III

Evvie did not lie in bed long after returning to her mother's house. She sat in shadowy corners, unseeing. Milk sometimes would be swallowed when brought to her; but eating required impossible effort.

"She don't hardly know me," said her mother. "Sometimes I'm 'most afeard of her. She might turn an' claw me with them hands like chicken feet. She's jest yeller skin an' bones, like a quare little old woman."

Judd did not come near her, and we heard of no inquiries on his part. But Cleve came out from Asheville and walked under my apple-trees.

"I cain't fight Judd," he said. "He's a heavyweight and I'm not. And I won't gun him. But I know where his blockade still is."

"Oh, Cleve, would you tell?"

"No, but it's hard not to. He'd go to jail, an' she could get her divorce."

"And he would be out again in six months, to go gunning for *you*. He wouldn't have your scruples. Besides, Cleve, if Evvie were free, you couldn't take on a burden like that."

"Burden! Mis' Dolly, I'd be willin' to carry Evvie with one arm and do my work with the other. You don't know how a man feels when there ain't but one woman fer him an' another man's got her—a man 'at wouldn't pull her out o' the fire! But I'm goin' back to Asheville, an' I won't try to see her. Here's my pocketbook. I want you to lend her father some money, and pay yerse'f out o' this."

He dropped the pocketbook and went, with his face oddly reddened after being so white. Evvie's doctor from Carson was paid; the parcel-post brought oranges, lettuce, and such to the Kanes' scant winter table. Gradually Evvie began to eat the food that interested her because it was unusual. Her eyes grew gentler and her glance rested intelligently on people and things. She would smile as her father told some pitiful joke, trying to ignore the fact that his daughter wasn't "jest right."

The growing baby exhibited family traits which made him a favorite. One day Evvie's wandering eyes fell upon him as he lay in my lap. Her glance stopped and became uneasy.

"Is that mommie's baby?" she said.

"No, he's your very own, Evvie, and as fine as they are made. Look! He has your big eyes, and just see how heavy! Let him lie on your lap a minute and you'll find out."

I started to lift him to her, but her look turned to swift terror and she shrank away. It was the beginning of health, however. A day or two afterward she asked me how long it would be before she died, and I knew she had begun to think about living.

"That depends on yourself, Evvie."

"Could I live if I wanted to?" she asked, with incredulous hope.

"You could be well in two months."

"After ever'thing?"

"Every single thing."

"Mommie don't want me home with a baby."

"Your mother wouldn't give up Bennie if Judd came with ten sheriffs to take him."

"Could Judd take him?" she asked, with vehemence that was full of promise.

"You left Judd, you know, and the law might let the father have the child."

"When he was so mean to me?"

"Oh! You think he was mean?"

"He'd leave me in that black holler by myse'f an' stay out all night huntin'."

"The law might think a wife ought to have the courage to put up with that."

"He knocked me inter the briars when I tried to foller him."

"M-m-m! How long was that," said I, touching the baby, "before your young man got here?"

" 'Bout a month. I told him I's afeard to stay in the shack, an' he said I wanted to foller him 'cause I thought he was goin' to Lizzie Barnes."

It was joy to me to see her eyes flood burningly with temper.

"That's where he was goin', too! He used to talk to her 'fore we's married. She'd come back from the cotton-mills in South C'lina with two silk dresses. They'd got up a big dance an' I knowed Judd was goin'. An' he knocked me inter the briars by the trail round the corn patch."

"The law might consider that," I said. "Don't worry about losing your baby. But first make sure that you want him."

"I b'lieve I could hold him a bit now if you'll set him here."

I laid the baby in her lap and slipped out to tell Mrs. Kane. In six weeks Evvie was helping her mother with the housework. Spring came, and she kept busy in the garden, or sat on the porch with her needle, making clothes for the preposterously growing Bennie. By June she was again intrenched in her loveliness; not quite so plump, but round enough, and with her old wild-rose color. By and by she was duly divorced. Judd, in South Carolina, made no protest. Evvie's perilous excursion seemed over, with no obvious reminder save the incredible baby. In a knee dress, and with hair thrown down her back, she seemed to be the child-sister of the youngster that scrambled about her.

"Your little brother will soon be big enough to go to school with you," said the new County Commissioner on his rounds, hoping to be pleasant.

Evvie stood mute and fiery red. "Don't tell him the baby's mine, mommie," she whispered later to her mother. It must have seemed strange to her—that bubbling other existence around her feet—and a little embarrassment was, I thought, quite proper.

With autumn and corn-gathering Judd returned. It was a good season in the woods for the blockaders, and Judd had made arrangements in the "South" for profitable sales. He announced that he was buying calves for the winter and wanted to lay in a supply of feed for them. I never heard of his purchasing any calves, but he went about getting a little corn here and there at the cheap harvest price. Perhaps some one told him that his boy was a lad to be proud of, for he came one day to see him. I had walked over to the Kanes with Cleve, and we were about to take our leave. Evvie shook hands with Judd quite prettily.

"Golly, Evvie, you've come back hard!" he said. "Let's set on the porch."

He had forgotten his son, but Evvie brought him out, then Judd had difficulty in maintaining indifference. He looked about and fixed on Cleve. . . .

"What you warmin' chair-bottoms round here fer, Cleve Saunders?"

"He's here," said Evvie, her cheeks pink-spotted, " 'cause he's the best friend the baby's got."

"I'm the kid's father, don't you fergit, an' I've got some rights. That divorce judge didn't put no paper 'twixt me an' the kid."

"You can see him whenever you want to," said Evvie, "so long as you don't make trouble fer anybody that's been as good to us as Cleve."

Their eyes met and battled—no doubt reminiscently— and Judd capitulated. "All right," he said.

From that time Evvie was sorely troubled by his visits. "I wouldn't mind his comin'," she said, "if he didn't keep aggervatin' me to live with him."

"Why don't you take Cleve, Evvie, and end the bother?"

"I don't want to marry," she said, with a shudder that was a broadside of confession. I was cheered. At least she would never be reconquered by Judd.

But the situation was pressing to a change; and finally it came. Judd was captured by Federal deputies. I went to Sam for particulars.

"They took him red-handed, stirrin' the mash," said Sam. "He fit like a bear, an' kicked the officer in the mouth. It'll mean the 'pen,' shore, an' Evvie'll be shet of him fer a while."

"Won't somebody bond him out?"

"His own folks don't think 'nough of him fer that. I hearn his own father say he wa'n't wuth a June bug with a catbird after it. Nobody's goin' to risk losin' a farm fer that thing."

I went home reassured. If Cleve would only pick up and woo furiously, instead of wistfully accepting mere smiles from Evvie, he could win, I felt, long before Judd's reappearance.

The sight of Evvie hurrying toward me gave me no uneasiness. She was lugging the child, in too much haste to let him toddle.

"Mis' Dolly," she began, "Judd's the baby's poppie, an' he's took. Nobody'll go his bond, an' ever'body's talkin' hard against him, an' him Bennie's poppie. I been thinkin' of that trouble 'way back, an' it wasn't all his fault."

"You fell into the briars, I suppose?"

"No, but I was aggervatin' him. I hated Lizzie Barnes an' her silk dresses, an' when he swore at me an' told me to go back, I picked up a rock an' if he hadn't jumped I'd a broke his head with it. I was ashamed to tell you then. I was wild mad, an' he ought to 'a' throwed me inter the briars. I wasn't any he'p to him in the field, an' when I got sick I wasn't any he'p in the house, like his mother said. I didn't do my part at all."

"You did all you could, Evvie," I said, with no effect on the tide pouring from her heart.

"An' way back, when we's livin' with mommie, I was aggervatin'. At first when he'd pout and wouldn't come to the table, I'd slip out with something fer him to eat, an' beg till he'd take it, but once when we had company an' he'd made me ashamed 'cause he went to the barn an' wouldn't come to breakfast, I got me a bundle o' blade-fodder an' took it to him. I told him if he wanted to live with the steers he could eat with 'em too. I was shore mean. An' Mis' Dolly, I want you to go to Carson jail an' see Judd, an' tell him when he comes back from the 'pen' I'll be ready an' we'll begin all over. He'll know I'll keep my word."

It was useless to remind her of pain that she could not recall; but I spoke of her father and mother. Would she break their hearts again?

"But Bennie!" she cried. "He's gettin' to look more like his father ever' day. If I'm hard on Judd now, how can

I look at my baby? Ever'body's against him. You're hard
as the others. Won't you go, Mis' Dolly?"

"No, I won't. You don't know what you are doing."

"Then I'll have to get somebody else to go."

Her message went to Judd by some busybody, and I
wired to Asheville for Cleve. When he arrived on the next
train I was at the station. "The thing to do, Cleve," I
said, "is to bail him out and let him come home."

Cleve, knowing so well the Evvie that eluded him, saw
the point at once. He also saw that neither he nor I
should figure as bondsman.

"The Copp boys are mixed up with Judd," said Cleve.
"I'll go to their dad, old Ham Copp, and scare him into
thinking that Judd may turn on 'em if he's not bailed out.
That'll start'll old Ham goin'. He'll know other fellers that's
been buyin' from Judd, and make 'em feel they'd better
help."

To be fair to Judd, neither of us thought that he would
ever turn informer, but the plan worked, the amount of
bail was made up, and Judd was free.

Evvie thought that he would come directly to her, but
first he went to Mossy Creek to see "the boys." They got
up a dance, and it would have been ungrateful of Judd not
to remain for it. When he reached Evvie his face was
swollen from drink, and his spirits were still riding high.
Friends had gathered at the Kanes' for the evening, and
Judd began to recount his triumphs in jail.

"They made me president o' their club soon as I got
there, an' kicked the other feller out. We had some regulations, you bet! Ever' feller that come inter jail had to pay
fifty cents fer tobacker. If he didn't, we'd hold court—
judge, jury, an' all—an' sentence him to a floggin'. We
laid it on him too. It was a purty good life if we'd had
more to eat. They wouldn't let us have whiskey nuther,
an' that was tough. They's all sorry to see me go, an' I

promised to smuggle in some hot stuff to 'em if there was any way. Mebbe I can work it with a mulatter girl 'at cooks fer 'em—right purty—color of a hick'ry leaf 'fore frost—she'll he'p me, you bet! I'll see her to-morr' when me an' Evvie go to Carson to hitch up. Some quare, ain't it, marryin' yer own wife? An' what about yer kid goin' on two at yer weddin'?"

Choking and helpless, I slipped away from the sound of his voice. Sam, walking home by my road, began to talk.

"Reckon you noticed Evvie in that corner while Judd wuz talkin'? Ef you'd 'a' cut off her head at the neck it wouldn't 'a' bled a drap."

I couldn't answer, and hurried on, finding Cleve, whom I was hoping to avoid, waiting on my doorstep. I brushed away my tears of failure and took him into the house. The flinty look I put on didn't help me any when the full light of the lamp fell on his face.

"There's twelve hours yet, Cleve," I said. "Evvie is not an utter fool!"

He wouldn't speak, and for over an hour sat by my fire, a humped reproach. I exhausted every consolation, even telling him that she wasn't worth it. Then he lifted eyes so full of mourning scorn that I became as silent as himself.

There was a tap at the door, slight enough to be Evvie's. I asked Cleve to go up to the kitchen loft and wait. When he was gone I opened the door and heard Evvie's voice.

"They's so many at our house to-night. Ever' bed's full. I thought I'd come over here to sleep. You don't keer, do you?"

"I'm glad to see you, Evvie. Come, warm a little, then jump into bed. You've been running."

"Yes, I's afraid. But I had to come."

Her little body was trembling as she sat down. I took up a book and read until she became quite still. We were in the kitchen, which once had been the "big room" of a pioneer house. Along with its hand-hewn beams and floor of puncheons two and three feet wide, it possessed the usual huge, ugly fireplace. In the corner at the right of the fireplace was a short flight of stairs with a closet under them. Here I stored the iron pots and hearth-ovens in which my predecessor had cooked her family dinners for fifty years. The closet had an opening half the height of a door. This was covered with a gay curtain.

I had held my book for ten minutes or more, when we heard sounds of talk and laughter from the road. I recognized Judd's voice. A loud knock followed. Instantly Evvie rose, stooped, and darting like a bee, vanished behind the little curtain of the closet. There was hardly room for her among the pots and old ovens, but she scuttled her way, and there was silence. I opened the outer door and Judd stood there with several companions.

"Me an' the boys are lookin' for Evvie. We started to have a reel at bedtime an' found she's gone. I 'lowed right away she'd skipped over here, bein' she's crazy 'bout you. Reckon I skeered her a little, talkin' so big about them jail fellers, but I'll make it all right. I'm goin' to be square with Evvie this time."

He began to peek around me.

"Why—ain't she here? She gone to bed?"

"No, Judd. Did you stop at Len's?"

"We hollered, an' she wuzn't there."

"You'd better go on to Sam's then," I urged, following, or rather leading him away. "Take the short trail by the hemlocks."

When they were certainly gone, I went in. Cleve and Evvie were sitting by the fire. Her arms were around his neck and she was crying steadily. Cleve's arms were determinedly in the right place. The next day they took the early train for Carson, and by noon were safely married.

Yesterday Evvie's mother said to me: "You ought to go over to Asheville, Mis' Dolly, an' see how Evvie keeps that little house primped up. There's ever'thing in it like I always wanted her to have. I reckon she's about fergot that shack in the holler."

I tell myself that it is as well with Evvie as life permits it to be with most of us; but she is only eighteen, chiselled in beauty and colored with youth; and I try not to wonder what would happen if she should ever fall in love.

JAMES BOYD

JAMES BOYD was born July 2, 1888, in Dauphin County, Pennsylvania. From the time he was thirteen, he spent much of his time in North Carolina on the estate of his grandfather, who had come to the Sandhills from the North.

After graduating from Princeton in 1910, he spent two years in England at Trinity College, Cambridge. During World War I, he served overseas and participated in the St. Mihiel and Meuse-Argonne actions. Back in America, he was advised to go south immediately, for his health had been impaired by the war. In 1919, he settled in Southern Pines on land which had belonged to his grandfather. After building a comfortable home overlooking the town, he began to try his hand at serious writing. His first published short story was "Old Pines," which came out in the *Century Magazine* in March, 1921. He had allowed himself five years of apprenticeship but was delighted that the allotted period was not necessary. Once he met John Galsworthy, who read some of Boyd's material and advised him to turn to novels. Galsworthy told his New York friends, "Keep your eye on James Boyd."

For the next four years, he carried on research in North Carolina history. The result was a powerful novel of the state during Revolutionary times, *Drums* (1925). Following the success of this book, he wrote *Marching On* (1927), a historical novel of the Civil War in North Carolina. His other books are *Long Hunt* (1930), *Roll River* (1935), *Bitter Creek* (1939), and the posthumous *Eighteen Poems* (1944).

Even more coveted than his position as one of the

foremost writers of American historical fiction was his reputation as a foxhunter. At Southern Pines, he was Master of
the Moore County Hounds. In 1927-28 he was president of
the State Literary and Historical Association of North Carolina. He was awarded the Mayflower Cup in 1935 for
Roll River, the most outstanding piece of writing by a resi-
dent North Carolinian during the year. In 1938, the
University of North Carolina conferred upon him the
honorary degree of Litt.D. Before America's entrance into
World War II, he was instrumental in the organization of
the Free Company, a group of American authors whose
purpose was to combat Axis propaganda and "to emphasize
what Americans have to be proud of and believe in."
He died February 25, 1944, at Princeton, New Jersey,
where he had gone to deliver an address on the South.

   "Old Pines" tells the story of a railroad, any one of the
numberless little lines which ran through the North Carolina
pine forests and flourished only so long as the pine trees
grew. It is also the story of a man's determination and faith.
It served as the title of *Old Pines and Other Stories* (1952),
in which Boyd's short fiction was first collected. About this
book of stories, most of which are set in North Carolina,
Richard Sullivan commented in the New York *Times*
Book Review that "the general feeling here is one of firm,
steady control and clear, objective vision."

Old Pines

JAMES BOYD

OLD MAN McDonald sat in the house of his ancestors watching his little railroad die. Its wabbling single track left the Great Southern in the town below him and, climbing with laborious eccentricity, passed near the composed and graceful portico and the old man himself, and meandered away through a ragged wilderness toward the vanished glories of an abandoned port. The old man's blunt figure at the base of a slender, quiet column stood out sharp and motionless. He was waiting, with his heavy gold watch in his hand, for the evening train to come by.

When he was young, the ruined scrub-clad hills that he could see to the east had borne a vast pine-forest stretching away to the sea—great dark trees, shoulder to shoulder, rising tall and true as masts and then, at the very tops, branching fancifully into Japanese designs. Through this as a boy he had run the rough survey for the right of way, blazing the solemn kings with a hardy impudence of which they took no note until too late, when the logging teams came in, and they tumbled stiffly down in impotent majesty.

In time a clean-cut swath wound its way through the forest, and McDonald set himself to gather a nondescript negro gang from the few scattered towns of the district. With

From *Old Pines and Other Stories* by James Boyd, published by The University of North Carolina Press. Copyright, 1952, by Katharine Boyd.

them he started to build the railroad to the coast, bossing them himself. They moved with unhurried and jocular ease, but they made the little rusty mules hump their backs in the stump-pullers while the scoops gently, but tirelessly, graded the red-streaked sand. As the road-bed took shape, the rails were laid and spiked down by buck niggers in groups of three, swinging alternately, in rhythm, with a coughing grunt at each stroke.

They kept working farther into the forest. The little eddy of movement sank into the unfathomed calm. The clink of sledge and the rattle of single-trees faded at birth into the dark maze. The gang made lean-to camps of pine-boughs, and sat close at night in front of a great fire. They had always a fiddle or two, and at the music one of them sometimes stood up, rocking gently, and began to shuffle softly in the dust, the great flat feet sliding delicately in a little circle with magic fascination. Then all at once the rest began to sing, and a song which had come from forests of mangrove and ebony vanished down aisles of cypress and pine.

He camped with them, going home now and then in a hand-car. As winter came, their spirits drooped, and they huddled around little fires all day. It did not pay to work then, but in three summers he had put the line through. He owed money on every nail and crosstie and knew he could not raise another penny anywhere. But the job was done, and in time he would make it pay.

So he went back to the white house his father had left him, and from his little office at one end he garnered the harvest of the halcyon turpentine days and watched his earnings, puffing mightily in their corpulence, steam by below his window—seeping hogsheads of tar and barrels of acrid rosin. Eastbound moved rotund drums of tobacco and cotton-bales to the seaboard port at the end of the road. But best of all he liked the evenings when the gangs of turpentine niggers rolled in, swinging their legs from the flat-cars and singing "Deep River."

He was now a man, self-reliant, but very shy. One day when he had gone down the line to the port and was watching the roustabouts spin the bales along the quay to where a Greenock tramp was nudging the piles, he saw a tall girl standing by the rail. Her face was homely, gentle, and, above all, strong. He knew at once that she was from the Highlands, where such women have been bred since the beginning. Culloden had sent the McDonalds across the sea two centuries before, but at the sight of her his blood went coursing back to the old clans. She saw it, and gave him a straight look without curiosity or fear.

Within a year she had come back to marry him and put his neglected garden to rights. She learned to run levels, and used to ride down the line in the cab or tramp through the forest beside him, knitting without looking down. They were happy with the deep stoic happiness of the Scotch, though at times she grew sad and lonely. She would go off by herself, and he could hear her in the distance singing the Skye boatsong:

"Speed, bonny boat, like a bird on the wing,
  'Onward' the sailors cry,
   Carry the lad that's born to be king
    Over the sea to Skye."

Her head would go up, and her low voice shiver with a defiant ring which took no reckoning of the poor ruined prince now crumbling in his grave as he had crumbled in his life generations before.

As the years passed, the pine-woods were slowly drained of their turpentine. The trees were still mighty, but each dark trunk bore a long pale herringbone scar, stretching as high up as the pullers would reach, at its bottom a little rough-hewed slot into which the precious sap oozed down every spring. The supply was failing, and the demand as well, for the iron and steel ships they were building now had small use for naval stores.

McDonald from his window watched the dwindling stream of freight. He had long since stopped paying off his debts and had begun to borrow again. He saw his earnings of years and, at last, the very life of his road slowly flowing away. It was as if the great forest from which that life had come was silently taking it back to itself again. He used to gaze out over the soft level floor of tree-tops not with any fear or depression, but wondering deeply and sturdily what he should do. At last he saw in the papers the news that he had long been waiting for. He looked on the waving, whispering tops that night with a certain shame and awe, and next morning he started North to talk with hard-faced men.

In six months the lumbermen came in, jovial, drunken vandals who descended roaring from the train and skirmished with all who appeared on the streets that night. Here and there along the road they set up their ramshackle sawmills, crazy sheds from which came shrill, purposeless toots, wisps of steam and, endlessly repeated, a high-pitched groan as each cradled log struck the spinning saw. Slowly the heaps of ruddy, golden sawdust grew until they seemed like the burial mounds of the old giants who had there been sacrificed. The log wagons rutted their twisting roads back into the hills, through the great raw stumps and the heaps of dying slash, ever seeking the quavering cry of "Timber!" and the crackle of branches and groan of the heart-pine which followed it. They came back, padding noiselessly over the bark and sawdust; only the complaining axles told of their mighty burden. The deer and the wildcat fled before them to the mountains of the west, and the little gray foxes crowded into the branches and lived precariously on the dark-furred swamp rabbits. Down by the sidings, heaps of rough-sawed lumber, a light, sharp yellow, shone in the raw light that now flooded for the first time those unaccustomed places. There were sturdy blockhouses of joist and scantling, and fan-shaped piles of sagging boards, while now and then a twelve-inch beam, destined for some distant, mighty task, basked its broad sides, still dripping from the saw.

The railroad flourished, and McDonald was happy again. The menace of the lean years had passed; he was once more paying off his debts; once more he had become a power in the land, a dispenser of prosperity to whom others turned deferential, hopeful faces; and above all he had now a child, a daughter, Flora. Small wonder he failed to see that his fortune was founded on nothing less and nothing more than the ruin of the country-side. Like the great pines that had fallen before him, he was in turn to stand, proud in the memory of countless frustrated storms, until disaster's unforeseen, keen edge should lay him low.

The first stroke came one evening in spring. He was sitting on the porch, his long square-tipped fingers were locked on his knee, and in the circle of his arms his little girl was curled up asleep like a puppy. Straggling pines barred the deep, rich sky; shadowy mocking-birds busied themselves after twilight insects; down in the yards he could hear the somnolent, metallic breathing of an engine.

His wife came to the door; even in the failing light he could see the startling pallor of her face. He would have sprung up, but she saw the child and stretched out a hand. "No," she said,—her voice was taut and whispering,— "it's come to me. The doctor said it would."

He could almost see the yearning glow of her eyes as they strained to make out his figure and the child's. The next instant she had slipped inside the house. All down his back the primeval hackles rose at the unseen menace of the enemy. He sat numb, while three chill, tingling waves of dread swept quickly over him. Then he raised himself by his will and, swinging the child into a chair, passed with quiet swiftness through the door. He found her on a wide sofa near a small ivory-shaded lamp. She was curled up cunningly, in the same way as the child outside, a position incongrous and touching in one of her years. She was dead, but at the last a faint flush had come back to her face, an exquisite afterglow. He came no nearer, but dropped on his knees like a peasant before a wayside shrine.

Now the struggle against failure began—a struggle as bleak and endless as the moors which had bred the McDonald stock. Almost imperceptibly timber became scarcer and poorer. Instead of the sinewy stringers of clear heart-pine, in time only shingles, slats, and crate-boards came out, the off-scourings of the forest. And across the waste lands spread the useless scrub-oaks in puny triumph over the old masters.

Along the coast the new ships of iron were bigger. Each year fewer of them could make the river port to the coast; slowly it withered away. The tall, serene houses of the old merchants and sailing masters passed shabbily into the hands of petty tradesmen. The tide of commerce receded, leaving at length only an impassive flotsam stranded in the town— negroes, Portuguese, some Swedes, and Yankees. One by one the ships lanterns over the doors of inns and drinking-places went out.

Of the railroad and its business nothing at length remained except a small traffic in grains and cheap manufactured goods that were carried by a single dingy engine over the crumbling line to the port and the scattered dead hamlets along the way. Nothing remained but that and old man McDonald himself. He used to sit on the porch every evening to see the only train come by. It would have been hard for a stranger to place him. More than anything else he might have been taken for a sheriff or a master engineer. His clothes were not those of a workman, but they could be worked in. His frame was heavy and block-like. At rest he seemed made of concrete, but he moved with a swiftness and certainty that had about them almost the beauty of machinery. When thus in action he appeared slighter and taller than he really was. His face was ruddy with a grim, humorous kindness that disconcerted small minds. His eyes were like the muzzle of his gun, steel-gray, with an impersonal threat in their black depths. His gray hair grew thickly in wind-tossed eddies, and he carried his head thrust a little forward, with the face upraised, like a seaman fronting a storm.

Now as he sat there holding his great, heavy watch in his hand he heard the distant whistle of the locomotive and saw the creeping smoke-serpent draw nearer over the tops of the trees. It ended in a curling black cloud as the fireman threw on more pine-knots. The next moment the grotesque front of the engine appeared round the bend. She was an antique wood-burner, with a funnel-shaped stack and a wide-spreading cow-catcher, like a prim old lady's crinoline. She passed with prodigious, woolly puffs and unearthly clankings, a string of box-cars clattering behind. Old man McDonald watched the negro train-hand shambling along the tops, setting the hand-brakes for the hill. The train descended into the town, clanging the engine-bell.

He looked at his watch to note her time. He always did this, although for many years it had not even faintly approached the schedule. Still, he liked to know every day how much was the deviation.

The night closed in with the suddenness of a stage scene. His old engine, lighting up the belly of her own smoke, moved to her berth in the yards; lights winked here and there in the town, and the casual noises of a slipshod existence floated up to where he sat. The frogs began their harsh, unvarying iteration. Suddenly, coming swiftly from far away, he heard a stirring sound of smooth power, then saw a streaming blaze of lights as the Great Southern express rushed in.   Her groaning brakes and shivering exhaust told of her might as she pulled up at the station.   She lay there, purring with iron sternness.   As the brakeman's lantern swung at the rear, she gave the first of the great, compact, measured coughs that were to send her on her way.   With a spasm she spun her drivers in a shower of sparks, and then, cresting the grade, hummed down the line.

Old man McDonald sat with the sound still ringing in his ears, thinking of the flimsy rattle of his makeshift train.   Inside he heard the gentle click of china and turned his head slowly.   His daughter, in the dining-room, was putting the supper things away.   Nothing had been changed in the house since that fatal night, nor ever would be, he thought grimly, as long as the two of them survived.   They still ate their fare, now plain and meager, off mahogany and plate.   He could see the old sideboard, whose lustrous, ruddy wood received deep into itself the reflection of the silver candle-sticks.   His mind wandered over the house, its sturdy furnishings of oak and pine, the foolish little odds and ends she had brought in and cherished with a childish care—earthenware vases, a wavy mirror with black-and-gilt frame, a rude print of Robert Bruce.   He thought with a pang of the cedar closet up-stairs where lay in even rows her beautiful dower linen. He took a sharp breath and threw up his head a little as he had a habit of doing at such times.

Through the window he could see Flora, a well-knit girl with a broad waist, but a quick, graceful carriage of the head.   Her face was very forceful, and at the same time had an open doglike friendliness that covered the unknown depths below.   She held a silver dish against her breast, polishing it round and round with a cloth.   She was whistling in a soft, measured sort of whisper, a habit of her father's.   He smiled as he watched her.   She looked up and grinned affably out toward where he sat.   "Coming out, Father," she said in the soft, but rugged, way of the Scotch Southerner.

Soon she appeared and sat on a chair beside him, and both looked out over the lights of the town for a while.

"Tired?" he said.

"Middling," she answered. "I oiled the big table today." They talked without looking at each other. He considered her remark for a moment, then said:

"The house looks mighty nice; everything—mighty nice."

This was spoken in a ruminating tone, as a soliloquy. By this device old man McDonald saved his own self-respect and spared her the intolerable mortification of having to receive a compliment. But it was perilous ground, and she quickly changed it.

"Are you going down the line tomorrow?"

"I reckon not. I was just looking at those two old engines in the yard. Expect I'll have to go over them. They are plumb rusty—both. Plumb rusty," he repeated after a long pause.

She moved slightly, but did not speak. Old man McDonald could not know that his words had suddenly flooded her with a strange, grotesque, yet passionate, longing to pick him up and rock him like a baby in her arms. She did, indeed, start impulsively to touch his worn sleeve in pity, but came to herself before she had done so. He sat, with no feeling of pity for himself, oblivious of his escape.

They talked no more. Here and there in the town the lights were going out. They rose and went to bed.

Early next day he started work. The yard, such as it was, lay in an unfrequented field that had been his father's. It was skirted by young pines, and along it, laid on the old furrows, ran two sidings. They were filled with the last crumbling relics of the old man's rolling-stock: a string of box-cars with bulged and gaping sides; the blank, dust-filmed windows of a coach; a miraculous caboose of local construction that looked a little like a stranded tug, a little like a suburban villa; and at the farther end the engines, so incrusted and immovable that they seemed to be two petrified antediluvians plunged through eternity in their vast bucolic reverie.

But despite their appearance they had been well cared for and could be easily put in running order. Old man McDonald began inspecting the first of them. His square figure heaved itself nimbly all over her, like a black bear in a grove of trees. Then he set to work.

First, he took the wooden cover off the stack and the housing off the cab and stowed them in a box-car. Then with waste and a bucket of turpentine he cleaned the paraffin from the bright work, and touched up a few rusty places with emery-paper. He filled the oil-cups from a long-nosed can, and put oil-soaked waste in the packing boxes. After that he went tapping around with a copper hammer in search of loose bolts, tightening a nut now and then with his wrench. He was by nature a mechanic, and that part of the job gave him much pleasure. He whistled to himself with the same laborious whisper of his daughter. He crawled underneath, and remained invisible for a long time, tinkering with the link motion and eccentric block. Only his musical breathings could be heard, as if the engine herself were already getting up steam. At last he emerged, solemnly content and heavily coated with grease and rust-flakes.

Matters now became serious, for he swung the arm of the near-by water-tank, and, coupling on an extra length of hose, began to fill the boiler. He mounted to the cab and peered intently into the fire-box, listening to the water muttering around the tubes and watching for leaks. A few small rivulets trickled down the back, but he knew the heat would close them. From the wood-pile he brought in pine-knots and hard wood and started his fire; then he delved into his pocket for corn-bread and sat down on the fireman's seat to wait. From time to time he gazed out the window at the dense oily smoke mounting straight in the still air, or looked impatiently at the steam-gage, though he knew well that it would be an hour before it registered. He soothed himself by lighting his pipe with elaborate preparations and settled down to smoke. At length, quite unexpectedly, the indicator swung to 5. "Five pounds' pressure," he muttered, hurriedly knocking out his ashes. He opened the steam-cocks one after the other. The bottom two spluttered scalding water, but the highest cock hissed a sharp, clear jet of steam. He shut it off and waited intently, not excited, but quietly and deeply moved.

As she warmed up, the engine appeared miraculously to come to life. The stolid, dead surfaces began to glisten with the melting oil. In the cab, where the heat was greatest, the metal, so senseless an hour ago, seemed almost to pulsate and twinkle.

He fixed his eyes on the gage. Slowly she climbed to 50. He opened the steam-cocks again; only the bottom one showed water. More quickly the hand swung up to 100. He opened the cylinder drain-cocks, and a splashing, feathered fountain of steam and water shot down along the rails. 120. He pulled back the throttle half an inch; the cylinders filled, and the forced draft whispered deeply in the smoke-box. He waited no longer, but leaned out the cab window and opened the throttle. Slowly the drivers began to move; with the snort of a bison she turned them over; steam jets hissed beside the ponies; twice more, and she struck her stride, and carried the old man, grim and bright-eyed, out on the line.

From that time on he worked more and more on the road himself. It made him happy to be doing things with his hands again, and it reminded him of the old days, now more glowing and unbelievable than ever, when he had made the road out of nothing by the power of his strength and love. But in the evenings, when the unique, consuming single-heartedness with which he always labored had left him, he felt the slow pressure of fate and dreaded a future more incredible than the past—dreaded it all the more because he could not quite conceive it. He was being ruined; he could see that without shifting his seat, and Flora would go down with him to whatever obscure disinheritance awaited ruined men. That was where his hurrying thoughts paused. He had never before considered ruin long enough to picture what became of the men it overtook, still less their women. His imagination had gone other ways, always building, building.

As for seeing himself without the road, it was harder still. He would think about it tenaciously until at times he ceased to believe in his own existence. He was always glad when Flora came out to sit silently beside him and restore him to his world.

So he went on, working harder by day and more puzzled in mind at night. He saved at every possible point. He was not man of affairs enough to believe that if ruin was inevitable, it should, at least, by judicious financing, be converted from slow prostration into an abrupt, majestic cataclysm. He simply fought doggedly, directly, to keep things going.

He had no one working for him now except the fireman, a certain John Henry Moorehead. John Henry, as he was invariably called, was a limber youth of great seriousness, punctuated by outbursts of irresistible mirth. He came to his chief one day.

"Mr. McDonal'," he said respectfully, " 'spect I better quit."

"Why, John Henry, nothing wrong, is they?"

"No, sir; I've always been well used."

Old man McDonald was distressed. The departure of John Henry would be a welcome relief financially, but he was fond of the boy.

"Why, son, I'm sorry."

"I've got to go. But if you ever need me,"—he shyly

stretched out a great hand,—"I'll come," he said, and turned away.

From this time on the old man ran the train himself, with his decrepit negro gardener to fire for him. Little by little all the rest of his rolling-stock was abandoned, and he settled down grimly to keeping the one train in order, and running it every day to hold his franchise. When he was younger he used to like to get the best there was out of an engine, and he knew how, too; but now he crept along, easing her down a mile before the stations and starting her by imperceptible degrees. He was hanging on to the last possible margin of safety. One morning as he waited beside the engine while she was being fired up the thought came to him that every bolt and plate in her stood between Flora, still a child, and some outer limbo beyond his horizon. When night came he would try again to picture it. He put a hand on the cylinder as if it were a talisman, and climbed into the cab.

That evening he sat straining into the dark, his hands curled over the arms of his chair like lion's paws, powerful, yet helpless. He was not afraid, but he hoped intensely to see for an instant what the future held, so that he might know how he should act. The darkness, blank at first, seemed after a while to weave with a motion that slowly took shape. At last he recognized it. It was the weaving of branches of great pines. Everywhere he looked the night seemed filled with those dark, tumultuous seas. The old pines, he thought, the old pines that were no more, come back to see his fall.

Suddenly he heard a brisk and hard-heeled step on the walk—the step of a Northern city-dweller. The next instant a dark little man had passed across the shaft of light and was wringing his hand.

"Mr. McDonald? Yes? This is Mr. Weiler. Well, Mr. McDonald, how are you now? Pretty good, yes? Good!"

He beamed affably, as though they were two old friends
reunited after a trying separation, and made a sort of em-
bracing gesture with his free arm. Then swiftly he drew up a
chair to a confidential distance, and at the same time produced a cigar. Old man McDonald noticed that both waist-
coat-pockets were stocked with imposing rows of Havanas,
like a duck-hunter's ammunition. He declined the cigar, and
watched, mildly fascinated, as Mr. Weiler replaced it carefully and gave the pocket a dapper pat. It was absorbing
to follow the pudgy agility of those hands, and he found
himself a little disconcerted to hear Mr. Weiler remark in
beaming tones:

"Certainly this is a fine location you got here, Mr. Mc-
Donald—and an elegant mansion and so forth."

"Well, sir, we're comfortable."

"Indeed, yes. I noticed it first thing I came into town. I
was greatly imposed, and I said to the conductor, 'I bet that's
where there lives a Southern gentleman.' Yes."

"What did he say?"

Little did the old man know how demoralizing was this
simple question to Mr. Weiler's fictitious recital. But Mr.
Weiler rallied.

"Oh, he said, 'Mr. Weiler,'—we had become fast friends,
—'Mr, Weiler,' he says, 'let me tell you something. It certainly is.' "

This was said with an air of gentle solemnity which, after
an impressive pause, swiftly passed into one of profound
concern.

"I was waiting all the afternoon to see you, Mr. McDonald, because I heard that in the day you are engaged with
your business affairs. So I did not come till now."

"Yes, sir, I was running the engine."

For a moment Mr. Weiler did not reply. When he did, it
was with the sober weight of a business man. Slowly he
opened a discussion of general trade conditions in the North

and spoke of bad times in a way that showed his responsibility for much that had been done to restore public confidence.

Old man McDonald listened closely, not always able to follow, but interested in this intimate view of a life so foreign —a life where men sat by telephones and made fortunes from the adventurous labors of other men, whose names they never knew, who were hired thousands of miles away to drill Persian wells, tap Congo rubber-trees, or seine the Northwest salmon streams. These men at telephones built railroads that they never saw, bought them, and sold them among themselves like mule-traders on court day. He knew all this before, but now it first seemed real; more real, indeed, than Mr. Weiler himself, whom he could not help feeling a fabulous creature, an emissary from Bagdad. He reflected that, despite appearances, these men could perform some service; but at the same time it seemed much easier than in his world to make money without performing any.

"And now, Mr. McDonald, I would like to make you a proposition."

"Proposition." Mr. Weiler pronounced the word with a delicate, yet sonorous, impressiveness that was hypnotic, and clearly inspired and fortified Mr. Weiler himself. It was the only word in his vocabulary that retained much trace of foreign accent, though he used it most of all.

His proposition was to buy the road for a good price, all things considered; to buy it as old junk. Old man McDonald's head sank now, his hands curved stiffly. Mr. Weiler went on to outline glowingly the acts of Providence which had made such a uniquely liberal offer possible. He was representing an iron foundry that was short of ore on account of mine-strikes. They had decided to buy junk not from the dealers, whose practices he described, illustrated, and epitomized, but direct, through the medium of the frank, open, dependable Mr. Weiler. Old man McDonald listened motionless as Mr. Weiler warmed to his theme. In a sense Mr. Weiler was an artist; men very like him had come to America and become great violinists, etchers, sculptors. He loved business dealing as an art, irrationally, exultantly, for its own sake. He was carried away, and his voice flowed hypnotically on, melodious and full of passionate conviction not in the truth of his words, but in the artistry of his method.

The sale of the road, so inconceivable an hour before, became gradually a possibility, then finally loomed as the fortunate golden escape from the inexorable force of events. Mr. Weiler, quietly persuasive, yet intensely, electrically alive, was putting the finishing touches to his work.

Inside a door swung sharply.

"Who was that?"

"That was Flora, my girl."

The old man breathed, and heaved himself in his chair; he felt as though he were struggling back to dry land; then he moved his feet apart slowly one after the other.

"Well, sir, I'll think about it. Won't you come inside?"

But Mr. Weiler, watching, knew that the moment had passed, and after selecting an expression from his stock of farewells which he conceived to be dignified, yet intimate, left the house. He was to return the next night.

Old man McDonald heard the clicking, incisive footfalls die away. At that distance Mr. Weiler seemed merely precise and active in a futile way. He was certainly inferior to the easy-going, but determined, men of the country; but up there on the porch he had shown a flash of peculiar power which they lacked. Was it simply the effect of his strangeness? The old man wondered in what that strangeness lay. He had traded with all sorts of men, Yankees, too, and always before he had read them well and relied on his judgment of them more than on written agreements. He wanted to understand Mr. Weiler before he did anything else, but

he felt incapable of fitting him into the scheme of life as he
knew it. If Mr. Weiler resembled anything, it was the little
foreign man who years ago ran a pawn-broking and sailors'
slops business down by the docks. But Mr. Weiler was far
bolder and more elegant. He had, however, the same fat,
quick hands and eyes at once sad and greedy.

At last old man McDonald turned from the problem and
began to think of the business aspect of such a sale. Mr.
Weiler had made it seem not only inevitable, but a peculiar
triumph of sagacity and good fortune. All of that conviction
did not depart with the tap of Mr. Weiler's heels. The old
man knew it would be a good trade and leave him able to
live decently, provided he were able to finance the road's
debts along the involved, but apparently honorable, lines
suggested by Mr. Weiler. Above all, there was no feasible
alternative. He must anchor himself to that, to that and the
picture of Flora, silent, brave, but touchingly helpless,
watching him board up the front door and then quietly setting out with him for—nowhere. The thought bowed him
forward into the darkness, but he returned to it again and
again, and clung to it to steady himself against the tides of
hope and memory that might now carry him to disaster as
irresistibly as they had before carried him to success.

Flora came out. She moved Mr. Weiler's chair away a little and sat down.

"Who was that, Father?"

"I don't just know."

"A Yankee?"

"I couldn't tell. Maybe. I reckon so."

"I heard what he was saying."

"He wants to buy the road."

"I know—for junk. Do you reckon you'll sell?"

"It's a mighty good chance. I expect there won't be another."

Their talk ended—ended, as always, where most talk

would have begun. They sat on, the old man engulfed in
the struggle and the girl frightened not at the event, but at
herself, for she had made up her mind.

He must be getting old, he thought, so fast the fragmen-
tary memories hurried through his mind. He lost the thread
of reasoning, and surrendered to them at last. He had a
glimpse of one of his old work gangs side by side along the
rail, hunching their backs all together in short lifts, shifting
the track; then he was sloshing along the wharf side against
a norther, going to meet a Greenock tramp for which he had
waited a year. He heard the click of the switch-points as his
first engine, with him at the throttle, came off the Great
Southern track to his own, and he felt the tug of the last
car when the trestle crackled down. And through it all, now
faint, now clear, came the murmur, mournful, strong, of
pines in the deep-sea wind. He rose as if he were breasting
it, and Flora followed him.

The next day passed in a dream of agony. His steady,
well-knit mind was working like a beaver, buttressing itself
against the poundings of his heart. By supper-time all was
settled, but only once before in his life had he ever felt so
tired. His daughter joined him afterward without clearing
the table.

She looked at him. He turned his gaze to her childish face
and saw the unbelievable woman in her eyes. Confused, he
shifted it to the fading hills.

"I'm going to sell. It's the only thing."

"Father, don't!"

That shivering ring! He had never thought to hear it
again. The old words sounded in his brain:

> Carry the lad that's born to be king
> Over the sea to Skye.

But he shook his head.

"We can't keep her running. What's going to become of
you? I wouldn't if I could help it."

"I wouldn't whether I could help it or not. That man!"

He grinned.

"I expect he's honest."

But while he was laboring the point, her mind went back
to her desire.

"Did you want money when you were young?"

"Not much."

"Did mother?"

"No."

"You wanted to make the road run, and she wanted to
help you."

"I reckon so."

"Well, that's what I want." She just touched him on the
sleeve; then she started in. At the door she turned. "That
man!" she said darkly, then disappeared. He could hear a
short laugh trailing behind her.

Profound and painful adjustments were taking place in
old man McDonald's mind. He had thought out his decision
and taken it to protect his daughter, and now in some un-
fathomable manner she made him seem ever so slightly
ludicrous and trivial. He might have been her small child
whom she had detected being corrupted by a bad little boy.
That was the way she had treated the business. But there
had been nothing patronizing; he admitted that. And there
had been something else that he would not forget.

She had grown up without his knowing it. He must have
been asleep not to see it before. Suddenly the memory of
John Henry flashed into his mind, and he recalled a hundred
little circumstances to which he had been blind. John Henry had gone away to make some money before he asked her.
Perhaps he had asked her. Well, he was a good boy.

Punctually, Mr. Weiler came. He performed the same
ritual with the cigar, then started to talk. That afternoon old

man McDonald had seen him looking over the road, but he
was too familiar with it himself to realize that an inspection
by a stranger would make its sale seem a foregone conclusion. Mr. Weiler had no doubts of the outcome, but he was
irresistibly impelled to finish his speech of the night before.
This he did.

"Ain't that so, Mr. McDonald?" he ended, with a perfo-
rating gesture of the index finger.

"I reckon so. But, Mr. Weiler, I don't believe I'll sell."

Mr. Weiler scarcely paused, but plunged again into the
discussion in order to straighten matters out as he could
easily do. But he did not get far.

"No, sir, I reckon I won't sell."

It was said in a shy and hesitating tone, but Mr. Weiler
recognized, with a dreadful acuteness, that behind it lay centuries of a grim Northern breed. He was struck speechless in
a way that he had never been before. He was frantic at being
so abruptly balked without even the chance to show his
cleverness. Yet in his despairing rage one idea persisted
above all others. That was to make a stately final impression
on old man McDonald.

After a heavy silence Mr. Weiler rose and stood rigid.

"I am certainly astonished. I made this expensive trip
thinking that of course you would be interested in my magnificent proposition. Good-by."

He bowed from the hips and vanished.

The next morning dawned in a sudden brilliant flash, and
old man McDonald rose up in his bed and began to pound
his chest mightily as he remembered the night before. Suddenly he felt his heart miss a beat, then two, and as he tried
to get to his feet he seemed to slip and plunge into a pool of
black oblivion. He sank back to the pillow, and raising one
arm with an effort of will, he knocked on the wall.

Behind his steadfast, even gaze in the last two days there

had raged a battle as intense, as merciless, as destructive in
its sphere as any struggle which men commemorate by statu-
ary and legal holidays. His body, square and hardy, but toil-
worn to the core, had given way.

For a week he lay there, and no train ran. No words
could tell more than that of his suffering. The future was
hopeless. He had missed his chance. Perhaps he could get
Mr. Weiler back, but it would be a bitter defeat. He would
write and tell him.

"Dear sir: I beg to advise you that, owing to my heart
having unexpectedly got bad"—something like that. He
reached for a financial newspaper to find the address of the
firm. As he turned the pages a head-line caught his eye.
"Southern Harbor Development Co." New Orleans, probably. They were growing fast down there. A familiar name
stared at him from the column of type. He began word by
word to read the lines. His great hands gripped the paper
till it trembled; then two tears twisted down his lined face.
They were going to dredge the port at the end of the line.
The old-time railroad days would come again. He pounded
on the wall with both fists.

"Flora! Flora!"

Standing by the bed, she read the paper that he thrust
silently into her hands.

"Take that down to the bank and ask them if they'll keep
me going for a year."

"Father," she murmured, and shyly patted the worn, gay
quilt.

"Honey," he said, "go on along," and turned his face to
the wall.

She came back beaming, and panting like a terrier.

"They say they will if it's so."

He grinned dryly, and then eyed her solemnly.

"They's a great future for this yer road," he announced,
and leaned back, contented.

For a week he lay there like some strong, inoffensive animal driven to bay for causes he could not understand. Friends at the bank were to take charge of starting the road again, and the old man was filled with forebodings of their well-meaning incompetence.

One morning Flora was sitting in the room, going over his papers and letters, trying to help him all he would let her, for he had tired rapidly in the last few days. His face was still ruddy, his mouth the same straight line; but he could not hide the great weariness in his eyes. The papers rustled, her voice murmured as she read, and the old man, gazing into space, seemed drifting far away. Then faintly, below the house, climbing nearer, they caught the familiar, lugubrious clanking and flat, shallow puffings of the old woodburner. She went to the window just as the little train lurched round the curve.

"Father, they've got her running again! She's all shined up. Two box-cars—and the caboose—and"—she scarcely breathed—"John Henry."

She gazed, rapt, at the train. Suddenly, she felt that he had moved. She looked around. He was standing beside her, incredibly old, his eyes blazing, the great gold watch trembling in his hand. He turned toward her with a touch of formal deference.

"By God! sir—" She never knew whether in that final movement he failed to recognize her, or whether at last he saw her for what she was. "By God! sir—on time!" And old man McDonald slipped quietly to the floor.

LUCY DANIELS

As GRANDDAUGHTER of Josephus Daniels, journalist and historian and biographer, and as daughter of Jonathan Daniels, also journalist and historian and biographer but novelist too, Lucy Cathcart Daniels took to writing quite naturally. At the "ripe old age" of fifteen, she had a short story, "Good-bye, Bobbie," accepted by the magazine *Seventeen*. It appeared in the issue of December, 1949. She had, of course, been writing for a long time before then.

She was born in Raleigh in 1934, and there she grew up. At the George School in Bucks County, Pennsylvania, which she attended for three years, she was assistant editor of the yearbook. It was during this time that she began teaching herself to write. When illness kept her from a college career, she intently pursued her course of self-training. Later in New York, where she went for hospitalization, she took a job with *Reader's Digest*. Back home, well again and eager to work, she became a reporter for the *Raleigh Times*.

In 1956, her novel *Caleb, My Son* appeared. It was an immediate success. Actually, says Miss Daniels, "I wasn't writing the book to be published. I was still teaching myself to write." But when her father suggested that she send it to a publisher to see what would happen, his prediction that it would be published was correct. A racial study of the struggle between a conservative Negro father and his proud son, the book caught the temper of the times, disturbed as they were by the Supreme Court decision on school segregation.

In 1957, Lucy Daniels received a Guggenheim Fellowship for creative writing. Already she was engaged to be married to Thomas Patrick Inman, a newspaper photographer. Thus, at the same time, she began her first year of marriage and her "year off" writing on a second novel.

Later, writing activity moderated somewhat when, on December 17, 1958, a son was born, Patrick Benton Inman.

Her short story "Half a Lavender Ribbon" is one of a number she has written. In it the unrealized daydreams of a child have tragic consequences. It was published in the winter, 1958, number of the *Virginia Quarterly Review*.

Asked to express her ideas on writing, Lucy Daniels explained: "I have none. . . . I write about people—human people. . . . I think you simply write what you have to write."

Half a Lavender Ribbon

LUCY DANIELS

ALMA'S broad capable hands strained hard as she tied a square of blue denim around the small bundle. A drop of perspiration squeezed out of the deepest furrow in her low black forehead and trickled idly down her nose.

"There," she announced proudly as she finished. "That won't be too heavy fo' nobody. You jes' feel that." She slipped two fingers under the knot and let the bundle swing from them.

William watched and listened—as he always listened. But he made no gesture to take the bundle from her. What difference did it make how heavy it was? He would have to carry it anyway. Besides, he was on the opposite side of the bed, and it was too hot to prop himself up with his crutches and get over there. So, he just sat still on the edge of the cane-bottomed chair and listened.

His good leg was braced against the floor, and his short shriveled one rested on the bottom rung of the chair. As Alma spoke, his thin fingers gripped the seat, and his large black eyes made a piercing study of her face. When she put the bundle down, though, and grinned at him, he did not smile back. He didn't look away, but he could not pretend to be happy. As always when afraid or angry, he could only make his eyes distant, his face empty of all expression.

By permission of the author.

Alma did not like that look. It made her uncomfortable, just as William's shriveled leg did, and the way he had of almost never speaking. Because of that look, she and her daughters and even some of the neighbors told each other that William was strange. They said he had caught the madness from old Nanny or been born with it, as with his shriveled leg, because of the ugly circumstances of his birth.

Alma felt sorry for the boy, and she tried to be kind. But even so, inside, that look, that silence, disturbed her. They made her feel as if in some way the child was superior, as if he was looking right into her mind.

Today especially she needed him to speak, to reassure her with some show of emotion. And now when he did not, the strained grin disappeared from her face. "Well, th' ain't nothin' t' be afraid of," she snapped with annoyance. "You plenty big enough. Lot o' boys half yo' size would give they eye teeth t' see New Yawk City."

William did not answer. He shifted his eyes to the floor and ran his right hand along the chair's rough caning. He tried to imagine that he was racing in one of the white boys' fast cars, the blue one with the top down, tearing furiously over the road. Then he tried to pretend it was two weeks ago and that old Nanny was still alive, still sitting there, crocheting and telling him stories.

William did not want to listen to Alma. She had been to New York—"Fo' a whole yeah, an' when I won't yet seventeen." He had heard her describe it many times— the big city and all she had done there. But William was only nine, and seventeen seemed very old to him— very old and far away. He could not bear for Alma to talk about it now.

And she did not. Still uneasy in the silence, she began once more to go over the directions for his trip. "You won't need no money," she said. "I got the ticket already.

But I'm givin' ya a whole dollah anyway—just in case.
A quatah in yo' shoe an' three mo' sewed in yo' pants an'
yo' sweat shirt." She glanced at him irritably. "You bettah
mind what I tell you, boy. I ain't gonna say it again."

William's expression was no more vacant than usual,
but his mind was far away. He had been pretending that it
was old Nanny talking to him instead of Alma. She was
telling him about the spirits and how he must do whatever
they said. As usual, he tried to ask her what her spirits
looked like, but, as usual, because she was deaf, she went
right on talking without hearing. Then she told him about
his grandmother—Alma's sister and Nanny's other daughter. He was just figuring it out again—how old Nanny must
be, when Alma broke in.

"I say, listen, boy. You be sorry if you don't."

"I am."

"Well—. So, I give you money, but that don't mean
you gotta spend it. Money don't grow on trees in New
Yawk no mo' than heah. This what I'm givin' you ain't t'
be spent—'cept in emergency."

William did not ask what emergency there might be.
He already knew and expected it as almost a certainty.
Alma had written his mother to meet him in New York,
and everybody—even Alma—knew she never would.

William had never seen his mother—Vinie Bowen; at
least he could not remember ever having seen her. But
all his life he had heard about her—heard plenty from
Alma and Alma's boy, Hiram, even from Alma's married
daughters and the neighbors. And all his life he had
learned through their words to think of her as only a
frightening threat.

Vinie Bowen? Yes, everybody knew about Vinie Bowen.
That "struttin' black gal" who had got herself into trouble
with a no-good killer right out of the state penitentiary.
Many remembered how she had bided her time in Miss

Alma's house and then, before the baby had even been weaned, had run off and left him.

William knew all this and more; about how lazy she was and still just a little hussy. She was living in New York now—and working, according to the Christmas cards which came to Alma each year. Alma always sneered over that card. "Working, ha!" she would say. "I can imagine at what! She jest hopin' I send her a Christmas present." Then, after copying the address off the envelope, she always threw the card away instead of propping it up on the mantel with the others.

"Boy, you heah what I say about the money?"

"Yes'm."

"An' what you gonna do when you get t' the station in New Yawk?"

He hesitated, wiggling the toes on his good foot. "I'm gonna follow the crowd."

"Wheah you goin'?"

"Trav-trav'ler's aid."

"What you gonna look fo'?"

"A lady—a lady wid a ribbon—a purple ribbon." He spoke the words precisely, coldly, with his tongue, but not with his mind.

His mind was out in the street with the white boys in one of their shiny cars—the blue one again, because it was the owner of the blue one who had spoken to William once. The boy—really he looked like a man, but his voice sounded soft and high like William's own—the boy was saying to him, "Here, kid, you steer for a while; I'm tired. Go fast. But watch out for the cops. Don't go near any cops." Then the sleek white steering wheel was in his hands, and they were off. Like a streak, faster, faster, faster—by places William had never even seen before because of his leg. Then around corners, zoom—zoom—! And back again to Wade Street. William waved to Hiram as they zipped by

and to Miss Marion next door and to old Nanny. After
that the white boy—

"An' s'posin' she don't come?"

No answer.

"William, you ain't list'nin'! You bettah min', boy! . . .
S'posin' she don't come? What you gonna do then?"

"Who?"

"Yo' ma, o' course. The lady wid the purple ribbon.
What you gonna do?"

"Wait."

"How long you gonna wait?"

"Till somebody ax me what I waitin' fo'. Then I tell
'em."

"All right. You jes' remembah that. I ain't goin' ovah it
again." The quiz was finished, and Alma stood up satisfied.
She started for the door, but then, sighing wearily, turned
to check the things laid out on the bed.

William's eyes followed her tall ample body stealthily.
As far as Alma was concerned, everything was settled.
But for William there was one more question, one more
thing he wanted reassurance in, but which he could never
ask Alma.

When his mother did not come, when he had answered
the people who asked him about it, what would happen
then? They would not send him back to Alma because he
would not tell them about her. It would be useless to.
Once Alma made up her mind about something, nothing
could stop her. And this time she had made up her mind
to send him away.

Actually William knew what would happen, actually he
only wanted to be told he was wrong. Children who had
no parents and no home were sent to orphanages. Hiram
had told him about that. Though Hiram was Alma's
youngest boy, he was going to college and knew everything.
He had said that orphanages made children work for their

food and clothes and that in an orphanage everybody had everything alike.

William couldn't bear the thought of that. His heart had always frozen with terror whenever they told him he should be grateful to Alma, whenever they reminded him that without her he himself would have been nowhere else but in one of those orphanages.

"Well, boy, I'm goin' outdo's an' tend my sweet potatoes. Whyn't you come an' play till suppah time?" Alma had finished checking the things on the bed, and she did not want to leave him alone in the house. William knew why. It had only been this way for the past ten days, since old Nanny had died and they had opened her trunk. Alma was afraid—especially now when he was going away—that he might take something.

"I'll go out soon," he replied. "Befo' Hiram do. Lemme jest set heah an' cool a minute."

Alma scowled at him impatiently, but she said, "Aw right then; jest mind you go out. You won't be able to aftah suppah. You have to come in then t' take a bath an' get ready t' go."

"Yes'm." The reply came automatically from his lips drawn tight and thin across his teeth. He kept his eyes on the grey weathered floor boards and only knew by the shuffling footsteps and then by the slamming of the screen door that Alma had finally gone out and left him alone.

His eyes rose from the floor then, but he did not stand up immediately. He just looked around the room, trying to recall how it had been before, trying to blot out all the changes of the last ten days.

Ever since he could remember, this had been old Nanny's room. He had sat here with her hour after hour when all the others were off at work or at school. At first he had been just a little boy who got into everything and wee-weed on the floor. Even now he could still feel the sting of her hard hand against his bottom.

But later when he was older—old enough to go to school if Alma would have let him—they had had wonderful times together. She was stone deaf by then so that he had to tug her apron and lead her when the phone rang or somebody was at the door. Also the spirits had begun to plague her more—telling her not to trust Alma or not to touch food or to change the hiding place for the key to her trunk, sometimes sending her clear across town to accomplish some mission or to wait for some message. Then it had been his job—William's—to get her to eat and, above all, to keep her at home and off the streets.

He had resented that in the beginning. Alma had made excuses to people for his not going to school. "That child cain't walk all that far wid only one leg," or "It wouldn't be no use noway. He can't learn; he just ain't right in the head." And he had known, even then, that it was just her way of keeping him home to nurse Nanny.

But with time he had actually become glad to stay home. He still longed to make friends and to see new things, but he knew deep inside that the other boys would have laughed and pointed at his leg.

In all the world only old Nanny did not realize he was different from everybody else. He began to prefer her room to any place else. And though her deafness had prevented any two-way conversation, she told him stories the whole time she was crocheting.

Now, however, as he looked around, William scarcely recognized the room. So many things were missing—the little ten-cent store prints with make-believe gold frames, the yellow crocheted bed spread which Nanny had made herself, even the bright patchwork quilt.

Nanny's trunk—a dilapidated black metal one—was still there in the corner between the two windows. But always—as far back as William could remember—that trunk had been locked with the key hidden where only Nanny could find it. And now it was open, its lid thrown back and, William knew, many of its contents removed.

That reminded him of himself. Like everything else that had belonged to Nanny, he was being given away. Only the valuable things, only the things which Alma needed or wanted would be kept. And he, of course, was of no use to anyone.

This thought was not new. He had felt it brooding over him ever since the morning when he awakened to find Nanny dead in the bed beside him. And he had known it to be a reality since yesterday afternoon when Alma told him she was going to send him to his mother in New York. But William's lips quivered now for the first time, and he felt a sudden fire leap to his eyes.

He reached down then for his crutches. He could hear Hiram moving around in the next room, and he knew he would soon have to go out. Supporting himself on the back of the chair, he stood up and moved slowly towards the bed.

There—laid out carefully—were all the things for his trip. The cloth-tied bundle of sweat shirts and overalls, a pair of drawers and an undershirt, his brown shoe, and finally—William's hands went tight around the handles of his crutches when he saw—finally, there was a piece of lavender ribbon tied in a bow and with a safety pin stuck through it.

William felt an overwhelming horror for that piece of ribbon. Alma had taken it out of Nanny's trunk only four days ago. He had seen her cut it in half and put the other part in an envelope with a letter to his mother. Then she had put two stamps on the envelope and walked all the way to the post office to send it air mail.

At the time William had not known what the letter was about or why the piece of lavender ribbon. But he had known it was important. And because it was addressed to Miss Vinie Bowen, his mama Vinie to whom no one ever wrote, he had been both curious and afraid.

But he had not asked. Alma was a good woman. She worked hard; she went to church every Sunday; she never failed to say grace before dinner. She even did kind things sometimes like having fried chicken because he and Hiram liked it. Yet, William had never been able to ask her anything about his mother.

He reached across the bed now and touched the piece of ribbon. Little goose pimples sprang up on his arms, but he rubbed his fingers against the tiny ridges, and his eyes memorized the soft lavender color. That was how he would know his mother—if she came. As soon as he saw a lady with a piece of that ribbon, he must go up to her and say, "Excuse me, ma'm, but are you Miss Vinie Bowen? Because if you are, I'm your boy."

Hiram came in then while William was still looking at the ribbon. "Whyn't you go outside an' play?" he said. "You know Ma don't like you in heah alone."

Surprised, the boy drew his hand back quickly from the piece of ribbon. He felt just then as though his thoughts and feelings were all spread out in the open like the things on the bed. And he could not bear for Hiram to see. "O-okay, okay," he stammered impulsively and befuddled. "I's only waitin' fo' you."

Hiram was kind then. He had heard the sudden catch and the quiver of defense in William's voice. "Co'se, I don' mind," he added. "Only she won't lemme leave the house 'thout you goin' out. An' I got a date wid Alice at the drug sto'."

William made no answer.

" 'Sides," Hiram added softly after a short silence.

" 'Sides, it ain't gonna do you no good t' stay in heah an' think on it. She ain't gonna change her mind now."

"No." William looked hard at the floor. He cleared his throat as if he were going to speak, but changed his mind and didn't. Then he turned abruptly and started for the door.

It was cooler on the porch. Though the sun still beat down, though the thermometer in the doorway said ninety-two, a faint breeze stirred the tops of the trees. William sat down on the front steps well within the lengthening shadow of the roof. He leaned on his elbow and watched Hiram amble slowly off down the street.

He would have liked to go to the drug store too—or anywhere to escape the night coming on and his own going away forever. He began to wish the white boys would come in their wild racing cars. Alma did not like the cars. Whenever they came by, she got mad and made William come into the house. "They gonna be a terrible accident," she always predicted. "Mind what I say, they gonna be a terrible accident one o' these days." But just once before he went away, William wanted to ride in one of those cars. If they came by, he intended to wave and ask them for a ride. Especially the blue one.

William had spoken to the blue one—that afternoon when the car killed their rooster and Alma called the police. The police had not come, of course. They had said they couldn't bother with streets like Wade Street where the people wouldn't even pay enough to have the road paved.

But the driver had had to stop anyway, because, besides killing the rooster, he had run over a nail. And it was then, while Alma was inside on the telephone—that William had spoken to him. That is, the driver of the blue car had spoken to William. He had talked about the car and about how hot it was and about what a crazy fool

Alma was to think she could stop him and his friends from racing.

Now, William's eyes followed Hiram to the bend in the road, then came back to the sun-cracked red clay yard. He could hear Alma's voice from out back talking to Miss Marion over the fence. They were talking about him. He knew that, but he did not strain to hear. He knew everything they could say. He had heard it and shaken with the terror of it many times. Now it didn't matter any more.

He could still remember Alma's voice tight and trembly with weariness as it said, "You bettah mind, boy. They comes a limit. I'll be sendin' you right up no'th to yo' ma."

Or even worse, the conversations he had overheard from the parlor nights when he could not sleep. First the talk of money and of the cost of groceries or clothes or maybe even something like a doctor's bill. Then Alma's voice high and clear and all alone—" 'Cou'se, if I didn' have that boy or Mama, it'd be diff'rent. All them pills fo' Mama costs money, an' then I still gotta worry half the time if she gonna staht out aftah them spirits an' git runned ovah in the street."

These words rang clearly in William's head as he sat there on the steps wiggling his toes in the red dust. But it was what came next, the way Alma spoke of Nanny and of himself that had always put the gnawing hollowness in his chest.

"An' sometimes I think it be jest as well a car do hit her," that came to him now. "She ain't doin' nothin' but makin' misery fo' herself as well as ever'body else. . . . 'Sides, if I didn' need him to mind 'er while I'm t' work, I could send William up to Vinie.

"I done had enough, I tell ya. Ain't faih, this family dumpin' ever'thing on top o' 'good ol' Alma.' "

After hearing those conversations, William had lain

awake half the night wondering if Alma would carry out
her threats. But eventually her words had proved to be
only words. And gradually the boy's dread of his mother
and of orphanages had eased a little, becoming more like
his fear of hell or of death—coldly terrifying, but so remote
that he could push it aside and think about something else.

Until suddenly now when it was no longer just a possibility, but a reality; not only close, but on top of him.
Hiram was right; there could be no escape now. William
knew that. And yet his mind would not rest. It kept in-
venting schemes for evading the inevitable horror of the
future.

He thought at first that he would just get off the train
tonight in the middle of some field before they even got to
New York. He would hide there until morning so that no
one would find him and send him to an orphanage. Then
he would go to town and spend his four quarters. He
would buy shoe polish and a brush and start polishing shoes
on a street corner.

There was one major fault in that plan though—William
was afraid of the dark. He hugged his knees to him now
and pressed his face against them to see if he still felt the
same. But he did, and he could only sit like that a minute
without looking up.

When he opened his eyes, he remembered that this was
the last time he would see these things around him and that
he must look carefully now to store them in his memory:
the giant sycamore tree hanging menacingly over the house,
so that each year when the hurricanes came Alma vowed
she would have it cut down; the red clay yard baked hard
and cracked despite Hiram's efforts to grow grass; the
tired, close smell of dust, crowded out now by the sharp,
insistent odor of fatback and greens; and finally, when he
rested his head on his knee, the sour stickiness of his own
perspiring flesh.

Mr. Berry walked by then on his way home from work and waved to Alma. William sat up straight to watch and to make himself remember what an old man Mr. Berry was and how his lunch box rattled more than anybody else's.

But then his eyes opened wide, and his fingers closed into hard little fists. For, just at that moment, he saw a cloud of dust at the end of the road and knew the white boys' cars were coming. His heart pounded in his chest, and Mr. Berry passed on down the street forgotten.

The yellow clouds came closer and closer, and then suddenly there were the cars. The red one, then the yellow, and then the blue. William did not stir until they were all past and the yellow clouds disappearing down the road behind them. But then such an excitement sprang up in him that he could not even remember the reason for it.

"They'll be back," he told himself. "They'll be back, and then'll be my chance." The blood hammered in his ears. His chance for what? He did not know exactly. A chance for a ride, of course, and perhaps for escape. But a chance for something else too, for something vague and hazy, which he could not picture clearly in his mind.

Anyway, it didn't matter that much. Only one thing mattered: here was his chance! William pulled himself up with his crutches and started quickly, if unsteadily, down the path to the curb. He stopped halfway there to listen for Alma, but as soon as he heard her voice droning mournfully from the back yard, he went on again relieved.

The excitement crowded up higher inside him. Even Alma was too busy to interfere with the cars today. Everything was going right now! Nothing could go wrong! Just like when you broke a wish bone and got the long end.

William glanced back in Alma's direction one more time and then sat down on the hot pavement. Drawing his good knee up before him and resting his cheek on it, he looked down the road in the direction from which the cars would come. "They'll come," he murmured low but urgently to himself. "They have to come."

The excitement would not be calmed. But now, too, somewhere in the depths of him a strange sadness rose— not just sadness either; a hint of fear. The piece of purple ribbon flashed before his mind, and then the memory that after tonight all this would be gone forever—the street and old Mr. Berry and the giant sycamore.

He did not have long to think, though. Soon he glimpsed the yellow clouds at the end of the road again. Hastily he stood up and glanced back at Alma. Then he stepped down into the gutter and took a few steps into the street.

All the while the yellow clouds came closer and closer until he could even glimpse the first car through the dust. His breath came quickly, and there was an iron knot in his chest. Now was his chance!

He edged closer into the road and waved one crutch. "Hey!" he called, "hey!" as loudly as he could. But the red car did not even slow down. His shouting was smothered under the roar of its motor, and the yellow dust whipped stinging into his mouth and eyes.

He did not cry. He went right on waving and screaming. But it was in that moment when the red car went zipping past him that the change came. All the while he was yelling, "Hey!" and edging into the street, but suddenly the thoughts of old Nanny's death and of the lavender ribbon and of his going away forever swept back over him. All of a sudden he was again aware of the nothingness awaiting him whichever way he turned.

But the time the next car—the yellow one—had ripped past, William was very near the center of the road. He left off waving and glanced back quickly at the big sycamore tree beside the weatherbeaten little house. Alma had left the back fence and was hurrying—almost running— towards the road. William could see she was calling. But the motor drowned out her words, and he did not worry about her interference now.   There was too little time.

He took three more steps to the center of the road and bellowed, "Hey! Stop! I want a ride!" But after that he was just too tired.

For a fraction of a minute he blinked hard-faced at the spinning wheels coming towards him. In that instant he remembered how their old black rooster had been crushed under those same wheels. And then there was the little piece of lavender ribbon taunting him again.

Not for long though. Soon he had forgotten even that. His eyes bulged wider and wider until finally the yellow dust stung too sharply and they shut of their own volition. So that he saw nothing any more—not Alma or the syca-more or anything. So that he did not even know when the blue car emerged from the clouds of dust and crashed full force against his small trembling body.

WILBUR DANIEL STEELE

DURING HIS two years in Chapel Hill (1930-31), Wilbur Daniel Steele wrote one of his finest pieces of fiction, "How Beautiful with Shoes." Seeking a quiet place for his writing, he had moved up from Charleston, South Carolina, where he had been living for a number of years. The move was almost a homecoming, for Steele had been born on March 17, 1886, in Greensboro, birthplace of O. Henry. Steele's life has been unusually mobile, even for that of a Methodist preacher's son: he went to kindergarten in Berlin, Germany, and to public school and college in Denver, Colorado. Since he wanted to be a painter, he went east in 1907 to attend art school, later pursuing his studies in Paris, Florence, and Venice. Returning to America, he married and settled in Provincetown, Massachusetts.

During the years that followed, he continued to travel—the West Indies, Bermuda, Ireland, France, England, North Africa. During World War I, he was a naval correspondent in Europe. Steele began to write stories in Paris while at the Académie Julian, but it was not until he returned to America that he decided on a career of writing instead of painting. In 1919, 1921, 1925, 1926, and 1931 he was honored by citations of the O. Henry Award Committee for the excellence of his short stories, a frequency which is proof of a remarkable record. *Land's End* (1918), *The Shame Woman* (1923), *Urkey Island* (1926), *The Man Who Saw Through Heaven* (1927), *Tower of Sand* (1929), and *Full Cargo* (1951) are volumes of his short stories. A representative collection is *The Best Short Stories of Wilbur Daniel Steele* (1946). His novels are *Storm* (1914), *Isles of the Blest* (1924), *Taboo* (1925), *Meat* (1928), *Sound of Rowlocks* (1938), *That Girl from Memphis* (1945), *Diamond Wedding* (1950), *Their Town* (1952), and *The Way to the Gold* (1955). He has collaborated in the writing of two plays, *Post Road* (1934, with Norma Mitchell) and *How Beautiful with Shoes* (1935, with Anthony Brown). Steele's home is at Old Lyme, Connecticut.

The story "How Beautiful with Shoes," written in 1932, is set in the North Carolina mountains, but it can hardly be classified as local-color fiction. The questions Steele asks are unmistakable and universal: Are love and poetry and religion and beauty not to be found in our sane, everyday world? Have they, somehow, become the keepsakes of those who have slipped beyond "reality"? If so, how "real" is the life left to us? As the story closes, Amarantha's primitive instincts bring her near an answer.

Though Steele has written other North Carolina stories, such as "Light," "Man and Boy" (previously titled "Town Drunk"), and "A Way with Women," his settings and theme are as varied as his travels.

How Beautiful with Shoes

WILBUR DANIEL STEELE

B Y THE TIME the milking was finished, the sow, which
had farrowed the past week, was making such a row
that the girl spilled a pint of the warm milk down the
trough lead to quiet the animal before taking the pail
to the well house. Then in the quiet she heard a sound
of hoofs on the bridge, where the road crossed the creek
a hundred yards below the house, and she set the pail
down on the ground beside her bare, barn-soiled feet.
She picked it up again. She set it down. It was as if she
calculated its weight.

That was what she was doing, as a matter of fact, setting
off against its pull toward the well house the pull of that
wagon team in the road, with little more of personal will
or wish in the matter than has a wooden weather vane
between two currents in the wind. And as with the vane,
so with the wooden girl—the added behest of a whiplash
cracking in the distance was enough; leaving the pail at the
barn door she set off in a deliberate, docile beeline through
the cow yard, over the fence, and down in a diagonal across
the farm's one tilled field toward the willow brake that
walled the road at the dip. And once under way, though
her mother came to the kitchen door and called in her high,
flat voice, "Amarantha, where you goin', Amarantha?" the

From *The Best Short Stories of Wilbur Daniel Steele*, published by
Doubleday & Co., Inc. Copyright, 1946, by Wilbur Daniel Steele.

girl went on, apparently unmoved, as though she had been as deaf as the woman in the doorway; indeed, if there was emotion in her it was the purely sensuous one of feeling the clods of the furrows breaking softly between her toes. It was springtime in the mountains.

"Amarantha, why don't you answer me, Amarantha?"

For moments after the girl had disappeared beyond the willows the widow continued to call, unaware through long habit of how absurd it sounded, the name which that strange man her husband had put upon their daughter in one of his moods. Mrs. Doggett had been deaf so long she did not realize that nobody else ever thought of it for the broad-fleshed, slow-minded girl, but called her Mary, or, even more simply, Mare.

Ruby Herter had stopped his team this side of the bridge, the mules' heads turned into the lane to his father's farm beyond the road. A big-barreled, heavy-limbed fellow with a square, sallow, not unhandsome face, he took out youth in ponderous gestures of masterfulness; it was like him to have cracked his whip above his animals' ears the moment before he pulled them to a halt. When he saw the girl getting over the fence under the willows he tongued the wad of tobacco out of his mouth into his palm, threw it away beyond the road, and drew a sleeve of his jumper across his lips.

"Don't run yourself out o' breath, Mare; I got all night."

"I was comin'." It sounded sullen only because it was matter-of-fact.

"Well, keep a-comin' and give us a smack." Hunched on the wagon seat, he remained motionless for some time after she had arrived at the hub, and when he stirred it was but to cut a fresh bit of tobacco, as if already he had forgotten why he threw the old one away. Having satisfied his humor, he unbent, climbed down, kissed her passive mouth, and hugged her up to him, roughly and loosely, his hands careless of contours. It was not out of the way; they were used to handling animals both of them; and it was spring. A slow warmth pervaded the girl, formless, nameless, almost impersonal.

Her betrothed pulled her head back by the braid of her yellow hair. He studied her face, his brows gathered and his chin out.

"Listen, Mare, you wouldn't leave nobody else hug and kiss you, dang you!"

She shook her head, without vehemence or anxiety.

"Who's that?" She hearkened up the road. "Pull your team out," she added, as a Ford came in sight around the bend above the house, driven at speed. "Geddap!" she said to the mules herself.

But the car came to a halt near them, and one of the five men crowded in it called, "Come on, Ruby, climb in. They's a loony loose out o' Dayville Asylum, and they got him trailed over somewheres on Split Ridge, and Judge North phoned up to Slosson's store for ever'body come help circle him—come on, hop the runnin' board!"

Ruby hesitated, an eye on his team.

"Scared, Ruby?" The driver raced his engine. "They say this boy's a killer."

"Mare, take the team in and tell Pa." The car was already moving when Ruby jumped it. A moment after it had sounded on the bridge it was out of sight.

"Amarantha, Amarantha, why don't you come, Amarantha?"

Returning from her errand fifteen minutes later, Mare heard the plaint lifted in the twilight. The sun had dipped behind the back ridge, and though the sky was still bright with day, the dusk began to smoke up out of the plowed field like a ground fog. The girl had returned through it, got the milk, and started toward the well house before the widow saw her.

"Daughter, seems to me you might!" she expostulated without change of key. "Here's some young man friend o' yourn stopped to say howdy, and I been rackin' my lungs out after you. . . . Put that milk in the cool and come!"

Some young man friend? But there was no good to be got from puzzling. Mare poured the milk in the pan in the dark of the low house over the well, and as she came out, stooping, she saw a figure waiting for her, black in silhouette against the yellowing sky.

"Who are you?" she asked, a native timidity making her sound sulky.

" 'Amarantha!' " the fellow mused. "That's poetry." And she knew then that she did not know him.

She walked past, her arms straight down and her eyes front. Strangers always affected her with a kind of muscular terror simply by being strangers. So she gained the kitchen steps, aware by his tread that he followed. There, taking courage, she turned on him, her eyes down at the level of his knees.

"Who are you and what d' y' want?"

He still mused. "Amarantha! Amarantha in Carolina! That makes me happy!"

Mare hazarded one upward look. She saw that he had red hair, brown eyes, and hollows under his cheekbones, and though the green sweater he wore on top of a gray overall was plainly not meant for him, sizes too large as far as girth went, yet he was built so long of limb that his wrists came inches out of the sleeves and made his big hands look even bigger.

Mrs. Doggett complained. "Why don't you introduce us, daughter?"

The girl opened her mouth and closed it again. Her mother, unaware that no sound had come out of it, smiled and nodded, evidently taking to the tall, homely fellow and tickled by the way he could not seem to get his eyes off her daughter. But the daughter saw none of it, all her attention centered upon the stranger's hands.

Restless, hard-fleshed, and chap-bitten, they were like a countryman's hands; but the fingers were longer than the ordinary, and slightly spatulate at their ends, and these ends were slowly and continuously at play among themselves.

The girl could not have explained how it came to her to be frightened and at the same time to be calm, for she was inept with words. It was simply that in an animal way she knew animals, knew them in health and ailing, and when they were ailing she knew by instinct, as her father had known, how to move so as not to fret them.

Her mother had gone in to light up; from beside the lamp shelf she called back, "If he's aimin' to stay to supper you should've told me, Amarantha, though I guess there's plenty of the side meat to go round, if you'll bring me in a few more turnips and potatoes, though it is late."

At the words the man's cheeks moved in and out. "I'm very hungry," he said.

Mare nodded deliberately. Deliberately, as if her mother could hear her, she said over her shoulder, "I'll go get the potatoes and turnips, Ma." While she spoke she was moving, slowly, softly, at first, towards the right of the yard, where the fence gave over into the field. Unluckily her mother spied her through the window.

"Amarantha, where *are* you goin'?"

"I'm goin' to get the potatoes and turnips." She neither raised her voice nor glanced back, but lengthened her stride. "He won't hurt her," she said to herself. "He won't hurt her; it's me, not her," she kept repeating, while she got over the fence and down into the shadow that lay more than ever like a fog on the field.

The desire to believe that it actually did hide her, the temptation to break from her rapid but orderly walk grew

till she could no longer fight it. She saw the road willows
only a dash ahead of her. She ran, her feet floundering
among the furrows.

She neither heard nor saw him, but when she realized he
was with her she knew he had been with her all the while.
She stopped, and he stopped, and so they stood, with the
dark open of the field all around. Glancing sidewise
presently, she saw he was no longer looking at her with
those strangely importunate brown eyes of his, but had
raised them to the crest of the wooded ridge behind her.

By and by, "What does it make you think of?" he asked.
And when she made no move to see, "Turn around and
look!" he said, and though it was low and almost tender in
its tone, she knew enough to turn.

A ray of the sunset hidden in the west struck through
the tops of the topmost trees, far and small up there, a thin,
bright hem.

"What does it make you think of, Amarantha? . . .
Answer!"

"Fire," she made herself say.

"Or blood."

"Or blood, yeh. That's right, or blood." She had heard
a Ford going up the road beyond the willows, and her attention was not on what she said.

The man soliloquized. "Fire and blood, both; spare one
or the other, and where is beauty, the way the world is?
It's an awful thing to have to carry, but Christ had it.
Christ came with a sword. I love beauty, Amarantha.
. . . I say, I love beauty!"

"Yeh, that's right, I hear." What she heard was the car
stopping at the house.

"Not prettiness. Prettiness'll have to go with ugliness,
because it's only ugliness trigged up. But beauty!" Now
again he was looking at her: "Do you know how beautiful
you are, Amarantha, *Amarantha sweet and fair?*" Of a

sudden, reaching behind her, he began to unravel the meshes of her hair braid, the long, flat-tipped fingers at once impatient and infinitely gentle. *"Braid no more that shining hair!"*

Flat-faced Mare Doggett tried to see around those glowing eyes so near to hers, but, wise in her instinct, did not try too hard. "Yeh," she temporized. "I mean, no, I mean."

"Amarantha, I've come a long, long way for you. Will you come away with me now?"

"Yeh—that is—in a minute I will, mister—yeh. . . ."

"Because you want to, Amarantha? Because you love me as I love you? Answer!"

"Yeh—sure—uh . . . *Ruby!"*

The man tried to run, but there were six against him, coming up out of the dark that lay in the plowed ground. Mare stood where she was while they knocked him down and got a rope around him; after that she walked back toward the house with Rudy and Older Haskins, her father's cousin.

Rudy wiped his brow and felt of his muscles. "Gees, you're lucky we come, Mare. We're no more'n past the town, when they come hollerin' he'd broke over this way."

When they came to the fence the girl sat on the rail for a moment and rebraided her hair before she went into the house, where they were making her mother smell ammonia.

Lots of cars were coming. Judge North was coming, somebody said. When Mare heard this she went into her bedroom off the kitchen and got her shoes and put them on. They were brand-new two-dollar shoes with cloth tops, and she had only begun to break them in last Sunday; she wished afterwards she had put her stockings on, too, for they would have eased the seams. Or else that she had put on the old button pair, even though the soles were worn through.

Judge North arrived. He thought first of taking the loony straight through to Dayville that night, but then decided to keep him in the lockup at the courthouse till morning and make the drive by day. Older Haskins stayed in, gentling Mrs. Doggett, while Ruby went out to help get the man into the judge's sedan. Now that she had them on, Mare didn't like to take the shoes off till Older went; it might make him feel small, she thought.

Older Haskins had a lot of facts about the loony.

"His name's Humble Jewett," he told them. "They belong back in Breed County, all them Jewetts, and I don't reckon there's none on 'em that's not a mite unbalanced. He went to college though, worked his way, and he taught somethin' 'rother in some academy-school a spell, till he went off his head all of a sudden and took after folks with an ax. I remember it in the paper at the time. They give out one while how the principal wasn't goin' to live, and there was others—there was a girl he tried to strangle. That was four-five years back."

Ruby came in guffawing. "Know the only thing they can get 'im to say, Mare? Only God thing he'll say is 'Amarantha, she's goin' with me.' . . . Mare!"

"Yeh, I know."

The cover of the kettle the girl was handling slid off on the stove with a clatter. A sudden sick wave passed over her. She went out to the back, out into the air. It was not till now she knew how frightened she had been.

Ruby went home, but Older Haskins stayed to supper with them and helped Mare do the dishes afterward; it was nearly nine when he left. The mother was already in bed, and Mare was about to sit down to get those shoes off her wretched feet at last, when she heard the cow carrying on up at the barn, lowing and kicking, and next minute the sow was in it with a horning note. It might be a fox passing by to get at the henhouse, or a weasel. Mare forgot her feet, took a broom handle they used in boiling clothes, opened the back door, and stepped out. Blinking the lamplight from her eyes, she peered up toward the out- buildings and saw the gable end of the barn standing like a red arrow in the dark, and the top of a butternut tree beyond it drawn in skeleton traceries, and just then a cock crowed.

She went to the right corner of the house and saw where the light came from, ruddy above the woods down the valley. Returning into the house, she bent close to her mother's ear and shouted, "Somethin's afire down to the town, looks like," then went out again and up to the barn. "Soh! Soh!" she called in to the animals. She climbed up and stood on the top of the rail of the cowpen fence, only to find she could not locate the flame even there.

Ten rods behind the buildings a mass of rock mounted higher than their ridgepoles, a chopped-off buttress of the black ridge, covered with oak scrub and wild grapes and blackberries, whose thorny ropes the girl beat away from her as she scrambled up in the wine-colored dark. Once at the top, and the brush held aside, she could see the tongue tip of the conflagration half a mile away at the town. And she knew by the bearing of the two church steeples that it was the building where the lockup was that was burning.

There is a horror in knowing animals trapped in the fire, no matter what the animals.

"O my God!" Mare said.

A car went down the road. Then there was a horse galloping. That would be Older Haskins probably. People were out at Ruby's father's farm; she could hear their voices raised. There must have been another car up from the other way, for lights wheeled and shouts were exchanged in the neighborhood of the bridge. Next thing she knew, Ruby was at the house below, looking for her probably.

He was telling her mother. Mrs. Doggett was not used
to him, so he had to shout even louder than Mare had to.

"What y' reckon he done, the hellion! He broke the door
and killed Lew Fyke and set the courthouse afire! . . .
Where's Mare?"

Her mother would not know. Mare called. "Here, up
the rock here."

She had better go down. Ruby would likely break his
bones if he tried to climb the rock in the dark, not knowing
the way. But the sight of the fire fascinated her simple
spirit, the fearful element, more fearful than ever now, with
the news. "Yes, I'm comin'," she called sulkily, hearing
feet in the brush. "You wait; I'm comin'."

When she turned and saw it was Humble Jewett, right
behind her among the branches, she opened her mouth to
screech. She was not quick enough. Before a sound came
out he got one hand over her face and the other arm around
her body.

Mare had always thought she was strong, and the loony
looked gangling, yet she was so easy for him that he need
not hurt her. He made no haste and little noise as he
carried her deeper into the undergrowth. Where the hill
began to mount it was harder though. Presently he set her
on her feet. He let the hand that had been over her mouth
slip down to her throat, where the broad-tipped fingers
wound, tender as yearning, weightless as caress.

"I was afraid you'd scream before you knew who 'twas,
Amarantha. But I didn't want to hurt your lips, dear
heart, your lovely, quiet lips."

It was so dark under the trees she could hardly see him,
but she felt his breath on her mouth, near to. But then,
instead of kissing her, he said, "No! No!" took from her
throat for an instant the hand that had held her mouth,
kissed its palm, and put it back softly against her skin.

"Now, my love, let's go before they come."

She stood stock-still. Her mother's voice was to be heard in the distance, strident and meaningless. More cars were on the road. Nearer, around the rock, there were sounds of tramping and thrashing. Ruby fussed and cursed. He shouted, "Mare, dang you, where are you, Mare?" his voice harsh with uneasy anger. Now, if she aimed to do anything, was the time to do it. But there was neither breath nor power in her windpipe. It was as if those yearning fingers had paralyzed the muscles.

"Come!" The arm he put around her shivered against her shoulder blades. It was anger. "I hate killing. It's a dirty, ugly thing. It makes me sick." He gagged, judging by the sound. But then he ground his teeth. "Come away, my love!"

She found herself moving. Once when she broke a branch underfoot with an instinctive awkwardness he chided her. "Quiet, my heart, else they'll hear!" She made herself heavy. He thought she grew tired and bore more of her weight till he was breathing hard.

Men came up the hill. There must have been a dozen spread out, by the angle of their voices as they kept touch. Always Humble Jewett kept caressing Mare's throat with one hand; all she could do was hang back.

"You're tired and you're frightened," he said at last. "Get down here."

There were twigs in the dark, the overhang of a thicket of some sort. He thrust her in under this, and lay beside her on the bed of ground pine. The hand that was not in love with her throat reached across her; she felt the weight of its forearm on her shoulder and its fingers among the strands of her hair, eagerly, but tenderly, busy. Not once did he stop speaking, no louder than breathing, his lips to her ear.

"Amarantha sweet and fair—Ah, braid no more that shining hair . . ."

Mare had never heard of Lovelace, the poet; she thought
the loony was just going on, hardly listened, got little sense.
But the cadence of it added to the lethargy of all her flesh.

*"Like a clew of golden thread—Most excellently ravellèd
. . ."*

Voices loudened; feet came tramping; a pair went past
not two rods away.

*". . . Do not then wind up the light—In ribbands, and
o'ercloud in night . . ."*

The search went on up the woods, men shouting to one
another and beating the brush.

". . . But shake your head and scatter day! I've never
loved, Amarantha. They've tried me with prettiness, but
prettiness is too cheap, yes, it's too cheap."

Mare was cold, and the coldness made her lazy. All she
knew was that he talked on.

"But dogwood blowing in the spring isn't cheap. The
earth of a field isn't cheap. Lots of times I've lain down
and kissed the earth of a field, Amarantha. That's beauty,
and a kiss for beauty." His breath moved up her cheek. He
trembled violently. "No, no, not yet!" He got to his knees
and pulled her by an arm. "We can go now."

They went back down the slope, but at an angle, so that
when they came to the level they passed two hundred yards
to the north of the house, and crossed the road there. More
and more her walking was like sleepwalking, the feet numb
in their shoes. Even where he had to let go of her, crossing
the creek on stones, she stepped where he stepped with an
obtuse docility. The voices of the searchers on the back
ridge were small in distance when they began to climb
the face of Coward Hill, on the opposite side of the valley.

There is an old farm on top of Coward Hill, big hayfields
as flat as tables. It had been half past nine when Mare
stood on the rock above the barn; it was toward midnight
when Humble Jewett put aside the last branches of the

woods and led her out on the height, and half a moon had
risen. And a wind blew there, tossing the withered tops of
last year's grasses, and mists ran with the wind, and ragged
shadows with the mists, and mares'-tails of clear moonlight among the shadows, so that now the boles of birches
on the forest's edge beyond the fences were but opal blurs
and now cut alabaster. It struck so cold against the girl's
cold flesh, this wind, that another wind of shivers blew
through her, and she put her hands over her face and eyes.
But the madman stood with his eyes wide open and his
mouth open, drinking the moonlight and the wet wind.

His voice, when he spoke at last, was thick in his throat.

"Get down on your knees." He got down on his and
pulled her after. "And pray!"

Once in England a poet sang four lines. Four hundred
years have forgotten his name, but they have remembered
his lines. The daft man knelt upright, his face raised to the
wild scud, his long wrists hanging to the dead grass. He
began simply:

> *"O western wind, when wilt thou blow*
> *That the small rain down can rain?"*

The Adam's apple was big in his bent throat. As simply
he finished:

> *"Christ, that my love were in my arms*
> *And I in my bed again!"*

Mare got up and ran. She ran without aim or feeling
in the power of the wind. She told herself again that the
mists would hide her from him, as she had done at dusk.
And again, seeing that he ran at her shoulder, she knew he
had been there all the while, making a race for it, flailing
the air with his long arms for joy of play in the cloud of
spring, throwing his knees high, leaping the moon-blue
waves of the brown grass, shaking his bright hair; and her

own hair was a weight behind her, lying level on the wind. Once a shape went bounding ahead of them for instants; she did not realize it was a fox till it was gone.

She never thought of stopping; she never thought anything, except once, "O my God, I wish I had my shoes off!" And what would have been the good in stopping or in turning another way, when it was only play? The man's ecstasy magnified his strength. When a snake fence came at them he took the top rail in flight, like a college hurdler and, seeing the girl hesitate and half turn as if to flee, he would have releaped it without touching a hand. But then she got a loom of buildings, climbed over quickly, before he should jump, and ran along the lane that ran with the fence.

Mare had never been up there, but she knew that the farm and the house belonged to a man named Wyker, a kind of cousin of Ruby Herter's, a violent, bearded old fellow who lived by himself. She could not believe her luck. When she had run half the distance and Jewett had not grabbed her, doubt grabbed her instead. "O my God, go careful!" she told herself. "Go slow!" she implored herself, and stopped running, to walk.

Here was a misgiving the deeper in that it touched her special knowledge. She had never known an animal so far gone that its instincts failed it; a starving rat will scent the trap sooner than a fed one. Yet, after one glance at the house they approached, Jewett paid it no further attention, but walked with his eyes to the right, where the cloud had blown away, and wooded ridges, like black waves rimed with silver, ran down away toward the Valley of Virginia.

"I've never lived!" In his single cry there were two things, beatitude and pain.

Between the bigness of the falling world and his eyes the flag of her hair blew. He reached out and let it whip between his fingers. Mare was afraid it would break the spell then, and he would stop looking away and look at the house again. So she did something almost incredible; she spoke.

"It's a pretty—I mean—a beautiful view down that-a-way."

"God Almighty beautiful, to take your breath away. I knew I'd never loved, Belovèd——" He caught a foot under the long end of one of the boards that covered the well and went down heavily on his hands and knees. It seemed to make no difference. "But I never knew I'd never lived," he finished in the same tone of strong rapture, quadruped in the grass, while Mare ran for the door and grabbed the latch.

When the latch would not give, she lost what little sense she had. She pounded with her fists. She cried with all her might: "Oh—hey—in—there—hey—in there!" Then Jewett came and took her gently between his hands and drew her away, and then, though she was free, she stood in something like an awful embarrassment while he tried shouting.

"Hey! Friend! Whoever you are, wake up and let my love and me come in!"

"No!" wailed the girl.

He grew peremptory. "Hey, wake up!" He tried the latch. He passed to full fury in a wink's time; he cursed, he kicked, he beat the door till Mare thought he would break his hands. Withdrawing, he ran at it with his shoulder; it burst at the latch, went slamming in, and left a black emptiness. His anger dissolved in a big laugh. Turning in time to catch her by a wrist, he cried joyously, "Come, my Sweet One!"

"No! No! Please—aw—listen. There ain't nobody there. He ain't to home. It wouldn't be right to go in anybody's house if they wasn't to home, you know that."

His laugh was blither than ever. He caught her high in his arms.

"I'd do the same by his love and him if 'twas my house, I would." At the threshold he paused and thought, "That is, if she was the true love of his heart forever."

The room was the parlor. Moonlight slanted in at the door, and another shaft came through a window and fell across a sofa, its covering dilapidated, showing its wadding in places. The air was sour, but both of them were farm-bred.

"Don't, Amarantha!" His words were pleading in her ear. "Don't be so frightened."

He set her down on the sofa. As his hands let go of her they were shaking.

"But look, I'm frightened too." He knelt on the floor before her, reached out his hands, withdrew them. "See, I'm afraid to touch you." He mused, his eyes rounded. "Of all the ugly things there are, fear is the ugliest. And yet, see, it can be the very beautifulest. That's a strange, queer thing."

The wind blew in and out of the room, bringing the thin, little bitter sweetness of new April at night. The moonlight that came across Mare's shoulders fell full upon his face, but hers it left dark, ringed by the aureole of her disordered hair.

"Why do you wear a halo, Love?" He thought about it. "Because you're an angel, is that why?" The swift, untempered logic of the mad led him to dismay. His hands came flying to hers, to make sure they were of earth; and he touched her breast, her shoulders, and her hair. Peace returned to his eyes as his fingers twined among the strands.

"Thy hair is as a flock of goats that appear from Gilead . . ." He spoke like a man dreaming. *"Thy temples are like a piece of pomegranate within thy locks."*

Mare never knew that he could not see her for the moonlight.

"Do you remember, Love?"

She dared not shake her head under his hand. "Yeh, I reckon," she temporized.

"You remember how I sat at your feet, long ago, like this, and made up a song? And all the poets in all the world have never made one to touch it, have they, Love?"

"Ugh-ugh—never."

"How beautiful are thy feet with shoes . . . Remember?"

"O my God, what's he sayin' now?" she wailed to herself.

> *"How beautiful are thy feet with shoes, O prince's daughter! the joints of thy thighs are like jewels, the work of the hands of a cunning workman.*
>
> *Thy navel is like a round goblet, which wanteth not liquor; thy belly is like an heap of wheat set about with lilies.*
>
> *Thy two breasts are like two young roes that are twins."*

Mare had not been to church since she was a little girl, when her mother's black dress wore out. "No, no!" she wailed under her breath. "You're awful to say such awful things." She might have shouted it; nothing could have shaken the man now, rapt in the immortal, passionate periods of Solomon's song:

> *". . . now also thy breasts shall be as clusters of the vine, and the smell of thy nose like apples."*

Hotness touched Mare's face for the first time. "Aw, no, don't talk so!"

> *"And the roof of thy mouth like the best wine for my belovèd . . . causing the lips of them that are asleep to speak."*

He had ended. His expression changed. Ecstasy gave place to anger, love to hate. And Mare felt the change in the weight of the fingers in her hair.

"What do you mean, I mustn't say it like that?" But it

was not to her his fury spoke, for he answered himself
straightway. "Like poetry, Mr. Jewett; I won't have blas-
phemy around my school."

"Poetry!   My God!   If that isn't poetry—if that isn't
music——" . . . "It's Bible, Jewett. What you're paid to
teach here is *literature.*"

"Dr. Ryeworth, you're the blasphemer and you're an
ignorant man." . . . "And your principal. And I won't
have you going around reading sacred allegory like earthly
love."

"Ryeworth, you're an old man, a dull man, a dirty man,
and you'd be better dead."

Jewett's hands had slid down from Mare's head. "Then
I went to put my fingers around his throat, so. But my
stomach turned, and I didn't do it. I went to my room. I
laughed all the way to my room. I sat in my room at my
table and I laughed. I laughed all afternoon and long after
dark came. And then, about ten, somebody came and stood
beside me in my room.

" 'Wherefore dost thou laugh, son?'

"I didn't laugh any more. He didn't say any more. I
kneeled down, bowed my head.

" 'Thy will be done! Where is he, Lord?'

" 'Over at the girls' dormitory, waiting for Blossom Sinck-
ley.'

"Brassy Blossom, dirty Blossom . . ."

It had come so suddenly it was nearly too late. Mare
tore at his hands with hers, tried with all her strength to
pull her neck away.

"Filthy Blossom! And him an old filthy man, Blossom!
And you'll find him in hell when you reach there, Blossom
. . ."

It was more the nearness of his face than the hurt of
his hands that gave her power of fright to choke out three
words.

"I—ain't—Blossom!"

Light ran in crooked veins. Through the veins she saw his face bewildered. His hands loosened. One fell down and hung; the other he lifted and put over his eyes, took it away again and looked at her.

"Amarantha!" His remorse was fearful to see. "What have I done!" His hands returned to hover over the hurts, ravening with pity, grief, and tenderness. Tears fell down his cheeks. And with that, dammed desire broke its dam.

"Amarantha, my love, my dove, my beautiful love——"

"And I ain't Amarantha neither, I'm Mary! Mary, that's my name!"

She had no notion what she had done. He was like a crystal crucible that a chemist watches, changing hue in a wink with one adeptly added drop; but hers was not the chemist's eye. All she knew was that she felt light and free of him; all she could see of his face as he stood away above the moonlight were the whites of his eyes.

"Mary!" he muttered. A slight paroxysm shook his frame. So in the transparent crucible desire changed its hue. He retreated farther, stood in the dark by some tall piece of furniture. And still she could see the whites of his eyes.

"Mary! Mary Adorable!" A wonder was in him. "Mother of God!"

Mare held her breath. She eyed the door, but it was too far. And already he came back to go on his knees before her, his shoulders so bowed and his face so lifted that it must have cracked his neck, she thought; all she could see on the face was pain.

"Mary Mother, I'm sick to my death. I'm so tired."

She had seen a dog like that, one she had loosed from a trap after it had been there three days, its caught leg half gnawed free. Something about the eyes.

"Mary Mother, take me in your arms . . ."

Once again her muscles tightened. But he made no move.

" . . . and give me sleep."

No, they were worse than the dog's eyes.

"Sleep, sleep! Why won't they let me sleep? Haven't I done it all yet, Mother? Haven't I washed them yet of all their sins? I've drunk the cup that was given me; is there another? They've mocked me and reviled me, broken my brow with thorns and my hands with nails, and I've forgiven them, for they knew not what they did. Can't I go to sleep now, Mother?"

Mare could not have said why, but now she was more frightened than she had ever been. Her hands lay heavy on her knees, side by side, and she could not take them away when he bowed his head and rested his face upon them.

After a moment he said one thing more. "Take me down gently when you take me from the Tree."

Gradually the weight of his body came against her shins, and he slept.

The moon streak that entered by the eastern window crept north across the floor, thinner and thinner; the one that fell through the southern doorway traveled east and grew fat. For a while Mare's feet pained her terribly and her legs, too. She dared not move them, though, and by and by they did not hurt so much.

A dozen times, moving her head slowly on her neck, she canvassed the shadows of the room for a weapon. Each time her eyes came back to a heavy earthenware pitcher on a stand some feet to the left of the sofa. It would have had flowers in it when Wyker's wife was alive; probably it had not been moved from its dust ring since she died. It would be a long grab, perhaps too long; still, it might be done if she had her hands.

To get her hands from under the sleeper's head was the

task she set herself. She pulled first one, then the other, infinitesimally. She waited. Again she tugged a very, very little. The order of his breathing was not disturbed. But at the third trial he stirred.

"Gently! Gently!" His own muttering waked him more. With some drowsy instinct of possession he threw one hand across her wrists, pinning them together between thumb and fingers. She kept dead quiet, shut her eyes, lengthened her breathing, as if she too slept.

There came a time when what was pretense grew a peril; strange as it was, she had to fight to keep her eyes open. She never knew whether or not she really napped. But something changed in the air, and she was wide awake again. The moonlight was fading on the doorsill, and the light that runs before dawn waxed in the window behind her head.

And then she heard a voice in the distance, lifted in maundering song. It was old man Wyker coming home after a night, and it was plain he had had some whisky.

Now a new terror laid hold of Mare.

"Shut up, you fool you!" she wanted to shout. "Come quiet, quiet!" She might have chanced it now to throw the sleeper away from her and scramble and run, had his powers of strength and quickness not taken her simple imagination utterly in thrall.

Happily the singing stopped. What had occurred was that the farmer had espied the open door and, even befuddled as he was, wanted to know more about it quietly. He was so quiet that Mare began to fear he had gone away. He had the squirrel hunter's foot, and the first she knew of him was when she looked and saw his head in the doorway, his hard, soiled whiskery face half upside down with craning.

He had been to the town. Between drinks he had wandered in and out of the night's excitement; had even gone a short distance with one search party himself. Now he took in the situation in the room. He used his fore-finger. First he held it to his lips. Next he pointed it with a jabbing motion at the sleeper. Then he tapped his own forehead and described wheels. Lastly, with his whole hand, he made pushing gestures, for Mare to wait. Then he vanished as silently as he had appeared.

The minutes dragged. The light in the east strengthened and turned rosy. Once she thought she heard a board creaking in another part of the house, and looked down sharply to see if the loony stirred. All she could see of his face was a temple with freckles on it and the sharp ridge of a cheekbone, but even from so little she knew how deeply and peacefully he slept. The door darkened. Wyker was there again. In one hand he carried something heavy; with the other he beckoned.

"Come jumpin'!" he said out loud.

Mare went jumping, but her cramped legs threw her down halfway to the sill; the rest of the distance she rolled and crawled. Just as she tumbled through the door it seemed as if the world had come to an end above her; two barrels of a shotgun discharged into a room make a noise. Afterwards all she coud hear in there was something twist-ing and bumping on the floor boards. She got up and ran.

Mare's mother had gone to pieces; neighbor women put her to bed when Mare came home. They wanted to put Mare to bed, but she would not let them. She sat on the edge of her bed in her lean-to bedroom off the kitchen, just as she was, her hair down all over her shoulders and her shoes on, and stared away from them, at a place in the wallpaper.

"Yeh, I'll go myself. Lea' me be!"

The women exchanged quick glances, thinned their lips, and left her be. "God knows," was all they would answer to the questionings of those that had not gone in, "but she's gettin' herself to bed."

When the doctor came through he found her sitting just as she had been, still dressed, her hair down on her shoulders and her shoes on.

"What d' y' want?" she muttered and stared at the place in the wallpaper.

How could Doc Paradise say, when he did not know himself?

"I didn't know if you might be—might be feeling very smart, Mary."

"I'm all right. Lea' me be."

It was a heavy responsibility. Doc shouldered it. "No, it's all right," he said to the men in the road. Ruby Herter stood a little apart, chewing sullenly and looking another way. Doc raised his voice to make certain it carried. "Nope, nothing."

Ruby's ears got red, and he clamped his jaws. He knew he ought to go in and see Mare, but he was not going to do it while everybody hung around waiting to see if he would. A mule tied near him reached out and mouthed his sleeve in idle innocence; he wheeled and banged a fist against the side of the animal's head.

"Well, what d' y' aim to do 'bout it?" he challenged its owner.

He looked at the sun then. It was ten in the morning. "Hell, I got work!" he flared, and set off down the road for home. Doc looked at Judge North, and the judge started after Ruby. But Ruby shook his head angrily. "Lea' me be!" He went on, and the judge came back.

It got to be eleven and then noon. People began to say, "Like enough she'd be as thankful if the whole neighborhood wasn't camped here." But none went away.

As a matter of fact they were no bother to the girl. She never saw them. The only move she made was to bend

her ankles over and rest her feet on edge; her shoes hurt
terribly and her feet knew it, though she did not. She sat
all the while staring at that one figure in the wallpaper,
and she never saw the figure.

Strange as the night had been, this day was stranger.
Fright and physical pain are perishable things once they
are gone. But while pain merely dulls and telescopes in
memory and remains diluted pain, terror looked back upon
has nothing of terror left. A gambling chance taken, at no
matter what odds, and won was a sure thing since the
world's beginning; perils come through safely were never
perilous. But what fright does do in retrospect is this—
it heightens each sensuous recollection, like a hard, clear
lacquer laid on wood, bringing out the color and grain of it
vividly.

Last night Mare had lain stupid with fear on ground pine
beneath a bush, loud footfalls and light whispers confused
in her ear. Only now, in her room, did she smell the ground
pine.

Only now did the conscious part of her brain begin to
make words of the whispering.

"*Amarantha,*" she remembered, "*Amarantha sweet and
fair.*" That was as far as she could go for the moment, except that the rhyme with "fair" was "hair." But then a
puzzle, held in abeyance, brought other words. She wondered what "ravel Ed" could mean. "*Most excellently
ravellèd.*" It was left to her mother to bring the end.

They gave up trying to keep her mother out at last. The
poor woman's prostration took the form of fussiness.

"Good gracious, daughter, you look a sight. Them new
shoes, half ruined; ain't your feet *dead?* And look at your
hair, all tangled like a wild one!"

She got a comb.

"Be quiet, daughter; what's ailin' you? Don't shake your
head!"

"But shake your head and scatter day."

"What you say, Amarantha?" Mrs. Doggett held an ear down.

"Go 'way! Lea' me be!"

Her mother was hurt and left. And Mare ran, as she stared at the wallpaper.

"Christ, that my love were in my arms . . ."

Mare ran. She ran through a wind white with moonlight and wet with "the small rain." And the wind she ran through, it ran through her, and made her shiver as she ran. And the man beside her leaped high over the waves of the dead grasses and gathered the wind in his arms, and her hair was heavy and his was tossing, and a little fox ran before them in waves of black and silver, more immense than she had ever known the world could be, and more beautiful.

"God Almighty beautiful, to take your breath away!"

Mare wondered, and she was not used to wondering. "Is it only crazy folks ever run like that and talk that way?"

She no longer ran; she walked; for her breath was gone. And there was some other reason, some other reason. Oh yes, it was because her feet were hurting her. So, at last, and roundabout, her shoes had made contact with her brain.

Bending over the side of the bed, she loosened one of them mechanically. She pulled it half off. But then she looked down at it sharply, and she pulled it on again.

"How beautiful . . ."

Color overspread her face in a slow wave.

"How beautiful are thy feet with shoes . . ."

"Is it only crazy folks ever say such things?"

"O prince's daughter!"

"Call you that?"

By and by there was a knock at the door. It opened, and Ruby Herter came in.

"Hello, Mare old girl!" His face was red. He scowled and kicked at the floor. "I'd-a been over sooner, except we got a mule down sick." He looked at his dumb betrothed. "Come on, cheer up, forget it! He won't scare you no more, not that boy, not what's left o' him. What you lookin' at, sourface? Ain't you glad to see me?"

Mare quit looking at the wallpaper and looked at the floor.

"Yeh," she said.

"That's more like it, babe." He came and sat beside her; reached down behind her and gave her a spank. "Come on, give us a kiss, babe!" He wiped his mouth on his jumper sleeve, a good farmer's sleeve, spotted with milking. He put his hands on her; he was used to handling animals. "Hey, you, warm up a little; reckon I'm goin' to do all the lovin'?"

"Ruby, lea' me be!"

"What!"

She was up, twisting. He was up, purple.

"What's ailin' of you, Mare? What you bawlin' about?"

"Nothin'—only go 'way!"

She pushed him to the door and through it with all her strength, and closed it in his face, and stood with her weight against it, crying, "Go 'way! Go 'way! Lea' me be!"

BERNICE KELLY HARRIS

BERNICE KELLY was born in Wake County on October 8, 1893, of many generations of sturdy Wake farming people. Her childhood was a happy one, for it was filled with box parties, revivals, baseball games, funerals, Sunday schools, Easter picnics, and friendships with innumerable country cousins and neighbors. The Bible, *Pilgrim's Progress,* and the *Progressive Farmer* were among her favorite readings. Her early education was received at Mt. Moriah Academy, a flourishing rural school of the day. Before she was ten years old, she had decided to be a poet like Longfellow and had written many melancholy verses. A year later, she had abandoned poetry in favor of fiction and at twelve composed a novel "filled with death-bed scenes of consumptive heroines and heartbroken lovers in whose arms the dear dying reclined as they breathed their last."

After one year at Cary High School, she attended Meredith College, from which she graduated. Then for twelve years, she taught high-school English, most of the time in Seaboard, Northampton County. In 1919, she studied playwriting under Professor F. H. Koch of the Carolina Playmakers and for many years thereafter was associated with amateur theatricals in her own community and at Chapel Hill. The best of her one act plays written during these years were published in 1940 as *Folk Plays of Eastern Carolina.*

In 1926, she married Herbert Kavanaugh Harris, a farmer and businessman. Abandoning her school teaching, she entered wholeheartedly into the social and church affairs of the Seaboard community. When interest in playwriting waned, she contributed human-interest bits to the Norfolk *Virginian-Pilot*. From reading the feature stories which she had been sending in to the Raleigh *News and Observer*, Jonathan Daniels inquired why she did not write a novel. The result was *Purslane* (1939), which was an immediate success both in America and England, where it received high critical praise. For this story of the lives of the humble people in a farming section in Wake County, she was awarded the Mayflower Cup by the State Literary and Historical Association. She was the first woman to receive this award, given at that time for the most distinguished North Carolina book of the year. Six other novels of the small-town and rural North Carolina scene have come from her pen: *Portulaca* (1941), *Sweet Beulah Land* (1943), *Sage Quarter* (1945), *Janey Jeems* (1946), *Hearthstones* (1948), and *Wild Cherry Tree Road* (1951). She has also written a number of full-length plays and television dramas, most of them based on characters in her novels. *Bernice Kelly Harris: Storyteller of Eastern Carolina* (1955) is a brief biography by Richard Walser.

Strangely enough, Mrs. Harris has not been a copious writer of short stories. "Bantie Woman" and "Yellow Color Suit," published separately in periodicals, are best known, though there are several in *Portulaca* used as illustrative work of its author-heroine. "The Lace Cloth" has never before appeared in print. "I think," wrote Mrs. Harris, "it has a message for our times—and any time. The image of Order—of Liberty, indeed—is being shadowed these days by so many hard-shelled interpretations of it. The entity gets lost in the welter of opinions."

The Lace Cloth

BERNICE KELLY HARRIS

EULALIA walked slowly through the long hall that divided the rooms of the old home place.

She paused at the door of each room to savor the order she had achieved inside, to enjoy in prospect its impact on Margie, to see it with the eyes of the whole Neal family who would assemble early this evening for the Re-union.

Its affirmation was as apparent as the motto on a family coat of arms would be.

For the first time since her husband's death, Eulalia did not feel aimless. Her objective had now become Family, specifically the youth, her brothers' children, who so vitally needed a sense of continuity and of the spiritual essence of order. So, during her turn in the family plan of alternately taking care of their bereft father in his country home, she had been projecting her aim.

In all her fifty-six years, though, she had not been so tired. Still, she felt it was the rewarding exhaustion of creation. For the past days she had re-created the image of chaste sweet order that had been her family's way of life before Miss Tulie.

The other stepchildren, as well as Eulalia, had been outraged by Miss Tulie's disorder, entrenched long before a heart ailment provided excuse for it. They had been embarrassed before Margie, one of the fastidious Camerons

By permission of the author.

with a tangible coat of arms in their hall, because Margie's concept of the Neals had been so grossly distorted.

That empty aspirin bottle, dangling as hand-pull from the light switch cord, had been a particular offense among the disorder, symbolic of the break with nicety everywhere. There had been other glaring indignities. The dusty corners, cluttered with old spools and corncobs and drab nothings for children to make foolish playthings of, the heaps of dirty cotton littering the once immaculate guest room, the filthy specimens stashed away in hand-painted urns, the old stockings that tied doors shut when latches became slack, the pencil marks on plastered walls, the grubby drawings on the oilcloth table cover—That oilcloth, spread on the walnut dining table, had been for Eulalia the big indignity of Miss Tulie's residence, the ultimate break with a gracious way of life.

So, the lace cloth from her own immaculate store at home, spread now over the dining table for the Re-union supper, symbolized for Eulalia the spiritual content of the old sweet order. It would indicate to the youth of the family, who had known only Miss Tulie in their Grandfather's house: "From this you came. This is what you are." For the little children it would be implying, "Grandfather's is not a big playhouse in which to mark up walls or sneak in bugs and bones and dirty cotton or draw pictures on tablecloths." For the adults it would bring back the essence of Home. For the Old Man it would betoken a bright haven for his sunset. For Margie, importantly for Margie—

Margie's voice suddenly interrupted the reflections. "Eulalia! The family's here!"

Eulalia hurried out front to greet her sister-in-law. "I'm glad you're first, Margie."

"The others are outside digging graves," Margie said. "What?"

"The youngsters found some broken bird nests under the old maples and—"

Eulalia interrupted quickly. "I hope the family all noticed I've had the trees trimmed up and all the dead maple limbs lopped off!"

"About all they noticed was dead birds and broken nests. They're organizing quite a burial out there under the maples, with headstones and flowers and—"

"They'll have to be moved!" Eulalia said. "I've had the grove put in complete order, and it isn't going to be cluttered up again."

"Say!" Margie looked around in surprise as she moved forward into the house. "You've been doing things inside too!"

"I was just waiting for your reaction, Margie."

"Clean and polished," Margie mused, "and—and chaste. I feel like tip-toeing."

"You must have known how upset I've been over the drab confusion here, Margie, over its impact on you—"

"I've loved to come here," Margie mused on. "Miss Tulie had such a relaxing way about her, such a flair for entertaining talk. Why, she could make commonplaces sound interesting. I suppose we all just listened effortlessly and forgot about the disorder around."

"Disorder is wrong, it's downright ungodly!" Eulalia declared earnestly as she opened another room for Margie's inspection. "Its impact on the children has been terrible!"

"Well, they seemed to create their own magic out of it, or maybe out of doing as they pleased here."

"That's it!" Eulalia cried. "Do-as-you-please is the root of all the juvenile delinquency today. Order has certain authority in it, truth. That's the motto I'd write on a coat of arms, if I were designing one for the Neals. Order has the kind of continuity the universe has, the permanence! I tell you, Margie, the truth has been so distorted for the

grandchildren, the images so blurred. The image of their
own Grandmother has been false, of their Grandfather
living here amid this sordid untidiness. I've felt guilty
before them—and before you, Margie—that I didn't wade
in sooner!"

"Oh, but you did try, Eulalia. And once or twice I
tried to help you clean up here. But when we saw how
nervous and upset our efforts always made Miss Tulie—
And after all, it was her home."

"Nervous over the debris we might uncover!" Eulalia
said crisply. "It's incredible what I've found in this house
the past days. And the pencil marks I've washed off
plastered walls—! Some child wrote, 'This is a house,'
right here in the front hall!"

" 'This is a house,' " Margie repeated reflectively. "Maybe that child was groping toward an idea of continuity and
permanence, Eulalia, trying to articulate his feeling about
his Grandfather's place. Maybe it was a motto, on his level,
for a family coat of arms."

Eulalia was silent. The significance of all that she had
been doing here was not getting through to Margie yet.
She opened the door to the dining room. "Look!" she
bade. There was the summation. It all converged on the
dining table.

Margie caught her breath. "The lace cloth!" she cried.
Then involuntarily she laughed. "Forgive me, Eulalia,"
she said quickly. "It's not funny, of course. But when I
suddenly realized how much territory one Quaker lace
cloth has to cover—"

Her explanation was cut short by a little boy's cry from
the living room. Both women hurried there.

Junie was standing in the middle of the room, staring
in dismayed unbelief at the light fixture overhead.

"Somebody's took my 'lectric bottle down!" he cried
tearfully.

"It belonged down," Eulalia said. "It was untidy."

"But we don't have no 'lectric bottles at our house to turn on lights by, and Miss Tulie let me!"

"It was disorderly dangling there, ugly."

"It was pretty." Junie looked up through his tears at the emptiness overhead. "That 'lectric bottle was like—like taking hold of a hand in the dark and—and seeing the way all of a sudden. It was the first 'lectric bottle in the world for old folks like Granddaddy that stumble round in the dark, and I was going to invent—"

Eulalia interrupted Junie's plaint and sent him outside to play. Then she called the other women to help her and Margie organize the Re-union supper.

The women were so agape over the lace cloth and the beautiful order of the dining room that one let her casserole burn. Flaking off the burnt top, she nervously dropped buttered bread crumbs and made grease spots on the lace cloth.

"Tch! Tch! Tch! I'm all thumbs tonight, trying so hard," she apologized, "with the table so nice."

"Now if I go and slop this tomato juice over on the lace cloth—" another said.

"You just did," she was told.

They went into action with warm water and cold, with soap flakes and detergent, with wet towels and dry. Trying out their combined Household Hints on the lace cloth, they let the rolls burn.

"Try scraping off the burnt top," one suggested.

"No," Eulalia said firmly. "It's not that kind of supper. Put another batch of rolls in the oven."

A boy rushed into the dining room. "Where's the chain, Aunt 'Lalia?" he asked. "We got to keep the prison door shut, you know, and somebody's gone and taken our chain down!"

"Chain?" Eulalia was puzzled.

"Aw, it wasn't stockings. It was chains that kept the convicts shut up when they broke the law, and they be-long—"

"Listen, son," Eulalia interrupted quickly, "doors belong to be fastened by latches, not old stockings. They're improper, ugly."

"They're chains for our prison—!"

"This is no playhouse," Eulalia reminded him. "Go outside to play."

The boy went outside. Eulalia turned her attention back to the dining room. She told the women the lace cloth looked puckered where they had washed the stains out.

"We'll press it," they said.

They found the iron, plugged it in, heated it to warm. Each cautioned the presser not to burn the lace cloth.

Amid the ado, one of the husbands came to the door. "How about chow?" he asked. "Isn't it time to come and get it?"

"It's not that kind of supper, dear," his wife said, lowering her voice.

At that instant they became aware of scorched food. Another pan of rolls had been burned. As Eulalia turned to put in a fresh batch, a youngster cried out in angry protest from the hall.

"Where's my museum? Where's my specimens?" He rushed to the door of the dining room. "Where's my bones?" he demanded.

"What are you talking about?" Eulalia said.

"I'm talking about my fossils—my bones and rocks and bugs and snake skins and butterflies! Miss Tulie let me keep them in the big urn where it was safe and dry, and it's empty. Somebody—" he accused. "Somebody—"

"Hank," Eulalia broke into the accusation, "that was a hand-painted urn. Aunt Lydia painted it a long time ago, when she was here on a visit—"

"It kept my fossils dry and safe! I had bones enough to build a skeleton. And rocks with gold in them and maybe uranium."

"This is a home, not a museum," Eulalia said. "Old bones are filthy!"

"It's do-as-you-please land, like in stories. It *was!*" he added hastily.

"Do-as-you-please is wicked, Hank, in principle. You might please to yell FIRE in a crowded theater, just to see people rush out and do disorderly things in the darkness and—"

Hank did not wait to hear the conclusion. He dashed past the man, who was still standing there observing the women at work over the lace cloth.

"It's all pressed and ready," Eulalia was told as she turned back toward the table. "No stains show, see?"

"Say!" the man demanded from the door. "Are we having lace cloth for supper or vittles?"

Finally the Family gathered around the lace-covered dining table. Eulalia had her father brought in and seated. He protested he wanted to eat, as he habitually did in the summertime, on the front porch. There Miss Tulie had served him so many summers, had let him dawdle over his food as long—and as sloppily, Eulalia recalled—as he pleased. Questioned once about this front porch fixation, Miss Tulie had explained it was such a long walk from the porch to the dining room for an old man. Pressed further, she had admitted the tray meals relieved him of having to say grace at the table. He had lately been forgetting the words, repeated so many times without variation through his nine decades. Only last summer he had been unable to recall what came after "Give us grateful hearts, Heavenly Father," and had said tremulously and a little abashed to Miss Tulie, "You finish, Mama."

For all that, Eulalia felt that the Head of the House must be in place tonight, must say the blessing around the lace-covered dining table in the presence of Family. The distorted image of Father, of Grandfather and Great-grandfather, had to move back into proper focus, the true identity be reestablished. Part of it was to keep him immaculate before children and children's children. Eulalia pinned a white towel around his neck.

One little boy cried out in protest, "Granddaddy's got on a bib!"

"A bib, just like a baby!" another chimed.

The old man was abashed. "Take it off!" he cried tremulously. "Take it off!"

"After supper, Father," Eulalia said gently, but firmly. "We're going to have the blessing now. Bow your heads, children. All right, Father." She stood near to prompt.

" 'Give us grateful hearts, Heavenly Father, for these and all Thy kind blessings,' " the Old Man repeated, without any need of prompting. Eulalia glanced with satisfaction at Margie, who was beginning to see for the first time the authentic image of the Neal Family. But she had to bow again. For the Old Man began improvising. He talked to Deity as though He were there, as though He understood all the family's inarticulations beyond their phrasing. "And let us walk in kindness and peace, one with the other," he concluded. "And when we have served our time here, take us to our bright home in heaven, where Mama is."

Children and grandchildren blinked their eyes after the Amen, cleared their throats. A minor note, strange and poignantly untidy, had intruded into the order of this Family Re-union. Everyone tried to become bright and chatty at once, following Eulalia's lead. But the old free and easy fellowship did not come through. There was constraint around the lace cloth. Mothers hovered over children restrainingly. Wives cautioned husbands not to spill casserole sauces on the lace cloth. Men who at home ate easily and casually from damask and Madeira linens were strangely self-conscious around the family board to-night. All were tentative, even timid, about spooning garden peas out of mushroom sauce, as though wary of lace at the old home.

The tentativeness merged into tension. The dismay Eulalia saw on Junie's face when he discovered that the aspirin bottle was gone from the light switch was reflected a little on adult faces. The new nicety was like a presence. The Family was sensitive to it, but not at home with it.

There was a chorus of cautions, of warnings around the table.

"Watch, son! You'll spill tea—Oh, you've turned over your glass of tea on the lace cloth!"

"Tch! Tch! Tch!"

"Quick! A towel!"

"Tea will stain."

"Won't it bleach out?"

"But it would spot the lace cloth."

"Try buttermilk, room temperature."

"Try cold water."

"Try a paste of mild soap flakes."

Amid the ado, the culprit was feeling oddly abashed over what had hitherto been routine mishap. "Aw-w! I like the flowered cloth best," he said.

"Me too!" the other children chorused.

"I could land my corncob jets on it. Miss Tulie let me."

"I could build spool towers this high—!"

"I made butterflies mongst the flowers, just as natural—"

"I drawed mottoes—"

Mothers bade the children hush and finish their supper.

"Say *drew,* not drawed," one added resolutely.

"I can go crawl in a hole, if it's such a disgrace to spill tea on a cloth—"

That suddenly gave the children an idea. "Our tunnels!" they shouted. "We can crawl in them!"

"Our igloos!"

"Our mountains!"

"Our snow man!"

They dashed out. Soon they were back.

"Somebody," they cried accusingly, "Somebody has destroyed our tunnels!"

"And our mountains."

"And our igloos."

"Where's our cotton?" they demanded as one.

Eulalia was gentle with them. "That dirty cotton did not belong in there. It used to be our guest room, where Aunt Lydia stayed when she came down from Virginia to visit, where the minister slept when he stopped with us, where the schoolteachers—"

"Aw, that was *then!*"

"*Now,* we can make igloos there, if we please. *Could.*"

"The only do-as-you-please land in the world. And it's gone."

"Doing as you please brings disorder," Eulalia told them earnestly. "And disorder is wrong. And ugly."

"We made pretty mountains."

"And tunnels."

"And snow men in July."

"And museums—"

"All right, children. This is how it was here, how it's going to be, orderly and clean and chaste. From this you came. This you are."

They were silent an instant. Then they organized. "Let's go outside!"

"In the dark!" they said.

After supper the women did not relax. There was no

cozy recounting of commonplaces, no effortless listening to entertaining talk. Instead, mothers were tensely keeping up with children. Since the materials for creating foolish playthings were gone from dusty corners, it was necessary to direct play, to invent sitting-down games against unruly impulses, to tide the youngsters over the strange lost interval.

Once Junie went back to the living room and stood under the light bulb, staring up as though the electric hand just had to be there at the end of a string.

There had never been such an orderly gathering. Boys who had been noisy among their igloos were quiet somewhere in the darkness of outside. Youngsters who had been gleeful in their do-as-you-please land sat regimented in the front room, putting no spirit in the sitting-down games. Women who had been free of responsibility at the old place as nowhere else in the world were on duty. Men began to ask from the porch what time it was. The Old Man wanted to go to bed earlier than ever before at re-unions.

Eulalia had a sense of the Family's waiting for time to pass.

Before nine o'clock they were heading toward their cars in the grove. Oddly nobody seemed really at home, here where the essence of Home was coming through so significantly. At least there was Margie, perceptive and fastidious Margie, who would be aware of the significance.

Margie was the last to leave. "Goodbye, Eulalia," she said. "You had a nice Family Re-union."

Some subtle reservation in Margie's manner prompted Eulalia to speak outright. She so needed reassurance from Margie. "Tell me, Margie, didn't the lace cloth signify beyond the territory it covered, now didn't it?"

"Maybe the oilcloth did too," Margie said cryptically.

"What on earth do you mean?"

"Well, I mean—haven't you been destroying an image

that signified too? Mightn't Miss Tulie's physical disorder
have had something of spiritual content too? Mightn't
a 'bright heaven' be composed of patience and understanding and kindness, even if the walls are not all jasper and
the streets gold?"

"Order is right," Eulalia said almost plaintively. "Do-
as-you-please is wrong."

"Maybe," Margie nodded wearily. "The youngsters of
the family, with all their electric trains and other marvels of
technology to play with at home, created magic and wonder
out of drab nothings here and called it do-as-you-please
land. Creation may involve certain disorder. Birth does.
But if an identity evolves—" She spoke gently. "I truly
think, Eulalia, the old home place as the grandchildren have
known it has a precious identity. Maybe it has for us, too,
more than we know. One thing I know, I'm tired. And
you are. Can I help with the dishes or anything?"

"Everything's in order," Eulalia said, "except that I
have to soak the tea stains out of the lace cloth."

Left alone, Eulalia tried to recall the various Household
Hints the women had contributed, their remedies for tea
stains. She was so exhausted she did not want to move.
If she could do as she pleased, that lace cloth would go un-
soaked until she was less spent and drained.

Suddenly she felt alone. She became oddly more aware
of the loneliness than of the importance of the lace table-
cloth.

If only she could relax and listen effortlessly to commonplaces, if she could just be entertained without need of
response from her—!

There was a lack somewhere. Here at the old Home she
felt homesick.

Could it be, she thought in one startled flash, that she
was homesick for Miss Tulie's do-as-you-please land? And
for Miss Tulie?

NOEL HOUSTON

THOUGH NOEL HOUSTON'S first and greatest love was the drama, he was almost equally adept at articles, short stories, the novel, and scripts for radio, television, and motion pictures. He was also a liberal thinker, a great talker, and an inspiring teacher.

Houston was born in Lawton, Oklahoma, in 1909. Following his education in the public schools and college in Oklahoma City, he was for nine years a newspaper reporter. After his marriage, upon deciding to study playwriting at an eastern university, he sent letters of inquiry to Yale and the University of North Carolina. Yale invited him to register for a degree. From Chapel Hill, Paul Green sent him this message: "If you want to write, come on over, and take as many or as few courses as you like. Writing's the main thing." Houston was more interested in writing than in a degree. So with his wife Kay, he arrived in Chapel Hill in 1937 for a year—and remained permanently.

Soon he had written a number of plays based on incidents back in Oklahoma. Their caliber was such that he was awarded several fellowships in playwriting. In 1941, he built a home in Chapel Hill. "During the war," he related, "I conducted a class in playwriting for students seeking the master's degree in dramatic arts at the University; but my own interests, because of the influence of Professor Phillips Russell, began to change to fiction. I began writing stories for the *New Yorker* and subsequently for such magazines as the *American* and *Collier's*."

The Great Promise (1946), his only novel, was well received both in the United States and abroad. It dealt with the lusty days of the Oklahoma land lottery during the early years of the twentieth century.

Later, various other kinds of writing engaged him. In 1953, he was in Hollywood preparing a screen adaptation for Columbia Studios. In 1957, he taught creative writing in the Department of Radio, Television, and Motion Pictures at the University in Chapel Hill. Suddenly, after an operation, he died unexpectedly at Chapel Hill on September 9, 1958.

"Lantern on the Beach" appeared in *Liberty* on May 8, 1943. A fanciful story of World War II, it makes use of an old Nags Head legend, which the author knew well from having spent many vacations on the Outer Banks.

Lantern on the Beach

NOEL HOUSTON

HIGH on the ridge of the Seven Sisters dunes Eddie
Daniel glumly watched a tanker ply north three miles
off the Carolina shore. Eddie didn't think much of the war.
They said there was something everybody could do to help
win it, but that just wasn't so. There wasn't anything a
twelve-year-old boy could do.

His father tended the drawbridge over to Roanoke Island.
That was important. His sister worked in a munitions
factory up in Virginia; and his brother Harvey had been
shipping on tankers since 1940. Even his mother helped at
the Red Cross.

But for him and his pony, Tuney, there wasn't nothing.
Why hadn't he been born a little sooner? Then he could be
in the marines! Sure was terrible—being twelve and useless.

Eddie kicked angrily at the sand.

Just then a pillar of smoke climed into the sky above
the tanker and spread out like a black mushroom. The
boom of an explosion rolled in from the sea.

Eddie's mouth dropped open. This wasn't the first tor-
pedoing off the Outer Banks. There had been three ships
sunk between Buxton and Hatteras the past two days. But
this was the first Eddie had actually seen.

Down to his left, at the Nags Head Coast Guard Station,
the guardsmen were hastily trundling out the boats. People

By permission of Kay Houston.

were running out of stores and houses and converging on the beach.

Eddie ran and slid down the dune to the flat where Tuney was munching grass. He mounted the pony's bare back and galloped across the black-top highway to the shore. The three Nags Head boats had become white specks this side the column of smoke, which was spreading out as the oil on the ocean caught fire.

Five planes roared over from their inland base. They dropped patterns of depth charges beyond the smoke area. Eddie was so excited he could hardly breathe. If only he were old enough to be out there helping!

The first two rescue boats returned, rocking and charging through the surf. Eddie saw they held only the coast guard crews. But in the stern of the third boat lay three blackened figures. Two boatmen were holding them against bumping overboard.

When the boat was beached, a group of menfolk gathered around the guardsmen, lifting out the bodies. Standing at a distance above the tidemark were a dozen womenfolk. One of the women was Eddie's mother. When she saw him down at the water's edge, she shouted, "Eddie, you come up here with me."

Eddie didn't hear her. He couldn't hear anything. There was a roaring in his ears like a hundred nor'easters were churning the surf. For when George Bass of the third boat waded in, he reported to old Captain Knight: "Three men, sir, was all we could find. Two of them are burned to death and the third one dying. He's Harvey Daniel, by thunder."

And Eddie standing there heard him, and he looked, and it was his brother Harvey. His brother's face was black and drawn in torture and his body was oil-smeared and burnt; but Eddie could tell. He could tell.

They laid Harvey Daniel on his back, and Doc Anthony, who brought Harvey into this world, worked over him. But you could see doc didn't have any hope.

Eddie dropped to his knees beside his brother, still holding Tuney's reins. The tears rolled down his freckled face onto the sand. He tried to keep from crying out loud. A sob broke from his throat in spite of himself.

At that Harvey opened his eyes. He didn't seem to see clearly, but he forced a whisper. "Hello, Eddie."

Eddie couldn't answer. He just clenched his fists together and shook his head.

"I was standing . . . by the rail," Harvey whispered. "Lookin' towards our house. And I was thinkin' . . . if I could yell loud enough . . . I could holler hello . . . let you know . . . I was passin' by."

Eddie nodded. "Sure," he said. "Sure. I seen you. I was up on the dune."

Harvey Daniel's mouth worked hard. He made a croaking sound come out. "Right in our own front yard, Eddie. Right out there . . . where we used . . . to fish for blues." And his eyes were lit with bitter anger.

"You gonna be all right, Harvey?" said Eddie. "You gonna be?"

"Sure, kid." He looked past Eddie. "Got old Tuney with you. A good . . ."

And suddenly Harvey Daniel didn't say any more. His eyes stared blank at the sunny sky.

A pair of rough, strong hands lifted Eddie to his feet. Next thing he knew, he was walking down the beach with some one's arm around him. He looked up. Through misty eyes he saw it was his friend Old Man Si Denning.

"We'll just go down to my shack, Eddie, and set a bit," Old Man Si said.

Behind him Eddie heard a woman scream. It was his

mother. They had told her. A shudder passed through
Eddie's slight frame.

The old man and the boy cut away from the shore line,
their feet crunching the broken shells, and Tuney plodded
along behind. They came to Old Man Si's one-room shack,
set amid the tufts of salt grass.

Inside it was cool and dark and smelled of fish. Eddie sat
on the single bed, which was never made up. Old Man Si
put a pot of coffee on the kerosene stove. He sat at the
table and pushed back the dirty dishes. He scratched his
stubbly chin and looked at Eddie. Then he ran a hand
through his stiff gray hair. Eddie just stared straight in
front of himself.

Old Man Si coughed. "Now, if you was older, Eddie, I
could give you a shot of corn likker and that would help.
But we'll have some coffee anyway, and outside of that
you'll have to be a man all by yourself."

"I'm all right, Mr. Denning," said Eddie.

"Sure ya are."

Old Man Si rubbed the stump of his left forefinger. It
was cut off at the first joint. He wished he hadn't ever told
Eddie how he had lost that finger, so he could tell him now.

But of course he had told that to Eddie and to everybody
else he had ever met. How he was one of the natives
Orville and Wilbur Wright got to run alongside the airplane
to steady it that day it took off, up the way at Kitty Hawk.
How his finger got caught between two wires at the end of
the wing and was nearly yanked off when the craft rose in
the air. "The world's first airyplane accident," Old Man
Si proudly told strangers.

When he judged fishing conditions were right, Old Man
Si staked a long net to the shore and ran it out, then took
his haul to Manteo. Generally, though, he didn't judge conditions to be right. Then he and Eddie would sit around,
and he would tell Eddie tales of old times on the Banks.

He wished he could think of a story to tell Eddie now, something to buck him up. But though he racked his brain it seemed as if he had told Eddie, at one time or another, about every story he ever knew.

He coughed again, uneasily. "Course now, you know, Eddie, all of us are seafarin' folk, and we know what the sea is like off here, all the way from Kill Devil Hills to Hatteras. Turn yer back on it a minute and it'll git ya. We know that, and we're prepared for it, and we take it like men if our time comes. Ain't that right?"

Eddie didn't say anything. Old Man Si got up and found two cups and poured coffee. He set a cup on the stool beside Eddie. He held his cup in both hands and took a deep draught.

"Pretty good coffee, boy. Try some."

Eddie's forehead was drawn in a frown. He was trying to figure out something.

"A man couldn't count the shipwrecks off this coast, all the way back to Spanish galleons. Graveyard of the Atlantic, these shoals is called," Old Man Si added, talking gently. "Nearly ever'body along here is descended somehow from shipwrecked sailors. You know that."

Eddie nodded. He spoke slowly, thinking out loud: "It wasn't the sea that done it to Harvey, Mr. Denning. It was that thing out there, layin' out there waitin' to kill our folks. Like Harvey said, killin' right in our own front yard."

"You're right about that, Eddie."

"If I was only older, I could be flyin' a plane, or I could be on a destroyer, and I could sink that submarine."

"You'll be older one of these days, and then you can do it."

"But not soon enough, Mr. Denning. The sub that got Harvey will be gone."

"I reckon it's gone now."

"Do you think it is?"

Old Man Si reconsidered.

"Well, no, I don't. I figure, since the flyin' lads didn't give any indication they got it, it's still hangin' around out there some'eres. It's got four ships round here in three days, and it ain't likely to leave while the huntin's so good."

"That sub just can't be let to get any more, Mr. Denning," said Eddie earnestly. "It just can't!"

Old Man Si shook his head.

"And it's got to pay for what it did to my brother." He clenched his fists. "There ought to be a way I could do it. I could get in a boat and go out there and I . . ."

"Now, we might as well be sensible, Eddie," Old Man Si interrupted.

Eddie scowled bitterly. Being with the gentle old man had dried his tears. In the place of sorrow was a frustrated anger that he could not be his brother's avenger. Just being twelve years old—that was the trouble.

Old Man Si didn't know what to say, except to fall back on his stories. He cleared his throat.

"Speakin' of how people have to be brave— Now, when Sir Walter Raleigh's folks come sailin' in to Roanoke Island, they was in three boats that wa'n't much bigger than lifeboats on a passenger liner of today. They had a hard time, but Virginia Dare was born the first year, and—"

"Yes, sir; I know about that," said Eddie.

Old Man Si stopped and thought a moment. He beat off on another tack.

"I remember the night the Northeastern run aground off Diamond Shoals. That was a storm, if ever there was one. The Buxton lads trundled their boats down to the shore, and one of the men said to old Captain Etheridge, 'Ain't no use goin' out there, cap'n—we'll never come back.' And old Captain Etheridge, his whiskers blowin' in the gale, he hollered back—"

Eddie, staring out the door, broke in automatically: "He hollered: 'The regulations don't say a damn thing about comin' back; they just say we got to go.' "

Old Man Si was confused. "Yep, that's right. That's what he said. That's the kind of men they used to produce along here."

Neither of them spoke for a few minutes. Then Old Man Si sniffed and cocked an eye out the window. The look confirmed what his nose had told him. A change in the weather coming. That reminded him of something to tell Eddie. He leaned back in his chair, hitched his thumbs in his belt, and chuckled.

"Now the way Nags Head got its name is an interestin' thing, Eddie. Nags Head. Back there a century or more ago, they was land pirates along here and—"

"Yes, sir," said Eddie respectfully. "I know about that."

Old Man Si frowned at the dirty dishes on the table. Just wasn't no way he could comfort the boy, looked like.

Eddie sighed and got up. "I guess I'd better go home," he said.

As Eddie rode slowly up the beach in the failing light, he noticed the wind had shifted to the northeast and was rising. Whitecaps were breaking to the horizon and heavy gray clouds were gathering out at sea.

Except for the scurrying fiddler crabs, the beach was empty where the crowd had gathered and Harvey Daniel had died. The ocean rapidly erases all signs of its tragedies. Perhaps that's so it can lull even the wariest, and strike them quick and hard just when they feel surest of themselves.

When Eddie got home, he learned Harvey's body had been taken to Manteo. His mother stood with her back to him at the kerosene stove, turning chops in a sputtering frying pan. His father, a big man, with the cuffs of his frayed blue shirt rolled halfway to his elbows, sat at the

table, holding his head in his mottled red hands. The room
was gray, almost dark.

"Hang the blackouts so I can turn on the light, Eddie,"
his mother said calmly.

Eddie went into each of the four rooms and fitted frames
covered with heavy tar paper into all except the land-
ward windows. He fastened them there with screen hooks.

When he had finished, his mother turned on the bulb
that hung from the center of the kitchen. The light beat
down on his father's head, turning his gray hair silvery;
but his face, cupped in his hands, was in shadow. Eddie
wondered if he was crying. He wanted to run to him and
put his head in his lap. But he knew he was too old
for that.

Suddenly his father smote the table with both fists and
lunged up from the table. He faced the east window as
if he were looking right through the blackout frame out to
where Harvey's tanker had been torpedoed. He cried out
in a voice which frightened Eddie, it was so agonized and
strange.

Eddie's mother went to his father and put an arm around
his waist. "Don't, Mark," she begged.

"We're—I— There ain't nothin' I can do," he groaned.

Eddie had never seen his father writhe under strong
emotion before. He felt stifled. "We ain't the men we
used to be," his father went on. "There was a time when
the men on Nags Head knew what to do."

Eddie stood stunned, a great white sheet of lighting in
his brain, blinded by the revelation which had struck him.
"A time when the men on Nags Head knew what to do."
And he heard Old Man Si Denning's voice, as if the old
man stood behind him, whispering in his ear, "An interestin'
thing—the way Nags Head got its name." And somehow
Harvey's black, burnt face was mixed up in it. "Got old
Tuney with you. A good —" Of course! Of course!

He didn't think out a plan step by step. He didn't have to. The whole plan was there, sprung to full life in an inspired instant, without Eddie's having to think about it at all.

The first spatter of the rising nor'easter's rain rattled across the roof like a ruffle of drums sounding marching orders. Eddie's parents' backs were to him. He grabbed the box of matches from the stove and scooted out the land-ward door.

Pitch-blackness had plunged over the Banks. The rain fell in sheets as he raced through the soft sand to Tuney's shed. Two hundred yards away the mighty, frantic surf spilled itself across the beach with the rumbling roar of an endless freight train.

Eddie bumped into the shed, then felt for the door latch. As he went inside, Tuney whinnied in fear until Eddie called to him reassuringly. In the light of a match, the boy and the pony looked at each other, their eyes shining with excitement.

"Steady, fella," said Eddie. "We've got work to do."

He took a big rusty lantern from the wall. Before the match flickered out, he examined the wick. Then, in the dark, he unscrewed the cap and thrust a finger into the container to make certain it was filled with kerosene.

He got down Tuney's bridle and put it on by memory, while the pony trembled in spite of comforting words. He struck another match. In a corner he found a piece of rope five feet long.

Once outside, Eddie leaped to Tuney's back, holding the unlighted lantern and rope in his right hand. The box of matches he had stuffed inside his shirt. He poked Tuney in the ribs with his bare heels. They crossed the black-top, swished through the grass of the flat, and Tuney unwillingly began to trudge up the dune.

When they reached the ridge, they were exposed to the
full force of the wind and rain. Eddie slid down. He led
Tuney a little way down the opposite side to comparative
quiet. There he struck match after match until he had the
lantern going. Carefully he adjusted the wick to give
maximum light. It threw back the darkness, startling
Tuney.

Quickly Eddie looped the rope around Tuney's neck,
then tied the lantern so that it hung like a brilliant pendant.
Tuney didn't like it, but submitted when Eddie spoke
sternly.

"Your ancestors did it," he argued. "Right on these same
dunes. And you can do it, too."

Doggedly, leaning into the sweeping rain, Eddie began
leading Tuney north along the backbone of the dune,
parallel to the sea.

"Help make this do it, Harvey," he muttered pleadingly.
"This has got to do it." And somehow he felt that Harvey
really was looking down on them, nodding approval.

Eighteen minutes later a coastguardsman, happening to
look landward from his beach lookout, saw the light back
there. Horrified, he ran to report to his superior. Together
they called Captain Knight from his house.

The shouting brought guardsmen from their houses in
the station area. All stared toward the oddly bobbing light
which moved northward relentlessly, seemingly suspended
in space not far above the ground.

"Arm yourselves and assemble here," commanded
Captain Knight. When the men returned, he said, "We'll
move in a body until I give orders to spread fanwise."

They shoved off toward the dunes, stumbling in the darkness.

The coastguardsmen were not the only persons to see the
oddly moving light. Out at sea, beneath the hard-running

waves, one Korvettenkapitän Clemens von Schilling peered intently into his periscope. He had picked up the light almost from the beginning, and he licked his thin lips nervously.

"Our information was right," he muttered to the lieutenant standing beside him. "That is our final tanker."

He chuckled harshly. "A good friend, whether he knows it or not, aboard there shows a light."

He rasped out terse orders: a run in.

"But—" remonstrated his navigator. "Without my sonic depth finder? *Es ist zerbrochen.* What of reefs and shoals?"

The Korvettenkapitän whirled. Exhaustion lined his face. He had been in the Atlantic more than eight weeks. His whole crew was worn out, inefficient. Two of the depth charges dropped by the planes that afternoon had nearly done for the sub. She was leaking. It was true, as the navigator said, that her delicate sonic devices had been knocked out. But the Nazi had two torpedoes left and he saw a new prey before his periscope.

"You heard my order!" he screamed. "That tanker is sailing safe, no? We are outside her, *ja?*"

"But—" the navigator whined. He got no further.

The Korvettenkapitän lashed out a hard fist to the navigator's jaw, and he went down. Breathing heavily, the Nazi glared into the faces of his crew. The white-faced men dropped their weary eyes, said nothing.

Suddenly Korvettenkapitän Clemens von Schilling felt a slow wave of fright mounting in his trembling body. He thought of home, his family, the little beer cellar at the corner. Cursing his *Heimweh* and his terror, he stood quivering beside the periscope, torn between lust for another kill and the whispering voice inside which cautioned him to start now for Deutschland.

Eddie and Tuney had gone more than a mile when black figures leaped out of the darkness from all directions. "Put up your hands!"

Eddie looked into the barrels of rifles. "Gee whiz!" he gasped.

"Why," exclaimed a guardsman, "it's only Eddie Daniel!"

"Who's with you, Eddie?" demanded Captain Knight.

"Gosh," said Eddie, "nobody but Tuney."

"Douse that light."

Two guardsmen extinguished it. On Captain Knight's orders, two more took Eddie by the arms. They went down the dune, Eddie kicking and protesting.

"I can't understand it, Eddie," said Captain Knight. "I just can't. Don't you know what it looks like— showing a light out to sea? Aiding the enemy!"

"I wasn't!" said Eddie, outraged. "I was trying to get it. The sub that killed Harvey."

"Ha!" said Captain Knight.

"If you had let me alone— You know how Nags Head got its name, don't you?"

"Of course. But this is not time for—"

"That's what I was doin'. The way land pirates along here used to do. The way they would put a lantern around an old nag's neck and walk her along the dunes on a stormy night. You know, Captain Knight. A ship out to sea would think it was another vessel sailing safe closer in, and it would come in closer, too, and pile up on the shoals. Then next day, when everybody had drowned and the storm gone down—gosh, you know!—the land pirates would row out and loot the ship. Gosh, Captain Knight—"

"Now let me get this straight."

"That's what I was doin'."

The alarm about the light had spread, and a good many people were waiting outside the station. At first the Bankers couldn't believe what Eddie had been trying to do. Then the full absurdity of one small boy, one Banks pony, and one rusty lantern trying to capture a great modern submarine began to soak in. They roared with laughter.

Eddie stood there in the dark circle of people, his own people, feeling more and more miserable. The rain beat down on him, but they were not all raindrops that coursed down his cheeks. He had thought he was doing a wonderful thing. Now he, too, saw how foolish he had been. He wanted to run somewhere and hide and never look anybody in the face again.

"Why, boy," said Captain Knight, "it's true land pirates wrecked many a ship doing exactly what you were doing; but these U-boats aren't old-timey sailing vessels."

Eddie wished he could explain he hadn't thought of that, hadn't thought at all—that it had been an inspiration, a flashing command, like a voice from heaven, like a voice from his brother Harvey.

A rough arm fell around his shoulder. He started to pull away. Then Old Man Si's voice said, "It's all right, Eddie." Old Man Si was there to see his misery, too. But the old man was gentle and understanding. Eddie snuggled close to the wet rubber slicker. Together they walked away in the darkness toward Eddie's house.

The boy felt an added twinge. This disgrace would be piled on his parents' sorrow.

"Imagine," he heard Jeff Beesum saying to the crowd— "imagine anybody being as dumb as that Eddie Daniel."

"Now that's enough," broke in Captain Knight sharply. He had a whiplash voice when he chose to snap it. "Eddie was trying to help his country—that's plain. Whatever else, he showed initiative and patriotism."

Everybody fell silent, feeling sheepish now for being grown-ups laughing at a small boy who had done his best to avenge his brother and save the lives of others of his countrymen. Especially they felt sheepish because the greatgranddaddies of several of those present had made a dangerous living using Eddie's scheme, and they had been men whom you wouldn't have dared to laugh at.

Captain Knight might have said more, but instead he grunted. For at that moment a red flare burst in the air not far off shore.

The flare had hardly reached its full brilliance before the captain was calling out orders. The guardsmen sprang into smooth, teamed action, as if pieces of a watch had suddenly all leaped into place and the watch started ticking.

"What is it, Mr. Si?" cried Eddie. "What is it?"

"Maybe it's—" shouted Old Man Si, and added fervently, "Oh, God, let it be!"

The horizontal beams of mobile searchlights darted over the angry whitecaps, then converged swiftly on one point.

Not more than six hundred yards out, the after half of a submarine angled out of the sea, its stern rocking and shuddering before the onslaught. Crawling aft, hanging on desperately, were half a dozen men.

Next morning—a clear, bright morning with a sea still running over the wrecked submarine, but the sky a clean and burnished blue—Eddie, his parents, and Tuney bringing up the rear trudged through the sand to the Nags Head Station.

This time, when Eddie hove in sight, everybody clapped and cheered. Eddie grinned. His father found his mother's hand and squeezed it, and her lip trembled with pride.

Lined up at the foot of the porch steps were six Nazis. A navy truck waited to take them to Norfolk.

Old Captain Knight, taking his pipe from his mouth, said to the Nazi commander, "Well, here's the boy and his pony that done it, like I told you. Just a regular American boy, Eddie is. We're going to get him a medal."

The Nazi glared at Eddie. He took a quick step forward and raised his arm to strike Eddie down.

Before anybody could move, Tuney, that old hero, extended his long neck and sank his teeth into the seat of the Nazi's pants.

Korvettenkapitän Clemens von Schilling jumped into the air, and his upraised arm gave a Nazi salute as he hollered "Heil Hitler!" at the top of his voice.

"Well," drawled Old Man Si, "they wanted total war. Man and boy, we'll hit 'em and bite 'em with everything we've got! Eh, Eddie?"

DORIS BETTS

FOR AT LEAST one North Carolina short story writer, there have never been enough hours in any day. Yet Doris Waugh, born in Statesville in 1932, has always somehow found the time to do what she wanted to do. At Statesville High School she was editor of the school paper, reporter for the local press, and special correspondent for an out-of-town newspaper. At the Woman's College in Greensboro, she was on the staff of the literary magazine; took creative writing courses under Frances Gray Patton, Peter Taylor, and Robie Macauley; was correspondent for a daily newspaper; did self-help work in the College News Bureau; maintained a Phi Beta Kappa scholastic average; and clerked in a jeweler's shop in downtown Greensboro. At the end of her sophomore year, she married Lowry Betts and moved to Columbia where he was completing his bachelor's degree at the University of South Carolina. In July, 1953, her first child was born; in August, she won a $500 College Fiction Contest conducted by *Mademoiselle* magazine; in September, she settled down in Chapel Hill where her husband entered the law school; and in November, she won the $2000 Putnam Fiction Prize for a manuscript of short stories.

The manuscript was published as *The Gentle Insurrection and Other Stories* (1954), its over-all theme being the loneliness and the need for understanding in the lives of a group of typical Carolina people. "The Sword" is a representative story from that book.

Meanwhile at Chapel Hill, Doris Betts worked for the *Chapel Hill Weekly,* found another job on the side, took

some courses at the University, kept up a home, had a
second child, and continued to write. In 1956, she moved
to Sanford, where her husband joined a law firm. Char-
acteristically, Mrs. Betts found an opening at the *Sanford
Herald*.

Her first novel, *Tall Houses in Winter* (1957), won for
her the Sir Walter Raleigh Award for distinguished work
in fiction by a North Carolinian. It is the story of personal
tragedy in a small Southern town. In 1958, she was granted
a Guggenheim Fellowship, permitting her a year's freedom
to write.

About "The Sword," Mrs. Betts said: "When I set out to
write it, I was consciously trying to construct short stories
on the basis of the Greek unities: one setting, three people,
a twenty-four-hour time-lapse. In prose, of course, one
can cheat on time with the flashback, which 'The Sword'
certainly does. But I hope that it shows the sense of dis-
cipline I intended and that the form is tight and taut and
healthy, like a ball." The story was chosen by Robert Penn
Warren for his collection *A New Southern Harvest*.

The Sword

DORIS BETTS

THE DAYS fell out of the sick man's life sluggishly, like dead coals slipping finally onto the hearth from an old fire. Every evening when he blew the lamp and raised the shade, Bert would stand in the dark thinking, This is the last one. Tomorrow he will be gone.

But the next morning, when Bert started awake in the leather chair and strained his ears for silence, he could still hear the tired in-and-out of breathing and his arms and legs would loosen in the chair as he listened to it.

Bert was almost never out of the sick man's room, until the smell of it seemed right to him and he could look at the flowers on the wall and not know if they were blue or green.

His mother would enter and leave the room all day long, standing with one hand curled around the bed rail and looking down at the sick man, her face set into awkward squares like blocks heaped up by some clumsy child.

"Is he any better, Bert?"

"No, I think he is about the same. Maybe a little weaker."

Then she would whisper it under her breath as if it hurt her mouth to make the words. "A little weaker . . ."

At first Bert had put out his hand to her, but she had not

From *The Gentle Insurrection and Other Stories* by Doris Betts, published by G. P. Putnam's Sons. Copyright, 1954, by Doris Betts.

seemed to notice, and after a while he stood at the window when his mother came in and stared at the leaves that tossed and shifted on the grass when the wind went by. She wanted to be left alone, he supposed. She had been left to herself for a long time now.

Always she would say hopefully, "Lester? How are you today, Lester?" But there was the suck and push of the old man's breathing and nothing else, and she would go away, watching her feet.

He had been sick for three weeks when Bert first came home, and he was still able to talk a little and smile and look around him.

He had been smiling when Bert came into the room that first day and put his coat on the leather chair and walked over to the bed.

"Hello, Father," Bert said.

The old man said slowly, "It's Bert, isn't it? Have you come home awhile, Bert?"

And he said, "Yes, Father. I've come home a little while."

But there were two more weeks gone now since that day and the old man still lay in bed—no longer smiling—and breathing in and out while Bert watched him.

This morning the doctor had come early, so that Bert was out of his chair before the sun was well into the room.

"Morning, Bert."

"Hello, Dr. Herman. You're early today."

"This is going to be a busy one. Did he rest last night?"

"Yes sir, he sleeps almost all the time now."

Only once during the examination had the sick man opened his eyes and then he had looked at the doctor without interest and closed them again.

"How is he, Dr. Herman?"

The doctor made a shrugging motion. "Holding his own. We're just waiting, I'm afraid."

Later, putting his things away, he had added, "I'm glad you've come home, Bert. Your father was always talking about you. He was very proud."

Was he? thought Bert.

Bert stood by the window and watched the doctor go down the walk, his black bag banging against his knee every other step. We're just waiting, the doctor had said. Once he stopped in the walk to tie his shoe and the wind rose in the oak tree—almost bare now—and came to flap the doctor's coat, impatiently.

After the doctor was out of sight, his mother came and stood by the bed and put her head against the post, as if she were tired of holding it up.

"Does the doctor think he is any better, Bert?" she said.

Bert said, "No, he seems about the same."

She sat down in the leather chair stiffly, leaning her head back, and he saw the hairs springing up from her braid like grass after feet go by.

She said to herself, "At first I thought he would get well. Even after the first week or so I thought he would get well."

"We both thought so," said Bert.

She said, "I wish he knew things. He'd be so glad you were home again. These last years all he could talk about before Christmas was that you would be home awhile. He looked forward to it so."

He looked forward to it, Bert thought. Always forward. What was I expected to do? The sick man moved and coughed and Bert went closer to the bed to see if he was all right. Nothing else was said, and after awhile his mother got up from the chair and went out to the kitchen.

No one else came in the rest of the morning, although Jubah put her head at the door once and smiled at him and Bert sat alone in the room and watched his father's face. He wondered how in five years features he had once known well could fold in upon themselves until the face was strange to him, with its pinched nose and sharp chin, and the cheeks that looked as if they had been pressed deep inside the mouth.

Sometimes Bert would try to remember how his father had looked a long time ago—when he had driven him to school on winter mornings, or across a hundred dinner tables, or on those few special times when he had gone hunting with his father and three other men. But all Bert could remember of those times was the bigness of the other hunters, and the early morning smell of woods and rain, and once his father stopping to put a hand against a poplar tree and smile.

His father had been a very poor hunter; he almost never made a successful shot. But he had been proud when Bert learned to shoot well. And when Bert began bringing home almost all the game, he could remember his father coming into the kitchen at dusk and calling, "Ruth? Come see what your son did!" And the rabbits would be spread on the table for his mother to exclaim about, while his father stood quietly at the sink, washing his hands.

After Bert became such a good shot his father complimented and praised him but gradually they went hunting less and less until one Christmas he had given his gun to Bert. "I was never much with guns," he said then. And after that, the two of them never went hunting again, and the gun was finally stacked away in some closet.

The only time Bert could remember his father's face clearly was that time he had come home from the army and they had sat up after the others were in bed—his father oddly expectant, with waiting eyebrows and a half-formed smile, and his own feelings of awkwardness and discomfort, until the two of them had fallen into separate silences and finally gone to bed. He remembered how his father had looked then.

At noon Mother brought the tray and they whispered at the sick man until he lifted his eyelids and looked at them, waiting, expecting nothing and yet seeming to expect anything.

Mother said, "It's lunchtime, Lester. Hot soup." And the sick man made a noise in his throat that might have meant yes or no, and might have meant nothing at all. She fed him slowly and all the time he never looked at the soup or the spoon or her hand holding it; he lay there watching her mouth with that funny look on his face.

Bert watched them for awhile, but he could not keep his hands still; they kept plunging into his pockets or picking at each other until he went to the window and made them into fists and leaned them against the glass. Sometimes the wind would catch a leaf and drive it against the glass where it paused and then tumbled off. Bert thought, My father is going to die, but he did not believe it. He believed the wind and the leaves and the window-glass; but he did not believe that about his father.

When the sick man had eaten, Mother came over to the window and touched Bert's arm; it startled him for a minute and he snapped his head over one shoulder and stared at her; then the muscles that had grown tight around his eyes and forehead let themselves go and he smiled.

She said, "He will sleep some more, Bert. Why don't you come sit out front with me?"

"All right," said Bert.

She whispered, "We'll leave the door open."

He took the tray from her and carried it out into the kitchen where he put it down on the table. His mother called, "Can you bring me a glass of water?" and he filled a glass at the sink and carried it into the front room to her.

She had put her feet up into a big chair and rested an arm against her eyes, and fine hairs were standing up out of her braid all over her head. Bert put the glass into her other hand, and she rubbed at her forehead with the arm and thanked him. He sat down opposite her.

She said, "I wish you'd let me stay with him, Bert. You've hardly been out of that room since you came home."

Bert shook his head. He had to stay with his father now. He had to do that much.

For a time neither of them spoke and he looked thoughtfully around the room. Here he had sat with his father when he came home from the army—his father had been in the big chair smiling, and Bert had sat just where he was now, moving his feet back and forth against the rug and looking now and then at his father thinking, What does he want of me?

His mother said, "At first I thought he would get well, Bert. I thought he would get well at first." For a minute Bert wanted to say, Did you like him? **Did** you really like my father? Do you know something I don't? But he didn't say anything; he just watched the movement in her face. He thought she was going to shed her first tears then, but she took her feet off the chair and moved around and shifted until the desire for tears went away. She looked suddenly like a brave little girl: a fat girl with chubby features and hair that would not stay in place. Bert wondered what she would do after the sick man died and if it would mean any real change in her life. Sometimes he thought he knew his mother very well and yet this thing he did not know. Does it mean a lot to her? Is there something in me that does not understand him? She'll just have me then, he thought, and he didn't feel quite so helpless for a minute. She's got to prepare herself.

Aloud he said, "Father is very weak now and his age is against him."

She said, "I know now he's not ever going to be well again. I know it and I don't know it all at the same time and that's a queer feeling, Bert, both at the same time."

When she said that, Bert felt his whole body tighten. His mother was right; that's the way it was for him too, maybe for everybody. Nobody believed it. The one thing that was glaring and obvious and unmistakable in the universe and nobody really believed it. Bert wondered if his father believed it now, waiting every day in bed to see if it were true.

He said, "Dr. Herman will be back tomorrow." He said it rapidly as if he had just thought of it, but it was because he couldn't think of anything else to tell her. "We're to call him if we need him for anything."

His mother said, "Yes," and drank the water very fast so that it must have hurt her throat to swallow so hard. Bert took the glass back into the kitchen.

He stacked the dishes off the tray into the sink and began to pour water on them from the kettle and then to wash them with a soapy rag. He thought, It seems to me now that if it were new again, I would be different than I was; but he didn't know exactly what he meant by that. Jubah came in from the back porch; she stopped in the doorway and stood there straight as a knife handle and watched him.

"What you doing, Mister Bert?" she said.

He said, "Dishes."

She came on into the kitchen and wiped her hands on a paper towel and threw it away.

"I'll do them," she said. "How's Mr. Lester?"

Bert watched her brown hands go down into the water and slush it up into soapsuds.

He said, "No different, Jubah. He just lies there but there isn't any change."

Jubah shook her head back and forth and made a tut-tut sound with her tongue. "Sometimes it comes up slow," she said.

When he went back into the front room, his mother looked as if she had been crying, but it was hard to tell. She had not cried before. That night he had come in from the station, she had stood in the hall holding one hand with another, looking something like a queen, he thought. She'd said, "I'm sorry to call you from your business, Bert. But it seemed best . . ."

He'd dropped his bag at the door and come to put his arm around her. "How is he?"

Just for a minute, she'd put her head down on his shoulder and rested it there and then she'd caught his arm in tight fingers and made a little smile. "He'll be glad you're here," she said.

Now, coming into the front room, he thought perhaps she had been crying, but he could not be sure. He sat down in the chair again and looked at her, trying to decide about it.

His mother said rapidly, "Do you know what Jubah said this morning? I was just walking through the kitchen and Jubah said—Death comes up slow like an old cat but after she waits a long time she jumps and it's all gone then—I was just walking by her and she looked up from the stove and said that, Bert, and I thought I would fall down right there to hear her say it."

Bert said, "Jubah talks too much," but he turned it over in his mind and looked at it in front and behind and on both sides. Death comes up slow like an old cat but after she waits a long time she jumps and it's all gone then.

He tried to remember what it had been like in the army, but he couldn't remember what he had thought about death then. He and Charlie used to talk about it sometimes, but always in terms of somebody else—the fellow in the next bunk, or the ship that left yesterday, or the list in the paper.

Charlie always said, "I don't believe nothing can hurt you till your time comes." He used to say it over and over, confidently, and Bert had listened just as confidently, because both of them knew their time hadn't come.

And it didn't seem to, because they got through all right and Charlie went home to his filling station in Maine and he'd never heard from him.

There'd been another boy, confident as they were, who said that ever since he was a kid he'd known he was going to die during a storm. Every time they had any kind of storm, he'd walk the floor smoking on a cigar, and jumping at the sound of thunder. They'd laughed at him.

"It's whenever your time comes," Charlie always told him.

But as it turned out Bert and Charlie had come home all right, and the other boy (funny that he couldn't remember his name) had died in Africa, they said, and there wasn't even a cloud in the sky.

But that didn't prove anything about what Charlie had said. It didn't prove anything except what his mother had said, that nobody really believed in it. Bert felt tired.

He frowned. "Sometimes," he began, "sometimes, Mother, I wish I could . . ." but he stopped there and didn't know what he wished. It had something to do with the old hunting trips and with his father and with Jubah, but he didn't know what it was. He put his head into his hands and smashed the palms into his eyes. He thought, I have known people and been known by people. That proves something, doesn't it?

His mother was looking at him. She said, "Your father loved you so, Bert." He kept his palms tight against his eyes where the pressure made him see sparks and gray wheels spinning and something like a Roman candle. He wondered, Was that it? Was that all it was all these years? And that made him tired too.

Bert said, "I'll see if he's awake now."

He tiptoed into the room and looked down at the sick man, who was awake—lying there with that look on his face. Bert looked down at him, at his faded eyes on each

side of the pinched nose and the mouth, bent in now as if
the corners had been tugged from the inside. Slow, he
thought, slow like a big cat, and for a minute he hated
Jubah for telling his mother about the cat.

The old man closed his eyes and Bert felt suddenly that
two doors had been shut against him and he no longer had
anything to do with his father. He came back into the front
room and sat down, then he got up and took a magazine
and sat again. He thought, I'm trying, damn it. I've always
been trying.

Big letters crawling crookedly on the magazine said
CHILDBIRTH, IT CAN BE PAINLESS. OUR GROWING TRAFFIC
DEATHS. RUSSIA AND THE ATOM. He leafed through it, not
reading anything.

Sometimes since his father had been sick, Bert had tried
to remember some vivid detail, some special time, some
conversation that had happened when he was a boy that
was important. That's where a psychologist began, with the
little boy, and he could say, "It is here that it began to go
wrong, when you were three, or seven, or nine." But Bert
could never find anything.

He remembered the time he came home from the army
only because it was so much like everything else that it
seemed important in itself.

His father and mother had met him at the train-station;
she had hugged him and Father had shaken his hand and
stood there smiling, looking at him curiously and—yes, he
was sure of it, warmly—until he stammered, "Well, let's go
home now." So they had piled into the Ford and gone
home, making a lot of noise on the road about souvenirs
and about old friends, and about what-he-was-going-to-do-
now.

And that night, when Mother and Aunt Mary had gone
to bed, and Jubah had called good night from the back-door
and thanked him again for the silk shawl, Bert and his fa-

ther had sat in this same front room; his father in the big chair, looking expectant, with his eyebrows up and an underdeveloped smile fooling with his mouth. Bert felt then the same way he did when he and his father came in from hunting and put the rabbits down on the kitchen table.

But his father hadn't seemed uncomfortable at all; he just sat across from him smiling, and Bert moved his feet back and forth against the rug thinking, What is it you want of me?

Finally he said, "You know, Father, I brought souvenirs to the others, but I didn't know what to bring you. I didn't know what you would like."

And his father had gone on smiling, looking at him out of a quiet face, his faded eyes making a question and yet not a curious question.

And Bert had said nervously, "So I just thought I'd give you the money, Sir, and let you get something you liked and wanted for yourself," holding out the envelope in a hand that was carved from wood or clay, but was not his hand.

His father had said slowly, "That was nice of you, Bert. Thank you very much," and had taken the envelope and turned it over and over in his hands, not opening it, just turning it over in his fingers.

After that the two of them had sat for a little longer until they fell into separate silences and went to bed.

Sometimes now, when Bert sat in the leather chair and watched his father breathe in and out, he would remember that night and try to think what else he should have done. The pistol? But his father had never been much with guns. Silk shawls or bits of jade? And what would his father have done with a Japanese sword or a rising-sun flag?

When his mother spoke now it frightened him because he had forgotten she was in the room.

She said, "What are you reading, Bert?" and he jumped and his eyes caught at the words in the magazine like fingers.

He said, "Childbirth. Painless Childbirth," and she almost smiled.

She said thoughtfully, "I remember the day you were born," but she didn't say any more. Bert tried to picture his father on that day. Had he been proud? Had he said perhaps, softly and to himself, "My son?"

Jubah called them to supper and Bert ate it automatically, watching Jubah's sharp hipbones shift when she moved about the kitchen. Jubah was very thin. She was almost as old as his father and she had been with them a long time. That was a funny thing, Jubah's loyalty to Mr. Lester. They were often laughing as if old and yellowed secrets were between them. I should have known Jubah better, Bert thought now, watching her go about the kitchen. Perhaps she would have told me.

Jubah said, "I'll stay over tonight, Mister Bert," and he didn't argue with her.

His mother said, "Your bed's fixed, Jubah," and she thanked her.

Later, when Bert blew out the lamp and raised the shade in the sick man's room he thought how tired he was, and he went to sleep quickly in the chair.

When he woke again, it was almost day and he heard the old man choking and wheezing on the bed and he knew this was the last day. He called his mother and they lit the lamp and stood by the bed while Jubah telephoned the doctor.

His mother didn't say anything or bend down to touch the sick man; she just stood there listening to him cough and the tears ran out her eyes and down her cheeks and fell off.

Now that it had come, Bert found his hands were trembling and the lamplight jiggled and splashed against the flowered wall every time his father made a noise with his throat, but even when he squeezed his eyes together they were dry.

Suddenly his father said, "Ruth," and she sat down on the side of the bed and took both his hands in hers and his eyelids flew up and he looked at her, until Bert felt he could not bear that look.

Bert put the lamp on the table and bent over the old man, feeling the hiccoughing begin in his throat and the tightness clamp across his chest. He put a hand against the old man's shoulder and said suddenly, "I should have given you the sword," and his voice was too loud.

The sick man's eyes flashed to him once, flicked his face and went away and he gargled a sound in his throat. His mother frowned at Bert and shook her head sharply.

"Hush," she said sternly. "Hush, he does not know anything," and the old man raised his head off the pillow stiffly and put it down again and was dead.

Bert backed out the door when Jubah came in; his mother had put her head down on the bed and begun to cry with a great sucking sound, and Bert went heavily into the front room and fell into the big chair, saying aloud over and over, "He is dead. He is already dead. He is dead."

He put his forehead down against his arm, but he could not even cry.

TOM WICKER

BEFORE HE WAS thirty-one years old, Tom Wicker had published five novels, almost one a year from the time he started writing. In between, he tried short stories and articles, too, though he was particularly eager to establish himself with the longer form. His main wish, always, was to keep writing—all the time.

Born in Hamlet on June 18, 1926, he went to the local schools before entering the University of North Carolina in 1944 as a Navy V-12 student. Later, after brief service on the West Coast, he returned to Chapel Hill and received a degree in journalism in 1947. There, under Professor Phillips Russell, he began writing in earnest. Publicity and newspaper jobs followed one another in Southern Pines, Aberdeen, Lumberton, Raleigh, and Winston-Salem. In 1949, he was married to Neva McLean of Rockingham.

Get Out of Town, issued under the pen name of Paul Connolly, came out in 1951 as an original paperback and sold almost a half million copies. Other "Connolly" novels are *Tears Are for Angels* and *So Fair, So Evil.* Fast-paced, strongly plotted, and full of suspense, these books are said by their author to be "thriller yarns." Long since, he had reserved the right to attach his real name to what he considered more serious fiction. In 1953, *The Kingpin,* a novel about North Carolina politics, carried Wicker's name, as did *The Devil Must* in 1957. All five novels, whether thrillers or serious works, skillfully recreated the atmosphere of North Carolina towns.

Meanwhile, Wicker had gone back into the Navy. During a two-year stint in Yokosuka, Japan, his daughter

Cameron McLean was born. Since 1951, he has been associated with the *Winston-Salem Journal,* with time out for his Navy service. In 1957, he was awarded a Nieman Fellowship to Harvard University, after a year as Washington correspondent for the *Journal.*

Like many of the characters in his novels, Tom Wicker made front-page headlines all over the country in 1957, when his canoe capsized and he was swept over the rocky seventy-six-foot drop of the Great Falls of the Potomac River near Washington. Though, previously, only one man had survived the experience, Wicker escaped injury.

"A Watermelon Four Feet Long" is a far cry from narrow escapes, fictional or otherwise. The story is printed here for the first time. Concerning it, Tom Wicker says: "This story is not autobiographical, but there *was* a watermelon four feet long in my childhood. I remember it as that long, anyway. My father—not the 'Father' of this story—found the magnificent thing on one of his trips as a railroad conductor. We did take it to the ice plant for cooling and there it met the fate described in this story. That broke my heart and my father's too. Otherwise, all is imagination or as much imagination as fiction ever can be. Most of the characters are lifted from my novel *The Devil Must.* The times, the town, the circumstances are fiction. . . . My father and I get on famously to this day; but I have never again had any use for an ice plant."

A Watermelon Four Feet Long

TOM WICKER

᪻

FATHER was touchy. He would go to work for somebody—I'm talking about after he had to close his cabinet
shop, when Mister H. P. Henderson's bank went broke—
and they would hit it off all right and then it would be pay-
day and maybe whoever it was would say to Father, "I owe
you twelve dollars." And Father would say, "That's right,
but there was them two co-colas you bought me." And the
man would say, "Oh, I ain't worrying about two co-colas."
Then Father would rip off something like, "Durned if I'll
take your charity." First thing anybody know, there went
another job. Or maybe a man would say to him, "That's
a pretty house over there, ain't it?" and Father would answer, "Well, you and me could have one like it if we was
willing to lie and cheat poor folks like so-and-so done to get
it." Of course, it would turn out every time that so-and-so
was the other man's cousin. And one Christmas, Father
even hit a fireman spang in the nose for bringing charity
toys to our house.

My sister Estelle used to say Father wasn't a bit hard to
get on with before my mother died. I don't suppose losing
his shop did him any good, either. I was just a little fellow
when I helped him take the sign down from over the door.
Edward Martin, it said, *Cabinetmaker.* While we were getting it loose from the angle-iron, some men came up in a

By permission of the author.

truck and carted the electric jigsaw away. We went home
and Father took his sign out to the woodshed and chopped
it up for kindling. Estelle cried but it didn't seem so sad to
me; it had been just a little shop and I thought maybe
Father would open up a movie house and get rich.

I had about given that up by the time Brooks brought us
the watermelon, two years later. I guess that was about
1934. Father hadn't been able to get a steady job, much
less keep it, and his odd work building fences and repairing
porch steps was all that kept us going. I don't reckon
Estelle could have managed if Karo syrup and fat meat
hadn't been so cheap.

"My land, Brooks," Father said, the day we got the
watermelon. "You take that thing downtown and get what
it's really worth. I never saw such a watermelon."

"I ain't either," Brooks said. "All summer I been meaning hit for you folkses, Mist Ed."

He had put the watermelon on the dirty gray floor of our
front porch and knelt beside it, one dark hand still and
tender on its green skin.

"I don't know," Father said. "Times are too hard for you
to be letting me have a watermelon like that for two bits."
He pushed open the screen door and went out on the porch,
squatting by the watermelon and thumping it with his forefinger. It gave off the sort of hollow sound he had taught
me to listen for in watermelons—the sound that meant it
was ripe and red inside.

"That time we was building Mist John's new stoop and I
step on that rusty nail," Brooks said. "Who was it load me
in the car and drive me to the doctor?"

Even Alton Henderson never had a watermelon like that,
I thought. Nobody in this old town ever had a watermelon
like that.

"Who was it loan me the money for lockjaw nockala-
tions?" Brooks said. "You just give me a quarter now, Mist

Ed, and take dis old watermelon for dis yere boy." He
smiled at me, a gold tooth flashing in the summer-morning
sun. Behind him, morning glories twined brilliantly on our
porch rail. It was just past seven o'clock and out on the
street Brooks's wife was sitting patiently in the wagon while
their motheaten mule cropped at the damp grass along the
curb. The wagon was loaded with peck and bushel baskets
of string beans and okra and tomatoes and field peas; when
they left our house, Brooks and his wife would go along
Oak Avenue, rapping on the porch floors of the big old
houses there, and offering their fresh produce a lot cheaper
than you could get such things downtown.

Father fished in his pocket and pulled out a quarter.
"Well, I ain't going to argue," he said. "I take this kindly,
Brooks."

Brooks took the quarter and stood up; his fingers lin-
gered on the watermelon. "Hit ought to make some right
smart eating," he said. "Mist Ed, you let me know when
you need help on another job."

Father laughed. It was a sound I had come to dislike,
harsh and high-pitched and faintly angry. "All the jobs I
get these days, a man don't need no help to do, Brooks. I
ain't had enough this summer to make one good day."

We took the watermelon out in the back yard after
Brooks left. My sister Estelle was sitting in a kitchen chair
under the wild cherry tree, shelling peas into a pan she
clutched between her knees.

"Where's that old washtub?" Father said. "We got the
granddaddy of all watermelons."

"My stars," Estelle said.

I ran for the washtub and carried it to the outdoor spigot
and filled it half-full of water. "Pop," I called, "I bet we got
the biggest watermelon in this old town."

"I bet so too," Father said. "That's enough water."

I twisted the spigot and he lowered the melon into the tub.

It was so long only the lower part would go in the water. The rest of it stuck up over the rim. I stroked it gently and I can remember to this day how the smooth, firm skin made my hand tingle and a shiver go up my spine.

"It's not going to get cold that way," Estelle said. "That's the biggest watermelon I ever laid my eyes on."

"Let's take it to the icehouse, Pop." We'll have the walk through town, I thought. Right through town carrying the biggest watermelon in the world.

Estelle got up and put down her pot of peas and came over and thumped the watermelon with her forefinger. "We could eat it the way it is. It sounds like it ought to be cut right this minute." She thumped it again.

"I ain't eating no warm watermelon," Father said. "I'd as soon eat dirt."

"Well, you better not take it down to that icehouse." Estelle bent and sloshed water up over the green skin. "That old man'd skin his grandma for a dime."

"Alf? I never knowed him to cheat a man."

"They'll all cheat you," Estelle said. "You know that, Pa."

He heaved the watermelon out of the tub and up on his shoulder. "I reckon Alf ain't going to try to cheat Ed Martin," he said.

"All right." Estelle went back to her chair and sat down and picked up the pot of peas. "You go on then. I don't like watermelon anyway."

"Come on, Pop," I said. "She's just bellyaching like always."

We went down the driveway, where grass and weeds were coming up in the ruts the T-model used to make. The screens on the windows were rusty and torn and the lawn was patchy as a sick dog's coat. "I got to fix this place up," Father said. "It's beginning to look like a white trash house." We went on out to the sidewalk the WPA had staked off. Father had said he would be in hell with his back broke before those bums would lay it across his lot, but it looked like they were going to do it. We went across it to the cracked and broken tar of the street and started toward town. Bird Dog Barnes came out of his house carrying an iron hoop and a piece of bent wire.

"Hey, Sandy," he called. I pretended I didn't hear him. Bird Dog trotted across the street, rolling the hoop in front of him with the piece of bent wire. He stopped suddenly, looking at the watermelon on Father's shoulder. He had staring blue eyes and a nose almost as wide as his mouth; it wiggled when he talked.

"Is that yours?" he said, his nose moving.

"Hello, Bird Dog," Father said. "You getting pretty good with that hoop, ain't you?"

Bird Dog stared at the watermelon. He was my age but he wore a pair of his father's cutdown overalls and they blossomed around him so that he looked much bigger. Bird Dog could handle a hoop better than any boy in town and he always seemed to have certain dark secrets I longed to share. But I had no use for him. Alton Henderson said Bird Dog was trashy and that was a good word for him.

"We better hurry," I said, pretending not to notice him.

"Yah," Bird Dog said, his nose wiggling furiously, "you got to hurry and suck up to Alton Henderson and them other pretty boys over to Oak Avenue. That's some watermelon you got there, Mister Martin."

"Maybe you can have a piece of it," Father said. "We'll see when we bring it back."

I looked over my shoulder. Bird Dog was still staring at the watermelon with his outsize eyes and I felt good about that. Over my dead body he'll get a piece of it, I thought. It's my watermelon, ain't it? The biggest watermelon in this town.

The tar was already hot and sticky under my bare feet and I picked my way along, looking for sandy spots I could step on. I thought about how I would announce the watermelon to Alton Henderson. I hoped Junior Fields and Billy Spencer and some of the other Oak Avenue boys would come over to Alton's so I could tell them about it, too.

"Maybe I'll ask Alton to come around and have a piece of it," I said.

Father looked down at me and his mouth worked curiously, as though he were tasting something sour. "We'll see," he said. "Maybe he won't want to come."

"Oh, I expect he'll want a piece of the biggest watermelon in town, all right."

We had to go right through town to get to the icehouse. Everybody we passed stared at the watermelon. I don't reckon another watermelon like that one has ever been seen in our county. Maybe not even in the whole state of North Carolina. Mister Cutlar Ray stopped us and said that himself and he was just about the biggest lawyer in town at that time. Mrs. Sadie Blue offered us fifty cents for it and I was scared to death Father was going to take it. I expect he might have if she hadn't been the richest woman in town. Mister Talking Billy Carrington called out to us when we were crossing Courthouse Square and wanted to know if it was a watermelon or a green shoat. Father said he sure-God wished it was a shoat but no such luck.

"I bet the boy don't wish it was a shoat," Mister Talking Billy said. "How 'bout it, boy?"

"I wouldn't take anything for it," I said. "I wouldn't even take a trip to Raleigh on the bus for it. You come around and have a piece of it with us this afternoon, Mister Talking Billy."

"I might do that," the old man said. "You got enough there to feed the whole dang town, look like to me."

We went on across the square and down Pine Avenue and three more people stopped us before we could get to the icehouse. By the time we got down to where the tobacco warehouses were getting ready to open for the season, Father had his chest stuck out like the rasslers we saw out to the fair one fall. He was walking so fast I almost had to run to keep up with him.

"I can't understand that Brooks," he told me. "Letting a thing like this go for a quarter when he could of got maybe a dollar just as easy."

Mister Alf was sitting on the loading porch when we came around the corner of the old whitewashed brick building of the City Ice and Fuel Company. Mister Alf had a colored helper named Joshua and he did all the work while Mister Alf just sat under the peg-board where the ice hooks hung, and gave directions. We stopped at the foot of the creaky wooden steps that led up to the loading porch and we could see that Mister Alf was napping. His straw sailor hat was pulled down over his eyes. The heavy wooden door that always looked like it was wet swung open and Joshua came backing out of the storage room, dragging a two-hundred-and-fifty-pound block of ice. He pulled it across the splintery porch floor to the crushing machine, then hung his ice-hook on the peg-board above Mister Alf's head.

"Hey, Alf," Father called.

Mister Alf rubbed a black-nailed hand over his face and all the way to the bottom of the steps I could hear it rasping against the gray stubble of his chin; then he pushed the sailor back and looked down at us. Joshua took an icepick out of a leather holster attached to his belt and began to pick at the block of ice.

"I be John Brown," Mister Alf said, "if that ain't the beatinest watermelon I ever laid my eyes on."

"How much you want to ice it down for me?" Father said. "I ain't got a tub'll hold it."

"Lemme see that critter up close." Mister Alf allowed his cane-bottomed chair to come down on all four legs, and Joshua chuckled, looking at the watermelon, too. The block of ice between his legs broke precisely in two from his picking. Father carried the watermelon up the steps and I scurried up after him, bending and scooping ice chips from around the crushing machine. Mister Alf leaned over, grunting, and thumped the watermelon. Joshua picked up one of the blocks of ice and dropped it into the crushing machine, then kicked an old enamel pan under the spout. Beyond the storage room and the little office where Mister Alf kept the supply of ice picks he sold for a dime each, I could hear the steady rushing fall of the brine through the ice-maker.

"I tell you," Mister Alf said. "A man brings a watermelon like that into my place, I ain't going to charge him to ice it down. It's a right down pleasure to have it on the premises."

"Well, I take that kindly," Father said. "Ain't nothing I love less'n a warm watermelon."

"Tell you what I bet I could do, though, Ed. I bet I could sit right here and not move no more than a finger and sell that critter for at least a dollar."

"No!" I cried, and almost choked on a chip of ice that slipped to the edge of my windpipe. Joshua began to turn the handle of the crushing machine, grunting rhythmically, and a steady stream of crushed ice poured from the spout into the enamel pan.

"Is that a fact?" Father said. He pounded me on the back. The chip of ice came free and I swallowed it. "Dollar, huh?"

"He wouldn't take a dollar for our watermelon," I said. "We wouldn't take a hundred dollars for it."

"I guess not, Alf." Father put his hand on my shoulder. Mister Alf tipped the straw sailor down over his eyes again.

"You, Joshaway," he said. "Carry that John Brown critter in the storeroom."

"YasSUH!" Joshua let go of the handle of the crushing machine. He looked delighted to be allowed to touch that green and glowing skin.

"We'll be back this afternoon," I called, as we went down the ricketing steps. "We'll be back for sure, Mister Alf." We went on back then past the warehouses and through town toward Alton Henderson's house. Father was still walking so fast I almost had to run to keep up. Good old Brooks, I kept thinking, good old Brooks, bringing us that watermelon. The biggest watermelon in this town.

Alton Henderson had this collection of model cars that was really fine. He had had to go all the way to Raleigh or Charlotte with his father to buy them. There were more than a dozen of them and all but two had real rubber tires. Alton would get the hoe out of the shed and take it and the box of cars out to where Mister Henderson had dug up one of his wife's flower beds and left this cleared space. Alton would draw off highways with the hoe-blade, a whole county full of highways right there in his backyard. He had this tin gas station he would put down at one crossing and he had a house or two that he took from his electric train set. He even had a place scooped out and lined with glass for a river, and there was a real drawbridge he could put down across it.

Father was tearing out the back of Mr. Henderson's garage that day, because Miz Henderson was just learning to drive. But Alton didn't even come out of the house until after dinner. He was carrying a pasteboard box full of cars.

"Junior and Billy are coming over in a little while," he told me. "Want to help get everything set up?"

I decided not to say anything about the watermelon until they arrived. Bird Dog would always try to pick a fight

with either one of them, but I didn't feel that way. I liked
Alton better—Alton would *talk* to you, most of the time
anyway—but Billy and Junior were all right. They didn't
mean to hog the cars. I was sure of that. But it did seem
like every time they came, pretty soon there wouldn't be
enough room for me around the little county in Miz Henderson's old flower patch. But that day, Billy and Junior even
let me have the Willys-Knight Whippet model.

"Listen," I said, the first time I thought they all could hear
me. "You know what we got at our house today?"

Junior hopped across the river, pulling a blue Olds over
the drawbridge. "I'm taking a thick old lady to the hoth-
pital. I'm breaking all thpeed laws but it'th a matter of life
or death."

"I'm a speed cop," Alton said. "I'll see you when you
cross that road down there and chase you."

"We got a watermelon four feet long!"

"I'm not going to thtop," Junior said. "You'll have to
try to thtop me but it'th my Chrithtian duty to keep going."

Billy Carter looked up at me, shaking his head. He had
funny brown eyes and he always looked as if he were going
to cry. "Watermelons can't be four feet long, stupid. Anybody knows that."

"What was that?" Alton let Junior's speeding car pass
the crossing unobserved. "What was that, Sandy?"

"I said old Brooks brought us a watermelon this morning
and it was four feet long."

"Aw." Junior looked disgusted. "You mean four
incheth?" He had had two front teeth knocked out in a
baseball game and the tip of his tongue was always poking
out of the hole when he talked.

"Nosirree. Four feet. That long." I stretched my arms
as wide as I could. "Mister Alf is icing it down for us at
the icehouse. We didn't have a tub big enough to put it in."

"Aw," Junior said. "Leth go thee it, then."

"I ain't going to see it." Billy turned his back on me. "He's just talking. Who ever heard of a watermelon that big?"

"I tell you what." My voice was calm but I felt like jumping up and down. None of them had ever paid so much attention to me before. "Hows about if everybody came around to my house after awhile? We could all have a piece."

"No kidding?" Alton picked up his Dodge model and blew sand off the tires. "You really got a watermelon four feet long?"

"Hope to die." I started to run toward the garage. "I'll tell Pop you're all coming."

"Aw," I heard Junior say. "Why don't he bring it around here?"

But I didn't care. Father and I owned the biggest watermelon in town. We owned a watermelon Mister Alf could easily have gotten a dollar for. And Alton and Junior and Billy were coming to my house. They would see. They would find out that I wasn't like Bird Dog and the other boys on Cooper Street. The would find out I wasn't trashy.

The sun had dropped below the treetops when we got back to the icehouse. Its last harsh light flickered through the leaves of the big trees and just over the roof of one of the tobacco warehouses, making my eyes smart. Mister Alf sat in his chair under the pegboard, fast asleep. Joshua sprawled on the steps of the loading porch, sucking on a big hunk of ice he kept flipping from one hand to the other.

"Get me my watermelon, Josh," Father said. "No need to wake up Alf."

Joshua took the ice out of his mouth. "Mist Alf," he called softly. "Here's Mist Ed done come back."

"No need to wake him up, I told you. Just go and. . . ."

Mister Alf's chair thumped down on the hollow floor.

He pushed back his sailor hat and stood up. His shirt tail billowed out around his fat waist.

"What'd I tell you 'bout that John Brown critter you brung in here, Ed Martin?"

"You got it iced down for me, ain't you?"

Mister Alf thumped his hand down on the porch rail. "I ain't no fool, if you are. I sold that watermelon for you, Ed."

I felt a stab in my throat as real as though a lump of ice had gone down my windpipe.

"*Sold* it?" Father said. "Why, Alf Butler!"

"Sold it is right. For a *dollar'n a half.*"

"You *sold* it!" I cried. "You sold our watermelon?"

"You don't mean it," Father said. "A dollar and a *half?*"

"Car drove up not an hour after you'd gone. This here woman's driving it and she says to me I'm looking for a goodsized watermelon. Wellsir. . . ."

"You didn't have any *right!*" I ran up the steps, leaping across Joshua's long legs in their tattered old overall trousers. "It was *ours!*"

"Wellsir, I seen my chance and I wan't the man to miss it . . . not Alf Butler."

I pushed at his hip with both my hands. "But it was *ours,* Mister Alf . . . make him get it back, Pop! Make him!" I thought of Alton and Billy and Junior coming around to our house. I thought of the way Father had stuck out his chest carrying it through town that morning.

"Sure 'nough, the minute that woman laid eyes on that John Brown critter she like to shuck her skin. Hold on there, I says to her, quicklike. It'll cost you a dollar'n a half to take it out."

"A dollar and a *half!*" Father said. "I never heard of anything like that in my life."

"I tell you, Ed, a man in trade he gets to know just how far he can push a price. He shorely does."

"Leave off that, Sandy!" Father said sharply, as I pushed Mister Alf again. Tears scalded my eyes and my chest swelled as though it would burst. I looked down at him, but he was paying no more attention to me.

"Seems like you might of asked me, Alf."

Mister Alf slid one hand into the pocket of his old wool trousers. "Ed, I had to close that sale on the spot or maybe not at all. A man in my line ain't always got time to do things the way he wants."

"Make him get it back, Pop! He didn't have any right to sell our watermelon . . . make him get it *back!*"

"Where's the money?" Father said, still not looking at me. Mister Alf cleared his throat.

"I tell you what's a fack, Ed, just any and everybody couldn't of done what I done for you. You spring a dollar'n a half price for a watermelon on just *any*body and see what you get."

"Where's the money?" Father said. He came up two of the steps to the porch and Joshua moved to the other side of the ice-crushing machine.

"Make him get it back, Pop," I said. "We don't want his old money."

"Now I got the money right here." Mister Alf took his hand out of his pocket. "What I was going to say was that taking only just what seems right and fair for my commission it was going to leave you six bits."

"Why, you cheap old goat!" Father came up the rest of the steps to the porch. Mister Alf moved quickly behind me. Father's face was white. I could see his teeth biting hard at his lower lip and he kept rubbing his hands on the front of his overalls. "You think I'd let you get away with that? Selling *my* watermelon without so much as a word to me and then trying to keep half the money?"

"Now listen here, Ed Martin . . . what you aim to do?"

"Do?" Father put his hands on my shoulders, still not looking at me, and moved me against the porch rail. Beyond him, Joshua slipped quietly off the porch. *"Do? I aim to collect my due."*

"I'll make it a dollar," Mister Alf said. "Nobody ain't never called me ungenerous in my life."

"Dollar'n a quarter," Father said. "You earned a quarter of it, skinflint."

"I'm surprised at you, Ed. I didn't think you'd treat a old man like he was just dirt. I thought better of. . . ."

"Dollar'n a quarter," Father said. "Give it here."

Mister Alf looked in his hand and picked out a quarter, then stuck out his hand to Father. "It's a John Brown crime the way folks look on a man in trade," he said. "I was just doing honest business."

"Honest business," I said. "Selling our watermelon."

The tears spilled out of my eyes and down my cheeks. There was a great emptiness in my stomach. It was as though the bottom had fallen out of something I had not even known was a part of me. I couldn't think about what Alton would say, or Billy or Junior. I couldn't think about anything. All I could see was Father standing there on the porch counting the money he'd got for the biggest watermelon anybody had ever seen. All I could see was the way the skin stretched over his jawbones and the way his eyes kept switching around, like a cat's do when you give him milk.

"Hush that whining, boy," Father said. "We can buy us a half a dozen watermelons with this here."

"I just want ours back," I said. "I don't want the old money."

Father looked away from the money, at Mister Alf, then at the peg-board over his head. "We can't get ours back anyway," he said. "You and me ain't had no business with anything that grand to begin with." He held out his hand. "Here."

He was offering me a dime. I hit his hand as hard as I could and the dime spun to the floor, flashing in the fading rays of the sun. Father's face went white again. His teeth clenched and the corners of his mouth pulled back and his eyes squeezed shut as though a sudden wind had blown sand in them. I stooped under the rail and leaped to the hard, rutted clay of the parking area in front of the ice-house. It was a long drop and I slipped when I hit the ground; small pebbles and cinders scraped the skin of my knees and hands. I heard Father cry out after me, but I scrambled up and ran around the corner of a tobacco ware-house. Joshua was peeping back around it, but I didn't stop. I ran with my face down, the sharp slap of my bare feet on the hot soft asphalt of Pine Avenue sending a jolt up my legs to my stomach and on to my head . . . *no right* I kept thinking *no right no right no right* but there was no right about anything. I looked at my dirty bare feet running through my world of no possession and no pride and no right, and I hated it. I hated my world and myself and, most of all, blindly running down those quiet evening streets in the last red glare of the sun, I hated my father, who alone could have made us something else.

They were sitting on a pile of old lumber Father had saved from a chicken coop he had built for Mister Carson Maynard. It was stacked under the rotting old oak at the side of our driveway and they were perched on it like pigeons in a row, Alton in the middle, waiting for me.

I ran around the corner of the house and stopped, look-ing at them. Behind me, across Cooper Street, I could hear the rusty scream of the old screen door of Bird Dog's house and the sharp slap of it back against the siding of the porch.

"Where'th that watermelon?" Junior said. He had brought a ball and glove with him and he tossed the ball up above his head and caught it without looking, carelessly, the way he did everything. He tossed it up again but this time it fell all the way to the ground and rolled toward me. In the twilit silence I could hear somebody running across the street and the faint whir of a rolling hoop.

"Can't we have some of the watermelon?" Alton said.

I bent and picked up the ball, not taking my eyes off them. Billy looked a little scared and more than ever as though he was going to cry. He slipped off the pile of lumber.

"How 'bout somma that old watermelon?" Bird Dog said, behind me. "Your old man said I could have a piece of it, too."

"I thought you said you had a watermelon four feet long," Alton said. "That's what you claimed around at my house."

I don't care what they think about me, I told myself. I don't care. Just so they don't find out he sold it.

I looked from one to the other of them, then at Billy edging toward the street. "We gave it away," I said. "We gave it to some poor people."

"Aw," Junior said, "I bet you didn't even have any watermelon four feet long."

"Yes, he did too!" Bird Dog said. "He's just trying to cut us out of having any, he just wants it all hisself. I seen that watermelon this morning with my own eyes."

I whirled toward him, the shameful tears flooding into my eyes again: "You're a liar! A liar!" If they just don't find out, I thought. If they just don't find out he sold it.

"Fight!" Junior said. "Thick'im, Bird Dog!"

I looked at his grinning face with its careless gaptoothed mouth and at the worried frown on Alton's face and the furious working of Bird Dog's broad nose. All the muscles in my body went tight as wound-up rubber bands. With all the strength I had, I threw Junior's ball across the corner of our house and down Cooper Street.

"Hey!" Junior said. "That'th my ball!"

"Oh, come on," Alton said. "I guess there isn't any watermelon." He and Junior walked slowly out the driveway to where Billy was waiting for them. Then they set off at a trot down the street toward Junior's ball.

Bird Dog walked up very close to me, his fists cocked in front of him. His breath was bad and his nose was working and sniffing as though I had left a scent for him to follow.

"Nobody calls Bird Dog Barnes a liar," he said.

"I'm not going to fight." I was not angry any more. I listened to the shouting voices of Junior and Billy and Alton as they hunted for the ball I had thrown down the street. I hoped they would be able to find it. "I'm sorry I called you a liar." I turned away and went back toward the house.

"Of all the yellow-bellied rats," Bird Dog called after me, "you're 'bout the *yell*owest!"

I went around the house to where our old Ford was sitting up on its two sawhorses, I climbed up on one of them and into the back seat. I lay down on the floorboards. There were a couple of Big Little Books there from the last time I had hid out, but I didn't read them. I just lay there looking up at the sky going dark and the way the clouds moved across it. After awhile, Bird Dog quit yelling and went back across the street. Father's heavy footsteps came down the driveway. The back door slammed after him. Then it was dark and I couldn't see the clouds anymore; not even the stars. Pretty soon, the back door slammed again and Father's footsteps came out in the yard.

"Sandy?"

I didn't answer. He went over to the old chicken coop and called for me again. Then I heard him coming toward the Ford. I shut my eyes.

"You out here, Sandy?"

I didn't say anything. I tried not to breathe. He was standing right beside the car. Maybe he was looking down into it. Maybe he could see me lying there on the floorboards.

"Don't you want some supper, Sandy?"

I could hear him breathing heavily and regularly, as though his chest hurt him. He stood there a long time. Then he went into the house.

After awhile, I got hungry and went in too. Father had gone by then; Estelle said she didn't know where. I had supper and went to bed.

That was a long time ago, of course, and Father is dead now. So is Alton Henderson, and I haven't seen Bird Dog Barnes or Junior Fields in ten years. Estelle is married and living in Chicago. Everything is changed. Everything keeps on changing. But I never have seen another watermelon like that one and I'll never forget the way Father looked counting that money on the porch of the icehouse. Maybe things would have been better for us if he and I had ever talked about that after I was old enough to understand. But we never did.

JOHN EHLE

JOHN EHLE (pronounced Ee-ly) was born in Asheville in
1925. At the Lee H. Edwards High School there, he became interested in writing, won national honors in public
speaking, and was soon professionally connected with a
local radio station as an announcer. During World War
II, he served as a rifleman in the 386th Infantry Regiment,
seeing action in Europe.

From Asheville-Biltmore College, he entered the University of North Carolina and received a bachelor's degree
in 1949. He stayed in Chapel Hill, working on an M.A.
in drama, and meanwhile was employed by the University
as a writer of radio scripts, nonfiction films, and historical
plays. A series called "American Adventures" was produced by the college Communications Center and later
aired all over the United States by the National Broadcast-
ing Company. As a result of these broadcasts, he received
six different awards. For several years he was assistant
professor of creative writing at Chapel Hill. In 1957, he
was called to New York University as a visiting associate
professor in the Communications Arts Group.

He has tried his hand at all kinds of writing. His novel
Move Over, Mountain (1957) is the hopeful story of
Jordan Cummings, a Negro in the town of Leafwood (not
unlike Chapel Hill in physical appearance). In it there is
no racial conflict—just the compelling narrative of a man
trying to get ahead. *The Survivor* (1958) is not a novel,
but the true story of a modern "man without a country":
Eddy Hukov, a former German SS who joined the French
Foreign Legion, then deserted and fled to Bangkok, where

without a passport he found he could neither work nor leave the country.

Concerning his earlier work, John Ehle said: "For two years, thanks to the University of North Carolina and to two national foundations, I had the privilege of writing about America and Americans. Twenty-six plays were thus prepared, each seeking to identify some quality characteristic of us and our country. One of those plays suggested 'Emergency Call,' the first story I ever wrote for publication. It still carries with it, as you will see, marks of its radio ancestry; almost all of it is told through dialogue. I hope it communicates my belief in the basic goodness of the people of our part of the world."

The original radio play was broadcast by NBC, as well as by the stations of the National Association of Educational Broadcasters, the Armed Forces Network, Radio Free Europe, and the Voice of America. In its short story form, "Emergency Call" appeared in the *American Magazine,* April, 1956, and has been published twice abroad. Later it was televised on the CBS and ABC networks.

Emergency Call

JOHN EHLE

IT WAS nine o'clock at night when the car coming down Patton Avenue hit little Sue Eaton. Her mother, Gail Eaton, tried to grab her hand and pull her back, but the child pulled free, and the long, black car struck her.

Sitting in the ambulance as it raced toward the hospital, Gail had one thought: *It was my fault. It wouldn't have happened if Charles had been there. It was my fault.* She could not force the idea out of her mind, hinged there as it was with the sickening fear that Sue was badly hurt. She thought of it as the internes, almost running, rolled the cot down the long corridor to the emergency operating room.

At ten o'clock a doctor came out of the operating room and ushered Gail into the doctors' lounge. He was a tall, gray-haired man of fifty, now very tired. His hands shook as he lit a cigarette. "It's worse when it's a child," he said. "Much worse. She keeps calling for someone; I think, her father."

"Oh." Gail rose abruptly and turned to the window. After a moment she said, "Sue was always fond of her father."

"Was fond of him? He's dead, then?"

"No. We've been separated a year."

The doctor inhaled deeply, thoughtfully. "Where is he?"

"Elizabeth City. He works on a newspaper there now."

By permission of the author.

The doctor watched her closely, looking at her reflection in the window glass. She was a beautiful woman with a childlike face. One would expect to find that she had dimples when she smiled, but she was not smiling now. Her eyes were dark with worry, and her lips moved nervously. Her hair needed combing, and her suit was badly wrinkled.

"Can you phone him?" the doctor said quietly.

Gail half turned from the window, hesitating.

The doctor spoke sharply: "I'm thinking of the child, Mrs. Eaton. The little girl is calling for her father. She is critically hurt, and he may help her."

"Can't I help her?"

The doctor's eyes were friendly, understanding; but they were firm, too. "She's calling for him, Mrs. Eaton," he said reasonably. He indicated a phone on the table. "You'd better call him now, from here." He turned to go.

"Doctor."

He stopped at the door.

"Doctor, if Charles does come, will it make a difference?"

"It could make *the* difference, Mrs. Eaton." He closed the door after him as he stepped into the corridor.

Gail looked after him for a moment, then moved slowly to the table and looked down at the telephone. It was hard to think clearly. Only the week before, her son, just turned six, a year older than Sue, had been sent to visit his father for two weeks. Now this . . .

She shook her head as if trying to clear her mind, picked up the phone, and dialed Long Distance.

"Asheville, Long Distance."

"Operator, I want to put in a person-to-person call to Charles Eaton, Elizabeth City, North Carolina."

"Do you know the number?"

"I'm sorry. I don't."

"One moment, please."

Gail heard a faint click, then, almost instantly, a distant voice: "Elizabeth City, Information."

"Number of Charles Eaton residence in Elizabeth City," the Asheville operator said.

"One moment."

Gail forced herself to think now of the words she must say to Charles, and a small sense of panic touched her. She had never found it easy or natural to ask help of others, and Charles had sometimes criticized her for it. In telling Charles what had happened, she would have to explain that it wasn't she who needed him.

"That number is 5-9887," the Elizabeth City operator said.

"Right," Asheville said. "What is your number, please?"

"What?" Gail said, startled. "Oh. 9-3589."

"And your name?"

"Gail Eaton."

A person has to live his own life, Gail thought. Charles was too much the other way, too willing to share his life with others, giving of himself and what he had. He had wanted to loan part of their savings to friends—that was just before they separated—one incident in a long series. She had asked Charles if he thought his friends would be as willing to help him if the situation had been reversed. He had said yes, and she had said no, and then some other things that she didn't really mean. But it had taken her a few days to realize she hadn't meant them, and by then it was too late. Charles was gone.

The Asheville operator interrupted her thoughts: "I'm sorry, Mrs. Eaton. 5-9887 does not answer."

Gail shook her head in disbelief. "What, Operator? It has to answer."

"Shall I try later and call you back?"

"No. He has to be there. The boy has to be there, at

least—a baby-sitter, or—" She stopped, expecting the operator to offer a suggestion.

Gail heard a nurse walk past the closed door and she paused, hoping the nurse would bring her word about Sue.

"Operator, perhaps a neighbor, one of Charles' neighbors," she said.

"Do you have their number?"

"I don't know anything about them. This is very important! Please."

"Is this an emergency call?"

"Yes!" Gail gasped. "Yes, Operator!"

"One moment."

Gail listened with increasing tension as the Asheville operator, efficient but unemotional, talked with the Special Service Assistant in Elizabeth City. There she was given the names of five other residents on Charles' block.

The second number answered.

"Hello." It was a man's voice, booming and vibrant in quality.

"This is Asheville, North Carolina. We have an emergency call for Mr. Charles Eaton at 415—"

"Yes, I know Mr. Eaton," he said.

"Do you know where he might be reached?"

"Sure. He's probably at home."

Gail bit her lip to keep from interrupting.

"His phone doesn't answer, sir."

"Well, that's not right, surely. His little boy is down here visiting him. I don't know what to say about it then."

"Just a moment, sir," the Asheville operator said. "Mrs. Eaton, would you care to leave a message?"

"No," Gail said emphatically. "Let me speak to him, Operator."

"All right."

"Hello. This is Gail, Charles' wife."

"Why, hello, Mrs. Eaton. It's good to hear your voice!"

"Thank you. I have to find Charles."

"Yes?"

"Our daughter Sue was just injured in an automobile accident."

"Oh, that's terrible!"

"She—she may die, I think. Do you understand?"

"Yes, I certainly do." Now he was speaking so low Gail could hardly hear him. "Just a minute, Mrs. Eaton; let me ask my son."

Gail waited, hearing the muffled voices in the background.

"Mrs. Eaton?" he said.

"Yes?"

"My son says Charles left here five days ago. Went on a trip with his boy."

Gail leaned forward weakly on the table. "Does he know where?"

"No, Mrs. Eaton. He doesn't know any more than that."

"But—" Gail was unable to comprehend it. "Surely—" She wanted to ask him to help her, to do something to help her, but it wasn't easy to ask.

"Mrs. Eaton, listen—let me ask around the neighborhood."

"Thank you, but what if—?"

"I'll call you back. What's your phone number?"

"9-3589 in Asheville."

"All right, I'll call you. Don't worry."

"Please hurry," she said anxiously.

"I will."

Gail slowly returned the telephone to its cradle and sat staring down at it, fighting back her tears. She didn't hear the doctor until he stood beside her.

"Your daughter is out of surgery," he said.

Gail stood shakily. "How is she? Is she all right?"

"She's is resting now. She's unconscious, but still mumbling something."

"About her father?"

"I think so.   You should get him here as quickly as possible, Mrs. Eaton." . . .

At 10:45, when Charles' neighbor had not called back, Gail asked the operator to try to ring the weekly newspaper near Elizabeth City, of which Charles was assistant editor and part owner. The telephone rang several times before someone answered.

"Hello," a man's voice said. He sounded annoyed, as if the call were an interruption. Behind his voice Gail heard the sound of machinery.

"This is Asheville, North Carolina," the operator said.

"Huh?"

"We're trying to locate a Mr. Charles Eaton on an emergency call."

"Just a minute, lady. Let me slam this door shut."

A moment later the machinery noises fell to a low background.

"All right," the man said. "What do you want with Eaton?"

"To find him, at once."

"Well, he isn't here."

"Do you know where he is?"

"No, sure don't."

"Let me speak to him, Operator," Gail said.

"Very well.   Go on."

"Hello, sir. This is Charles' wife, Gail Eaton."

"Oh? Well, how are you? This is Mr. Collins, the editor."

"It's very important that I find Charles."

"Well, all I know is that he came in last Monday morning and said that his boy had arrived and he was taking two weeks off. I told him he couldn't find a worse time in the world, with a special twelve-page issue coming out, but he said good-by. I don't know where he is, and I would be the last one to be told."

"Would he have gone to Nags Head? Isn't that close to you there?"

"He might have, yes, but it's not likely. He knows I want a story on the whereabouts of the Monitor—you know, that Civil War vessel that went down off Hatteras. If he went down there he'd feel called upon to write it."

"Perhaps that's what he is doing."

"On his own time? Well, maybe. 'Course, then he'll send it to a national magazine and I'll never see it. He's sold two articles lately, you know."

The editor started laughing then, almost to himself. It grated on Gail's nerves.

"Mr. Collins," she said suddenly, "Charles' daughter Sue was struck by an automobile earlier this evening, and I think she may die."

The laughter stopped.

"Now, how can I find Charles?"

There was a long pause. "Now, I'm sorry, Mrs. Eaton," he said simply, his voice shaking. "I had no idea. But I'll find him for you if I can. I'll get the radio stations and the TV station in Norfolk to put on announcements. How is the daughter?"

"I don't know, sir. Would you ask around your shop and find out if Charles mentioned where he was going?"

"Just a minute. Hold the line."

She heard the phone being laid down, then the door opened and the sound of the press grow high suddenly. Over the sound came the high-pitched voice of the editor:

"All right, close her down. Shut that thing off for a minute."

Gail listened as the press wound down.

"What you doin', Mr. Collins—you out of your mind?" a

voice said. Gail pressed the phone tightly to her ear so that she could hear.

"Charles' wife is on the phone. She's got to find him—tonight. Where is he?"

There was a long pause. Gail waited tensely.

"Where is he? I don't want him, but his baby's hurt."

Somebody said something that Gail didn't catch.

"Is that all you know?" the editor said.

There were more mumbled words.

"Anybody else?"

There was silence for a moment.

"All right. One of you get a picture of Charles and box it up—get it to the bus station and send it to the Norfolk TV station. I'll phone them. Another of you get in touch with the radio stations in this area, ask them to send out word for Charles Eaton to contact his wife in Asheville right away."

"What about the paper, Mr. Collins?" somebody said.

"Hurry! I want Charles found!"

The door slammed, the phone was picked up. "Hello, Mrs. Eaton—"

"Yes?"

"He's on the coast—somewhere at Nags Head, one of the men said."

"I see. Thank you. I'm sure I can find him at Nags Head." She said the words with great relief.

"I'll try too—as this madhouse permits. Good luck, Mrs. Eaton."

"Yes sir. Thank you."

Gail knew she couldn't count on Mr. Collins or the radio announcements. Mr. Collins had a paper to get out and it was too late for the radio announcements to reach Charles or the boy directly. They were probably in bed by now.

She dialed the Asheville operator. An idea glimmered

in her mind, and although she didn't think the operator would co-operate, it was worth trying.

"Operator, I would like to put through a person-to-person call to Mr. Charles Eaton at Nags Head, North Carolina."

"Does Mr. Eaton have a phone listed?"

"No, Operator."

"Do you know where he is at Nags Head?"

"No, Operator."

". . . Well, do you know anybody at Nags Head who might know?"

"I'm sorry, Operator."

There was a pause. "Mrs. Eaton, I'm no magician."

"I know," Gail said, "but I thought perhaps there was some way . . ." The operator said nothing. "Operator, I need your help. My baby is hurt and is calling for her father, and what I told you is all I know. Just Nags Head—and I'm not even sure of that."

After a moment the operator said, "Hold the line, ma'am." She dialed Elizabeth City.

"Let me speak to the operator at Nags Head."

"Yes, Operator."

"Nags Head." It was a tight, high voice.

"This is Asheville, North Carolina. I would like to put in a call to Mr. Charles Eaton, in care of the hotels and tourist courts at Nags Head and vicinity."

"What, Operator?" She sounded hurt and surprised.

"That's all the information I have, Operator. This is an emergency call."

"Well, I don't care what it is. This is a big beach too. This is sixty miles of beach, with tourist courts and—"

"Operator, we have to find Mr. Eaton. This is an emergency."

"I can't accept it, Operator."

"Operator, this call is in order."

"It isn't in order at all. You have to tell me which tourist court or hotel or tourist home. I go off duty in an hour."

"Aren't you to be replaced?"

"No. Elizabeth City handles local after midnight."

"Well, let Elizabeth City take over this at that time."

"They don't know anything about this beach up there."

"Well, Operator, the call is in order just the same."

"Well, it might be in order in Asheville, but it isn't in order here."

"Operator, Mr. Eaton's daughter was struck by an automobile and she's calling for him. That's important in Nags Head, isn't it?"

Finally there came a deep sigh from the Nags Head operator. "Operator, you wait—a time will come when somebody will ask you to check the hotels and tourist courts in Asheville, and you'll know how I feel. But I'll see what I can do. I'll call you back when I get a report."

"Thank you, Operator. My number is 17."

There was a click as the Nags Head connection was broken. Gail ran her hand over her eyes, as if holding back the tears. It was going to be all right. She was sure of it.

"That Nags Head operator tried to give us a hard time, didn't she, Mrs. Eaton?" the Asheville operator said. . . .

At 11:15 Gail tried to get in to see Sue. "No," the doctor told her bluntly. "She's in a state of severe shock. Not even you can go in now."

Thirty minutes later—after telling herself every minute that good news would arrive from the coast—the editor at Elizabeth City phoned.

"I been asking around," he said. "Charles was staying at the Carolinian Hotel at Nags Head."

"Oh. Then—"

"He checked out two days ago, Mrs. Eaton."

"Do they know where he went?"

"Not an idea in the world."

Gail gripped the phone tightly, her mind settling slowly under the weight of the moment, feeling a need for clear thinking and responding to it without panic. "If he went north from Nags Head, what town would he go through?" she asked.

"Elizabeth City, most likely."

"What if he went south?"

"Hatteras Island. But if he's on Hatteras he can't get off tonight. The ferries stop runnin' about midnight, I think —and the town is at the southern tip of the island."

"Where is the Monitor, Mr. Collins?"

"Huh?"

"The Monitor."

"Well—it's off Hatteras Island."

"Thank you," she said.

"What?" He seemed to be startled, as if he had lost her line of thought.

"Thank you very much, Mr. Collins."

She hung up quickly and dialed for the Asheville operator. "I want the Coast Guard station at Cape Hatteras," she said. A few seconds later she was talking to a Forrest Jenkins there. Behind him she imagined she could hear the sound of the wind and the water.

"And you say your husband is somewhere around here?"

"Yes, sir. And my daughter is calling for him, you see."

"Yes, ma'am. Does your husband have a boat down here?"

"No, sir."

"Does he fish much?"

"No, sir. He's a newspaper reporter, and he might be trying to find something to write about."

"Around here?" The young man seemed to be surprised.

"Yes, sir."

"Well, that's not much help—unless he's interested in

the Wright Brothers or the Lost Colony, but both of those
are up at Kitty Hawk and Manteo."

"Yes, sir, I know. And he has already left the Nags Head
area."

"I see. Well . . ." Gail could picture the young man leaning over the table in the main room of the Coast Guard
station, trying to figure out a way to help her. "I can radio
other Coast Guard stations along the coast hereabouts and
have them help, ma'am."

"Would you do that, please?"

"If it will help—sure."

"Is there somebody around there who is an authority
on the Monitor?"

"Ma'am?"

"The Monitor. A Civil War vessel."

"How do you spell that?"

"M-O-N-I-T-O-R."

"I'll ask around."

Gail couldn't think of anything else she could ask.

"Maybe Jude Rush would know," the young man said.
"He knows about ships along here. But he's up at Nags
Head, though; not down here."

"It's a wrecked ship."

"Well, most of them are, ma'am—along here. I'll ask
around."

"Yes, sir. Thank you, Mr. Jenkins."

Gail returned the phone to its cradle and walked to the
window. Down below, the parking lot of the hospital was
empty, and the lights were being cut off in almost all the
windows. The place was settling down for a few hours of
rest.

She had done all she could do. There was no other way
to find him.

As time went by she began to realize that the Coast
Guardsman wasn't going to find Charles. She knew that the

radio and television announcements had not found him, either.

Her mind kept going back to the Monitor.

At 11:50, ten minutes before the last ferry that night would leave Hatteras Island, she phoned Jude Rush at Nags Head, the man the Coast Guardsman had said knew about wrecked ships.

"Hello." It was a sleepy voice that answered.

"Hello. Mr. Rush?"

"Who is this? Susan, is this you?"

"Mr. Rush, this is Gail Eaton."

"Who?"

"You don't know me, sir. But I know you are an authority on shipwrecks along the Hatteras coast."

There was a pause. "What—?"

"Mr. Rush—please help me. Please."

There was a longer pause. "Susan? Is this a joke? It's very late, you know."

"This is Gail Eaton in Asheville, Mr. Rush. My husband is down in that section somewhere, I think, and I have to find him. Have you seen him?"

"Seen who?"

"Mr. Charles Eaton."

"Eaton? No. Don't know a man by that name."

"But, did somebody come to you to ask about the Monitor?"

"When?"

"In the last few days."

There was another pause. "Yes."

"Did he have a little boy with him?"

"I don't know. I didn't talk to him. I wasn't home."

Gail slowly took the phone down from her ear. She started to put it back on the cradle and give up. There was no way to do it, no way to find Charles, and the tragedy of it all was too much for her. But at that moment the doctor opened the door and came in, sighing heavily. He nodded to her encouragingly, indicating that Sue was holding her own. Gail put the phone back to her ear. If Sue could hold her own, she could, too.

"Hello," she said.

"Yes, ma'am. I thought the line went dead."

"No, sir." She couldn't remember the man's name. "Mister, who did talk to my husband?"

She saw that the doctor was watching her now with interest.

"Why, my wife answered the door. She just told me a man came here to talk about the Monitor and said he would be back. But he didn't return."

"Do you know where he went?"

"I never saw him, lady. But hold the line—let me wake up my wife."

Gail almost said no, instinctively, but reconsidered quickly. "Would you, please?"

She heard his footsteps trudging up some stairs and slowly fading away.

"You haven't found him yet?" the doctor said.

Gail shook her head, not looking up.

"I didn't know that. I talked to Sue just now."

"Yes?"

"She came to consciousness for a minute. I told her her father was on the way. I didn't know."

Gail nodded slowly, as if telling him she didn't blame him for saying that. She was afraid she was going to cry, and she didn't want to do that while he was there. She wished he would go outside again.

Finally she heard the footsteps of the man at Nags Head come slowly back down the stairs.

"Hello."

"Yes?"

"She didn't know, ma'am."

"I see," Gail said wearily.

"She said a man with a little boy tuggin' at him came here three days ago to ask about the Monitor, and he also asked her where he could find the wreck of the Carroll A. Deering —that mystery ship that landed in 1921."

"I see," Gail said listlessly, then looked up. "The Deering?"

"Yes, ma'am. Came ashore with nobody aboard, but with tables set for dinner."

"Where is the Deering, sir? At Nags Head?"

"No, ma'am. The Carroll A. Deering wreck is at Ocracoke Island, south of Hatteras."

"Could he have gotten to Ocracoke from Nags Head?"

"Yes, ma'am—if he had taken a boat or a plane."

"Thank you. I'll try to find him at Ocracoke."

"No trouble, ma'am. Good luck."

The doctor watched her carefully as she hung up. He came over to her. "You look very tired, Mrs. Eaton. I'll take over, if you like."

"No, I want to tell him myself." She picked up the phone.

The doctor said, "I don't think there are any phones on Ocracoke, Mrs. Eaton. I think you'd better lie down."

A chill gripped Gail.

"Asheville, Information," the operator said.

Gail hesitated a moment, then spoke slowly, distinctly: "Can you get through a call to Ocracoke Island, Operator?"

"I'll see. Hold the line."

The doctor went back to his chair and sat down, still watching Gail.

The operator said, "We can get a phone call through to the lighthouse there or the Coast Guard Station."

"I want to speak to the Coast Guard Station, Operator, and—"

The connection was broken.

"Special Operator interrupting. I have an emergency call for this number. Will you take the call?"

Gail was startled. "I beg your pardon? Is this Operator 17 in Asheville?"

"This is Special Operator in Morehead City, North Carolina. I'm interrupting with an emergency call for this number. Will you take the call?"

"What call, Operator? I was trying to—"

"It's a station-to-station call. Will you take it?"

"I'll—I'll take it, of course, but—"

"Hold the line, please."

"What is it?" the doctor said.

"I don't know. I don't know."

"Go ahead, sir," the operator said.

"Hello." It was a booming voice which Gail could not immediately place. "Mrs. Eaton?"

"Yes."

"This is your husband's neighbor, remember me?"

"Why—yes, of course—"

"I'm at Ocracoke, North Carolina. What do you think of that?"

"How—? At Ocracoke?"

"One of our friends got a card this morning from Charles at this place. But you can hardly get in here by phone and your line stayed busy—"

"I see."

"So I chartered a small plane. I just decided I would— never done anything like that before."

"Yes, sir." Gail began to cry, unable to keep back the tears.

"You should of seen us landing on the beach. Scared the devil out of me."

Her whole body was trembling now with the sobbing she had held so long.

"But I found Charles. He's here."

A moment later Charles was on the phone, his voice deep and confident. "Gail? Hello, Gail?"

Gail could hardly speak. She didn't want him to know she was crying. "Charles . . ."

The doctor got up and walked to the window, where he stood, looking out, his back to her.

"Flip told me about Sue. I'm flying out of here now."

"Charles, I tried to stop Sue, but—"

"I know, honey. I'll be there by morning. Is she all right?"

"Charles—"

"Don't cry, honey. I'm sure she'll pull through. The two of us, we'll help. You'll see."

"I want you here, Charles. I need you."

"Yes, darling. I'll be there. I'll be there, Gail."

For a moment she thought Charles was crying, too, and she couldn't stand that; she couldn't let herself believe it. She hung up the phone and buried her head in her arms.

Later she looked up. The doctor was still standing at the window. "It's all right," she said. "Charles is on his way. Everything is going to be all right."

The doctor turned from the window and nodded, smiling. "I'm sure it is, Mrs. Eaton."

"But I don't even know his name."

"I beg your pardon?"

"My husband called him 'Flip,' I think. Isn't that strange? I don't know his name."

"Whose name, Mrs Eaton?"

Gail shook her head. "I don't remember any of their names," she said, "and all of them wanted to help."

The doctor nodded slowly, understandingly. "Yes, that's the way people are, Mrs. Eaton. We can always count on that."

THOMAS WOLFE

OUTSTANDING AMONG ALL North Carolina writers is
Thomas Wolfe. During his lifetime he enjoyed a world-
wide popularity, and since his death, his literary reputation
has steadily increased.

Wolfe was born in Asheville on October 3, 1900. His
father was a stonecutter with a love for rhetoric, his mother
the keeper of a boarding house. With his senses alert to all
that went on about him, he grew up in the mountain city,
attended the local schools, and had a paper route. As
his father wished him to become a lawyer, he enrolled at
the University of North Carolina. There his interests turned
to writing; he was editor of the college newspaper, assistant
editor of the magazine, and one of the first members
of the Carolina Playmakers, a dramatic group established
by Professor F. H. Koch. After his graduation in 1920,
he went to Harvard to continue his study of playwriting
under George Pierce Baker, and in 1922, received an M.A.
degree. The following year he accepted an instructorship
in English at New York University and, except for occa-
sional visits to Europe, remained there till 1930. In
England in 1926, he rejected the theater as his literary
medium and began the writing of a novel.

Look Homeward, Angel appeared in 1929. An immediate critical success, the novel won him a Guggenheim Fellowship and he sailed for Europe to begin his next book. A
year later he settled in Brooklyn and for four years buried
himself in his work. *From Death to Morning,* a volume
of short stories, appeared in 1935, as did *Of Time and
the River,* the second novel. Thereafter, he spent much

time in Europe, writing incessantly. For the first time
since the publication of *Look Homeward, Angel,* he then
visited North Carolina and was widely acclaimed as the
state's most eminent literary artist. From an illness con-
tracted during a tour of the West, he died on September 15,
1938, in Baltimore. He is buried in Asheville near the grave
of O. Henry.

After his death, two more novels appeared, *The Web and
the Rock* (1939) and *You Can't Go Home Again* (1940),
followed by an additional volume of stories, *The Hills
Beyond* (1941). Other books include his letters to his
mother, early plays, poetic excerpts, and journals. In
1956 came the long-awaited *Letters of Thomas Wolfe,*
edited by Elizabeth Nowell. Among the studies which treat
the Asheville author are *Thomas Wolfe* (1947) by Herbert
J. Muller, *Hungry Gulliver* (1948) by Pamela Hansford
Johnson, *Thomas Wolfe: Carolina Student* (1950) by
Agatha Boyd Adams, *The Enigma of Thomas Wolfe*
(1953) edited by Richard Walser, and *Thomas Wolfe:
The Weather of His Youth* (1955) by Louis D. Rubin, Jr.

Wolfe's style is characterized by its gentleness as well as
its lusty power. As plot is rarely important in his books,
almost any chapter may be extracted and read as a short
story. Those pieces published as stories generally fall into
the scheme of the four novels. "The Lost Boy," the first
section of a story by the same name in *The Hills Beyond,*
would fit properly into the early chapters of *Look Homeward, Angel.*

William Faulkner lists Wolfe as the top American novelist among his contemporaries. His early death was, indeed,
the heaviest blow ever to befall North Carolina letters.

The Lost Boy

THOMAS WOLFE

LIGHT CAME and went and came again, the booming strokes of three o'clock beat out across the town in thronging bronze from the courthouse bell, light winds of April blew the fountain out in rainbow sheets, until the plume returned and pulsed, as Grover turned into the Square. He was a child, dark-eyed and grave, birthmarked upon his neck—a berry of warm brown—and with a gentle face, too quiet and too listening for his years. The scuffed boy's shoes, the thick-ribbed stockings gartered at the knees, the short knee pants cut straight with three small useless buttons at the side, the sailor blouse, the old cap battered out of shape, perched sideways up on top of the raven head, the old soiled canvas bag slung from the shoulder, empty now, but waiting for the crisp sheets of the afternoon— these friendly, shabby garments, shaped by Grover, uttered him. He turned and passed along the north side of the Square and in that moment saw the union of Forever and Now.

Light came and went and came again, the great plume of the fountain pulsed and winds of April sheeted it across the Square in a rainbow gossamer of spray. The fire department horses drummed on the floors with wooden stomp, most casually, and with dry whiskings of their clean, coarse

From *The Hills Beyond* by Thomas Wolfe, published by Harper & Brothers. Copyright, 1937, by Maxwell Perkins as Executor.

tails. The street cars ground into the Square from every portion of the compass and halted briefly like wound toys in their familiar quarter-hourly formula. A dray, hauled by a bone-yard nag, rattled across the cobbles on the other side before his father's shop. The courthouse bell boomed out its solemn warning of immediate three, and everything was just the same as it had always been.

He saw that haggis of vexed shapes with quiet eyes—that hodgepodge of ill-sorted architectures that made up the Square, and he did not feel lost. For "Here," thought Grover, "here is the Square as it has always been—and papa's shop, the fire department and the City Hall, the fountain pulsing with its plume, the street cars coming in and halting at the quarter hour, the hardware store on the corner there, the row of old brick buildings on this side of the street, the people passing and the light that comes and changes and that always will come back again, and everything that comes and goes and changes in the Square, and yet will be the same again. And here," the boy thought, "is Grover with his paper bag. Here is old Grover, almost twelve years old. Here is the month of April, 1904. Here is the courthouse bell and three o'clock. Here is Grover on the Square that never changes. Here is Grover, caught upon this point of time."

It seemed to him that the Square, itself the accidental masonry of many years, the chance agglomeration of time and of disrupted strivings, was the center of the universe. It was for him, in his soul's picture, the earth's pivot, the granite core of changelessness, the eternal place where all things came and passed, and yet abode forever and would never change.

He passed the old shack on the corner—the wooden fire-trap where S. Goldberg ran his wiener stand. Then he passed the Singer place next door, with its gleaming display of new machines. He saw them and admired them, but

he felt no joy. They brought back to him the busy hum of
housework and of women sewing, the intricacy of stitch and
weave, the mystery of style and pattern, the memory of
women bending over flashing needles, the pedaled tread,
the busy whir. It was women's work: it filled him with
unknown associations of dullness and of vague depression.
And always, also, with a moment's twinge of horror, for his
dark eye would always travel toward that needle stitching
up and down so fast the eye could never follow it. And
then he would remember how his mother once had told him
she had driven the needle through her finger, and always,
when he passed this place, he would remember it and for a
moment crane his neck and turn his head away.

He passed on then, but had to stop again next door before
the music store. He always had to stop by places that had
shining perfect things in them. He loved hardware stores
and windows full of accurate geometric tools. He loved
windows full of hammers, saws, and planing boards. He
liked windows full of strong new rakes and hoes, with un-
worn handles, of white perfect wood, stamped hard and
vivid with the maker's seal. He loved to see such things as
these in the windows of hardware stores. And he would
fairly gloat upon them and think that some day he would
own a set himself.

Also, he always stopped before the music and piano store.
It was a splendid store. And in the window was a small
white dog upon his haunches, with head cocked gravely to
one side, a small white dog that never moved, that never
barked, that listened attentively at the flaring funnel of a
horn to hear "His Master's Voice"—a horn forever silent,
and a voice that never spoke. And within were many rich
and shining shapes of great pianos, an air of splendor and
of wealth.

And now, indeed, he *was* caught, held suspended. A
waft of air, warm, chocolate-laden, filled his nostrils. He

tried to pass the white front of the little eight-foot shop; he paused, struggling with conscience; he could not go on. It was the little candy shop run by old Crocker and his wife. And Grover could not pass.

"Old stingy Crockers!" he thought scornfully. "I'll not go there any more. But—" as the maddening fragrance of rich cooking chocolate touched him once again—"I'll just look in the window and see what they've got." He paused a moment, looking with his dark and quiet eyes into the window of the little candy shop. The window, spotlessly clean, was filled with trays of fresh-made candy. His eyes rested on a tray of chocolate drops. Unconsciously he licked his lips. Put one of them upon your tongue and it just melted there, like honeydew. And then the trays full of rich home-made fudge. He gazed longingly at the deep body of the chocolate fudge, reflectively at maple walnut, more critically, yet with longing, at the mints, the nougatines, and all the other dainties.

"Old stingy Crockers!" Grover muttered once again, and turned to go. "I wouldn't go in *there* again."

And yet he did not go away. "Old stingy Crockers" they might be; still, they did make the best candy in town, the best, in fact, that he had ever tasted.

He looked through the window back into the little shop and saw Mrs. Crocker there. A customer had gone in and had made a purchase, and as Grover looked he saw Mrs. Crocker, with her little wrenny face, her pinched features, lean over and peer primly at the scales. She had a piece of fudge in her clean, bony, little fingers, and as Grover looked, she broke it, primly, in her little bony hands. She dropped a morsel down into the scales. They weighted down alarmingly, and her thin lips tightened. She snatched the piece of fudge out of the scales and broke it carefully once again. This time the scales wavered, went down very slowly, and came back again. Mrs. Crocker carefully put the reclaimed piece of fudge back in the tray, dumped the remainder in a paper bag, folded it and gave it to the customer, counted the money carefully and doled it out into the till, the pennies in one place, the nickles in another.

Grover stood there, looking scornfully. "Old stingy Crocker—afraid that she might give a crumb away!"

He grunted scornfully and again he turned to go. But now Mr. Crocker came out from the little partitioned place where they made all their candy, bearing a tray of fresh-made fudge in his skinny hands. Old Man Crocker rocked along the counter to the front and put it down. He really rocked along. He was a cripple. And like his wife, he was a wrenny, wizened little creature, with bony hands, thin lips, a pinched and meager face. One leg was inches shorter than the other, and on this leg there was an enormous thick-soled boot, with a kind of wooden, rocker-like arrangement, six inches high at least, to make up for the deficiency. On this wooden cradle Mr. Crocker rocked along, with a prim and apprehensive little smile, as if he were afraid he was going to lose something.

"Old stingy Crocker!" muttered Grover. "Humph! He wouldn't give you anything!"

And yet—he did not go away. He hung there curiously, peering through the window, with his dark and gentle face now focused and intent, alert and curious, flattening his nose against the glass. Unconsciously he scratched the thick-ribbed fabric of one stockinged leg with the scuffed and worn toe of his old shoe. The fresh, warm odor of the new-made fudge was delicious. It was a little maddening. Half consciously he began to fumble in one trouser pocket, and pulled out his purse, a shabby worn old black one with a twisted clasp. He opened it and prowled about inside.

What he found was not inspiring—a nickel and two pennies and—he had forgotten them—the stamps. He took the stamps out and unfolded them. There were five twos, eight ones, all that remained of the dollar-sixty-cents' worth which Reed, the pharmacist, had given him for running errands a week or two before.

"Old Crocker," Grover thought, and looked somberly at the grotesque little form as it rocked back into the shop again, around the counter, and up the other side. "Well—" again he looked indefinitely at the stamps in his hand— "he's had all the rest of them. He might as well take these."

So, soothing conscience with this sop of scorn, he went into the shop and stood looking at the trays in the glass case and finally decided. Pointing with a slightly grimy finger at the fresh-made tray of chocolate fudge, he said, "I'll take fifteen cents' worth of this, Mr. Crocker." He paused a moment, fighting with embarrassment, then he lifted his dark face and said quietly, "And please, I'll have to give you stamps again."

Mr. Crocker made no answer. He did not look at Grover. He pressed his lips together primly. He went rocking away and got the candy scoop, came back, slid open the door of the glass case, put fudge into the scoop, and, rocking to the scales, began to weigh the candy out. Grover watched him as he peered and squinted, he watched him purse and press his lips together, he saw him take a piece of fudge and break it in two parts. And then old Crocker broke two parts in two again. He weighed, he squinted, and he hovered, until it seemed to Grover that by calling *Mrs.* Crocker stingy he had been guilty of a rank injustice. But finally, to his vast relief, the job was over, the scales hung there, quivering apprehensively, upon the very hair-line of nervous balance, as if even the scales were afraid that one more move from Old Man Crocker and they would be undone.

Mr. Crocker took the candy then and dumped it in a paper bag and, rocking back along the counter toward the boy, he dryly said: "Where are the stamps?" Grover gave them to him. Mr. Crocker relinquished his clawlike hold upon the bag and set it down upon the counter. Grover took the bag and dropped it in his canvas sack, and then remembered. "Mr. Crocker—" again he felt the old embarrassment that was almost like strong pain—"I gave you too much," Grover said. "There were eighteen cents in stamps. You—you can just give me three ones back."

Mr. Crocker did not answer. He was busy with his bony little hands, unfolding the stamps and flattening them out on top of the glass counter. When he had done so, he peered at them sharply for a moment, thrusting his scrawny neck forward and running his eye up and down, like a bookkeeper who totes up rows of figures.

When he had finished, he said tartly: "I don't like this kind of business. If you want candy, you should have the money for it. I'm not a post office. The next time you come in here and want anything, you'll have to pay me money for it."

Hot anger rose in Grover's throat. His olive face suffused with angry color. His tarry eyes got black and bright. He was on the verge of saying: "Then why did you take my other stamps? Why do you tell me now, when you have taken all the stamps I had, that you don't want them?"

But he was a boy, a boy of eleven years, a quiet, gentle, gravely thoughtful boy, and he had been taught how to respect his elders. So he just stood there looking with his tar-black eyes. Old Man Crocker, pursing at the mouth a little, without meeting Grover's gaze, took the stamps up in his thin, parched fingers and, turning, rocked away with them down to the till.

He took the twos and folded them and laid them in one rounded scallop, then took the ones and folded them and put them in the one next to it. Then he closed the till and started to rock off, down toward the other end. Grover, his face now quiet and grave, kept looking at him, but Mr.

Crocker did not look at Grover. Instead he began to take some stamped cardboard shapes and fold them into boxes.

In a moment Grover said, "Mr. Crocker, will you give me the three ones, please?"

Mr. Crocker did not answer. He kept folding boxes, and he compressed his thin lips quickly as he did so. But Mrs. Crocker, back turned to her spouse, also folding boxes with her birdlike hands, muttered tartly: "Hm! *I'd* give him nothing!"

Mr. Crocker looked up, looked at Grover, said, "What are you waiting for?"

"Will you give me the three ones, please?" Grover said.

"I'll give you nothing," Mr. Crocker said.

He left his work and came rocking forward along the counter. "Now you get out of here! Don't you come in here with any more of those stamps," said Mr. Crocker.

"I should like to know where he gets them—that's what *I* should like to know," said Mrs. Crocker.

She did not look up as she said these words. She inclined her head a little to the side, in Mr. Crocker's direction, and continued to fold the boxes with her bony fingers.

"You get out of here!" said Mr. Crocker. "And don't you come back here with any stamps. . . . Where did you get those stamps?" he said.

"That's just what *I've* been thinking," Mrs. Crocker said. "*I've* been thinking all along."

"You've been coming in here for the last two weeks with those stamps," said Mr. Crocker. "I don't like the look of it. Where did you get those stamps?" he said.

"That's what *I've* been thinking," said Mrs. Crocker, for a second time.

Grover had got white underneath his olive skin. His eyes had lost their luster. They looked like dull, stunned balls of tar. "From Mr. Reed," he said. "I got the stamps from Mr. Reed." Then he burst out desperately: "Mr. Crocker—

Mr. Reed will tell you how I got the stamps. I did some work for Mr. Reed, he gave me those stamps two weeks ago."

"Mr. Reed," said Mrs. Crocker acidly. She did not turn her head. "I call it mighty funny."

"Mr. Crocker," Grover said, "if you'll just let me have three ones—"

"You get out of here!" cried Mr. Crocker, and he began rocking forward toward Grover. "Now don't you come in here again, boy! There's something funny about this whole business! I don't like the look of it," said Mr. Crocker. "If you can't pay as other people do, then I don't want your trade."

"Mr. Crocker," Grover said again, and underneath the olive skin his face was gray, "if you'll just let me have those three—"

"You get out of here!" Mr. Crocker cried, rocking down toward the counter's end. "If you don't get out, boy—"

"*I'd* call a policeman, that's what I'd do," Mrs. Crocker said.

Mr. Crocker rocked around the lower end of the counter. He came rocking up to Grover. "You get out," he said.

He took the boy and pushed him with his bony little hands, and Grover was sick and gray down to the hollow pit of his stomach.

"You've got to give me those three ones," he said.

"You get out of here!" shrilled Mr. Crocker. He seized the screen door, pulled it open, and pushed Grover out. "Don't you come back in here," he said, pausing for a moment, and working thinly at the lips. He turned and rocked back in the shop again. The screen door slammed behind him. Grover stood there on the pavement. And light came and went and came again into the Square.

The boy stood there, and a wagon rattled past. There were some people passing by, but Grover did not notice them. He stood there blindly, in the watches of the sun, feeling this was Time, this was the center of the universe, the granite core of changelessness, and feeling, this is Grover, this the Square, this is Now.

But something had gone out of the day. He felt the overwhelming, soul-sickening guilt that all the children, all the good men of the earth, have felt since Time began. And even anger had died down, had been drowned out, in this swelling tide of guilt, and "This is the Square"— thought Grover as before—"This is Now. There is my father's shop. And all of it is as it has always been—save I."

And the Square reeled drunkenly around him, light went in blind gray motes before his eyes, the fountain sheeted out to rainbow iridescence and returned to its proud, pulsing plume again. But all the brightness had gone out of day, and "Here is the Square, and here is permanence, and here is Time—and all of it the same as it has always been, save I."

The scuffed boots of the lost boy moved and stumbled blindly. The numb feet crossed the pavement—reached the cobbled street, reached the plotted central square—the grass plots, and the flower beds, so soon to be packed with red geraniums.

"I want to be alone," thought Grover, "where I cannot go near him. . . . Oh God, I hope he never hears, that no one ever tells him—"

The plume blew out, the iridescent sheet of spray blew over him. He passed through, found the other side and crossed the street, and—"Oh God, if papa ever hears!" thought Grover, as his numb feet started up the steps into his father's shop.

He found and felt the steps—the width and thickness of old lumber twenty feet in length. He saw it all—the iron columns on his father's porch, painted with the dull anomalous black-green that all such columns in this land and weather come to; two angels, fly-specked, and the waiting stones. Beyond and all around, in the stonecutter's shop, cold shapes of white and marble, rounded stone, the languid angel with strong marble hands of love.

He went on down the aisle, the white shapes stood around him. He went on to the back of the workroom. This he knew—the little cast-iron stove in left-hand corner, caked, brown, heat-blistered, and the elbow of the long stack running out across the shop; the high and dirty window looking down across the Market Square toward Nigger-town; the rude old shelves, plank-boarded, thick, the wood not smooth but pulpy, like the strong hair of an animal; upon the shelves the chisels of all sizes and a layer of stone dust; an emery wheel with pump tread; and a door that let out on the alleyway, yet the alleyway twelve feet below. Here in the room, two trestles of this coarse spiked wood upon which rested gravestones, and at one, his father at work.

The boy looked, saw the name was Creasman: saw the carved analysis of John, the symmetry of the s, the fine sentiment that was being polished off beneath the name and date: "John Creasman, November 7, 1903."

Gant looked up. He was a man of fifty-three, gaunt-visaged, mustache cropped, immensely long and tall and gaunt. He wore good dark clothes—heavy, massive—save he had no coat. He worked in shirt-sleeves with his vest on, a strong watch chain stretching across his vest, wing collar and black tie, Adam's apple, bony forehead, bony nose, light eyes, gray-green, undeep and cold, and, some-how, lonely-looking, a striped apron going up around his shoulders, and starched cuffs. And in one hand a tre-mendous rounded wooden mallet like a butcher's bole; and in his other hand, a strong cold chisel.

"How are you, son?"

He did not look up as he spoke. He spoke quietly, absently. He worked upon the chisel and the wooden mallet, as a jeweler might work on a watch, except that in the man and in the wooden mallet there was power too.

"What is it, son?" he said.

He moved around the table from the head, started up on "J" once again.

"Papa, I never stole the stamps," said Grover.

Gant put down the mallet, laid the chisel down. He came around the trestle.

"What?" he said.

As Grover winked his tar-black eyes, they brightened, the hot tears shot out. "I never stole the stamps," he said.

"Hey? What is this?" his father said. "What stamps?"

"That Mr. Reed gave me, when the other boy was sick and I worked there for three days. . . . And Old Man Crocker," Grover said, "he took all the stamps. And I told him Mr. Reed had given them to me. And now he owes me three ones—and Old Man Crocker says he don't believe that they were mine. He says—he says—that I must have taken them somewhere," Grover blurted out.

"The stamps that Reed gave you—hey?" the stonecutter said. "The stamps you had—" He wet his thumb upon his lips, threw back his head and slowly swung his gaze around the ceiling, then turned and strode quickly from his workshop out into the storeroom.

Almost at once he came back again, and as he passed the old gray painted-board partition of his office he cleared his throat and wet his thumb and said, "Now, I tell you—"

Then he turned and strode up toward the front again and cleared his throat and said, "I tell you now—" He wheeled about and started back, and as he came along the aisle between the marshaled rows of gravestones he said beneath his breath, "By God, now—"

He took Grover by the hand and they went out flying.
Down the aisle they went by all the gravestones, past the
fly-specked angels waiting there, and down the wooden steps
and across the Square. The fountain pulsed, the plume blew
out in sheeted iridescence, and it swept across them; an
old gray horse, with a peaceful look about his torn lips,
swucked up the cool mountain water from the trough
as Grover and his father went across the Square, but they
did not notice it.

They crossed swiftly to the other side in a direct line to
the candy shop. Gant was still dressed in his long striped
apron, and he was still holding Grover by the hand. He
opened the screen door and stepped inside.

"Give him the stamps," Gant said.

Mr. Crocker came rocking forward behind the counter,
with the prim and careful look that now was somewhat like
a smile. "It was just——" he said.

"Give him the stamps," Gant said, and threw some coins
down on the counter.

Mr. Crocker rocked away and got the stamps. He came
rocking back. "I just didn't know——" he said.

The stonecutter took the stamps and gave them to the
boy. And Mr. Crocker took the coins.

"It was just that——" Mr. Crocker began again, and
smiled.

Gant cleared his throat: "You never were a father," he
said. "You never knew the feelings of a father, or understood the feelings of a child; and that is why you acted as
you did. But a judgment is upon you. God has cursed you.
He has afflicted you. He has made you lame and childless
as you are—and lame and childless, miserable as you are,
you will go to your grave and be forgotten!"

And Crocker's wife kept kneading her bony little hands
and said, imploringly, "Oh, no—oh don't say that, please
don't say that."

The stonecutter, the breath still hoarse in him, left the store, still holding the boy tightly by the hand. Light came again into the day.

"Well, son," he said, and laid his hand on the boy's back. "Well, son," he said, "now don't you mind."

They walked across the Square, the sheeted spray of iridescent light swept out on them, the horse swizzled at the water-trough, and "Well, son," the stonecutter said.

And the old horse sloped down, ringing with his hoofs upon the cobblestones.

"Well, son," said the stonecutter once again, "be a good boy."

And he trod his own steps then with his great stride and went back again into his shop.

The lost boy stood upon the Square, hard by the porch of his father's shop.

"This is Time," thought Grover. "Here is the Square, here is my father's shop, and here am I."

And light came and went and came again—but now not quite the same as it had done before. The boy saw the pattern of familiar shapes and knew that they were just the same as they had always been. But something had gone out of day, and something had come in again. Out of the vision of those quiet eyes some brightness had gone, and into their vision had come some deeper color. He could not say, he did not know through what transforming shadows life had passed within that quarter hour. He only knew that something had been lost—something forever gained.

Just then a buggy curved out through the Square, and fastened to the rear end was a poster, and it said "St. Louis" and "Excursion" and "The Fair."

Date Due

gndef			